Praise for the Baby Boomer Mysteries

"Santangelo has come up with an intriguing premise, drawing on the much-publicized fact that the baby boomer generation will soon be facing retirement, and she develops it cleverly....We'll look forward to more Boomer mysteries in the years to come.... Pure fun—and don't be surprised if retired sleuths become the next big trend."
—*Booklist.com*

"*Retirement Can Be Murder* is a fun chick lit investigative tale starring Carol Andrews super sleuth supported by an eccentric bunch of BBs (baby boomers), the cop and the daughter. Carol tells the tale in an amusing frantic way that adds to the enjoyment of a fine lighthearted whodunit that affirms that 'every wife has a story.'"
—Harriet Klausner, National Book Critic

"*Moving Can Be Murder* is jam-packed with Carol's cast of best buds and signature Santangelo fun! The author has penned a magnificent cozy that will leave you panting from the excitement, laughing at the characters, and—no surprise here—begging for more."
—Terri Ann Armstrong, Author of *How To Plant A Body*

"With her Baby Boomer mystery series, Susan Santangelo documents her undeniable storytelling talents. *Class Reunions Can Be Murder* is an especially well crafted and entertaining mystery which plays fair with the reader every step of the way....An outstanding series."
—*Midwest Book Review*

"Can it be possible that Carol Andrews somehow attracts murders— or at least their discovery and subsequent solution—into her life? As this fun romp opens, Carol is simply attending the untimely funeral of her very hunky handyman. *Funerals Can Be Murder* is the fifth installment in Santangelo's *Carol and Jim Andrews Baby Boomer Mystery* series, and it doesn't disappoint. Another 'must-read'!"
—Anne L. Holmes ("Boomer in Chief"), National Association of Baby Boomer Women

"Susan Santangelo's *Baby Boomer Mystery* series never fails to delight. I always know I'll be in for several hours of enjoyable reading and quite a few laughs when I spend time with Carol Andrews, her irrepressible sleuth. *Second Honeymoons Can Be Murder*, the sixth book in this cozy series, is no exception. I'm already eagerly anticipating the next book. Santangelo needs to write faster!"
—Lois Winston, *USA Today* Bestselling Author of the Critically Acclaimed *Anastasia Pollack Crafting Mystery* Series

"In this sixth entry in Susan Santangelo's charming *Baby Boomer Mystery* series, Carol Andrews finds herself in TV Land when she and Jim consult on a reality show that takes them on a second honeymoon in Florida. But when the Sunshine State is overshadowed by a sudden death, Carol once again finds herself embroiled in a murder investigation—one that hits uncomfortably close to home. With a vivid supporting cast including Carol's best gal pals, snooty television execs, and a sketchy hotel concierge—not to mention the canine versions of Lucy and Ethel—Santangelo spins another delightful tale of murder and mayhem."
—Rosie Genova, Author of the *Italian Kitchen Mysteries*

"Susan Santangelo's latest *Baby Boomer Mystery*, *Second Honeymoons Can Be Murder*, keeps a smile on your lips and the pages turning one right after the other. What's not to like? An engaging mystery and laugh-out loud characters right to the very last page."
—Susan Kiernan-Lewis, Award-winning Author of the *Maggie Newberry Mystery* Series

"In *Second Honeymoons Can Be Murder*, Susan Santangelo treats us to a new adventure by amateur sleuth Carol Andrews, who accompanies her husband Jim to Florida for what promises to be a dream vacation and the beginning of a new career in reality TV...but the reality turns out to be the murder of her old school chum and new boss. The latest addition to Santangelo's *Baby Boomer Mystery* series gives us delicious new insights into her heroine's quirky personality, told engagingly as a conversation with the reader in Carol's inimitable chatty style. And that's not all—there's a recipe for Key Lime Pie that is, well, to die for."
—Carole Goldberg, National Book Critics Circle Member

Second Honeymoons
Can Be Murder

Every Wife Has a Story

A Carol and Jim Andrews Baby Boomer
Mystery

Sixth in the Series

Susan Santangelo

SUSPENSE PUBLISHING

SECOND HONEYMOONS CAN BE MURDER
by
Susan Santangelo

PAPERBACK EDITION
* * * * *
PUBLISHED BY:
Suspense Publishing

Susan Santangelo
COPYRIGHT
2016 Susan Santangelo

PUBLISHING HISTORY:
Suspense Publishing, Paperback and Digital Copy, 2016

Cover and Book Design: Shannon Raab
Cover Artist: Elizabeth Moisan
Cover Photographer: Lynn Pray

ISBN-13: 978-0692530528 (Custom)
ISBN-10: 0692530525

Publisher's Note: The recipes in this book are to be followed exactly as written. The publisher and the author are not responsible for a reader's specific health or allergy needs which may require medical supervision. The publisher and the author are not responsible for any adverse reactions to the recipes contained in this book.

This book is dedicated to Maryvonne and Jim Fouss, who've been on their second honeymoon for the last fifty years. And to Terri Ann Armstrong, who would have made a heck of a police detective!

Acknowledgments

Thank you to my wonderful family—Dave, Mark, Sandy, Rebecca, and Jacob. And especially to my husband Joe, who keeps me on my toes and inspires me every day.

A big thank you to my First Readers Club, including Marie Sherman, Sandy Pendergast, and Cathie LeBlanc.

Thanks to Elizabeth Moisan for once again coming up with terrific artwork for this book's cover.

Honeymoon Island really exists on Florida's beautiful west coast. It's part of the state park system, and couples can/do marry and have their wedding receptions there, although not in the resort setting described in this book.

There's a new puppy in our house, and her image is on the back cover. Her call name is Lilly, and her official AKC name is My Pulitzer Prize. (I hope y'all get the double reference.) Boomer is still the model for the front cover, however, and is adjusting to having Lilly in his life. Thanks to Lynn Pray and Courtney Cherrico, Pineridge English Cockers, Rehoboth, MA for breeding such wonderful dogs,

I am grateful to Sandra Tatsuno and Paulette DiAngi for providing the delicious Key Lime Pie recipes found in the back of this book.

To everyone at the Breast Cancer Survival Center, and cancer survivors everywhere, God bless! And to those who are continuing to fight the fight, never give up!

A big thank you to everyone from the Cape Cod Hospital Auxiliary, Barnstable Branch, and the Cape Cod Hospital Thrift

Shop. And to all my new friends in Clearwater, Florida, especially the members of the Clearwater Welcome Newcomer Club and my volunteer buddies from Morton Plant Hospital. For Carole Goldberg from *The Hartford Courant*, and Gwenn Friss from the *Cape Cod Times*, I appreciate your help more than you will ever know.

A special shout-out to Marti Baker, who's always in my corner, no matter what.

To all my friends and cyber friends from Sisters in Crime, especially the New England and Florida chapters, thanks for sharing your expertise with me. I always learn something new, and the support is fantastic.

To Shannon and John Raab, and everyone at Suspense Publishing, who help me in so many ways, thank you for coming with me on this incredible journey.

And to everyone who's enjoyed this series—the readers I've met at countless book events and those who have e-mailed me—thanks so much! Hope you enjoy this one, too. And keep those chapter headings coming!

Second Honeymoons
Can Be Murder:

Every Wife Has a Story

Susan Santangelo

The West Coast of Florida.

On The Beach.

"That feels wonderful," I said, snuggling closer into my husband's arms. This move was immediately followed by an image of Sister Mary Evelyn, the freshman health teacher at Mount Saint Francis Academy, scowling at me, and intoning, "A proper young lady NEVER allows her hormones to get the better of her in a public place. Girls, you must keep your knees together at all times. And always allow room for the Holy Ghost when you are dancing with a boy."

That killed the mood, all right. Good old Sister Evelyn. She was even haunting me from the grave. I pulled myself away from my husband's amorous embrace. "Stop that. Somebody might see us."

Jim rolled over on his side and gave me a look. "Carol, for heaven's sake. We're on our second honeymoon here in Florida. And we're on Honeymoon Island. It's paradise here." He gestured around at the pristine beach and powdery white sand. "I hope you remember what we did on our first honeymoon. It was a lot more than what we're doing now."

He waggled his eyebrows for emphasis, in case I didn't get his meaning. Which I definitely did. My education had progressed way beyond what I learned from Sister Evelyn.

I sat up and brushed the sand off my bathing suit. Truth to tell, it fit a little tighter than it did when I tried it on at Suits R Us in Fairport, Connecticut, last summer. But I hope you won't tell anyone I admitted that. Fortunately, from the way he was acting, Jim hadn't noticed there was a little more of me to love these days.

"Why don't we go for a walk along the beach?" I suggested to my paramour of thirty plus years. "That way, we won't feel guilty about ordering dessert back at the hotel."

"I went to a Jesuit school, in case you've forgotten," Jim said, rolling over and getting himself to his feet. With some difficulty, which I pretended I hadn't noticed. "Jesuits don't believe in guilt. At least, not where dessert is concerned."

I laughed and took my husband's hand. To help me up. I admit it.

"Why don't we walk that way?" I suggested, indicating a route that we hadn't tried before. "It looks pretty level, and it's in the direction of the parking lot, so if one of us gets tired, we're close to the car."

I squinted, then said, "Wait a minute, Jim. Do you see something bright?" I sniffed. "It smells like something's burning."

The next thing I remember, there was a loud *whoosh* sound. I'd never heard anything like it before.

Jim grabbed my hand and pushed me into the sand. "Get down, Carol."

"What? Why?"

"Our car's on fire. If the flames hit the gas tank, it's going to explode."

There was a deafening noise, then silence. I was lying face down in the sand, Jim on top of me. I opened my mouth to scream, but all that did was fill my mouth with sand. Ugh.

I heard the sound of sirens in the distance, then several emergency vehicles careened into the parking lot at once. As Jim and I struggled to our feet, I heard someone scream, "There's a person trapped in the car!"

I felt sick to my stomach, and it wasn't from the sand, either. Trust me, having a near death experience can do that to a person.

Weeks later, when Jim and I were safely back home in Fairport, I still had trouble figuring out how our Florida adventure turned into such a nightmare. Except for the tiny fact (which I conveniently ignored) that it all began because of one of my very brilliant ideas.

Chapter 1

God made man before He made woman to give him time to think of an answer to her first question.

"Good lord, Carol, I thought they'd never leave."

"Hush, Jim," I said to my husband. "Phyllis and Bill will hear you. At least wait until they cross the street and are in their own house before you start to complain."

Jim grunted, which I took as a promise of temporary good behavior, and started to clean up the remains of the desserts—leftovers of what was one of the most boring evenings I've ever hosted.

As if reading my thoughts, Jim said, "There's nothing as dull as looking at other people's vacation pictures. For hours. Why in the world did you invite them over? In all the years that we've been neighbors, we've never entertained them solo before."

"I had to, Jim," I said, picking up two dirty wineglasses and heading in the direction of the kitchen. "Phyllis cornered me a while ago at Will Finnegan's wake, and I had to get away from her. The only thing I could think of was to invite them both over here some night to share their vacation pictures. I was desperate. I stalled the visit as long as I could, but I finally ran out of excuses."

Perhaps some of you recall that encounter at Mallory and Mallory Funeral Home in the bucolic Fairfield County, Connecticut, town of Fairport that Jim and I have called home for most of our married life. If you don't, never mind. I'll fill you in another time.

"Promise me that we won't ever have to entertain them alone again," Jim said, depositing the tray of leftover pastries on the granite island in our kitchen. "I hope you saved the box for these."

"For your information, Mr. Smarty," I said, "I actually baked the brownies and the chocolate chip cookies myself. No box was harmed in the making of these desserts." Except for the box that the brownie mix came in, but I didn't need to share that detail with my husband. No sense in confusing the guy, especially at this late hour when we were both exhausted from feigning interest at all the pictures Phyllis and Bill had shared.

"I'll bet the oven was surprised," Jim said. "And happy to be used after such a long time."

I swatted him with the dishtowel.

"I didn't make the ice cream, just in case you were wondering," I added in a rare burst of complete honesty. "But I did make the ice cream bread. Which I haven't made in a long time. Not since Jenny and Mark started to date again." I gave Jim a smooch. "Thanks in part, to you, of course."

"Always happy to be of service," Jim said, with a mock bow.

Since his remark referred to a time when Jim was under suspicion for the death of his retirement coach, and our now son-in-law, Mark, was one of the policemen assigned to the case, I wasn't sure how to respond. Which proves how exhausted I was. I always have a snappy comeback armed and ready in my arsenal.

"I always thought Mark would be the perfect husband for Jenny," I said, rinsing the wineglasses and putting them in the drainer to dry overnight. (They're Waterford, and I'm always petrified I'm going to break one, so I let them air dry.) "Even way back when they used to do homework together at the kitchen table, I knew they were meant to be together," I said. "But I had to let them figure that out for themselves."

I never interfere in my children's lives, despite what you may have heard. And the fact that our second child, Mike, has chosen to live in Miami, Florida, far away from us in New England, is purely coincidental. I'm certain he only wanted to live in a warmer climate, not escape from his parents. Especially, me.

"Do you want me to walk Lucy and Ethel one more time before I go to bed?" Jim asked. "Where are they, anyway?" Our two English cocker spaniels love to sleep on our bed, and don't always like to share it with the humans.

"You must be kidding, Jim," I said. "I'm sure they're where they always are at this time of night. If you want to wake them up and take them out for a quick stroll, be my guest. I'll check the living room to be sure I've cleaned up everything."

Jim nodded and headed toward the bedroom. I wondered if I were taking a chance. He looked so pooped that he probably would just collapse on the bed next to the sleeping canines and go right to sleep himself.

Oh, well.

I saw that Bill had forgotten one of his precious photo albums on the coffee table, which one of us would have to return to him in the morning. Which would inevitably lead to another long conversation about their trip.

Rats. Maybe I could just leave the album on their front stoop and run away before they spotted me.

I ordered myself to stop thinking mean thoughts. Phyllis and Bill had no living family, and they'd just taken a great trip to celebrate their fiftieth wedding anniversary. They had no one to share the photos with, except us. It was very sad.

I picked up the photo album and a handwritten card fluttered to the floor. To read, or not to read? That, indeed, was the question.

Well, I could just take a quick peek. After all, there was no one around to stop me.

For my darling Bill: Thank you for making the last fifty years so wonderful. You have shown me the meaning of true love. I look forward to making more memories with you for a long time to come.

Always Yours, Phyllis

My cheeks burned with embarrassment. I felt like a voyeur. Well, probably because I was one. Who would have suspected that crotchety Phyllis Stevens would express such tender feelings for the man she bosses around every waking moment of his life? I snuck the card back into the photo album, left it on the coffee table as a reminder to return it in the morning, and took my aching bones to bed.

As I snuggled up to Jim and the two sleeping canines, I decided it was high time we took a fabulous anniversary trip of our own.

Chapter 2

*You have two choices. You can agree with me,
or you can be wrong.*

"I never thought I'd be jealous of Phyllis and Bill Stevens," I said
to Lucy and Ethel as I poured their breakfast kibble into matching
bowls, "but I sure do envy them that trip. Jim and I haven't been
away together—just the two of us—since Jenny was born. And that
was twenty-nine years ago."

I immediately regretted that I'd broadcast Jenny's age, even
though it was only to the two dogs. Some women are sensitive
about their age, and lie about it every time they're asked. Not me,
of course. I take the bull by the horns, so to speak, and lie about it
all the time, even if nobody asks me.

I figured that, since Lucy and Ethel were also females, they
could be counted on to keep Jenny's age a secret. But just to be
sure there was no misunderstanding, I added "People years are not
the same as dog years. So do not multiply twenty-nine by seven. In
case you were struggling to figure that out."

Naturally, both dogs ignored me, as they were too busy devouring
their morning kibble.

The table was littered with the remains of Jim's breakfast—a
cereal bowl with a few leftover raisins and bran flakes swimming in a
pool of milk, an empty coffee cup, and…blueberry muffin crumbs.
That darn Jim. He's supposed to be on a low-fat, low-cholesterol diet
since his little heart incident a while back. But every now and then,

when I'm not looking, he sneaks in something he's not supposed to have. Like a blueberry muffin.

Of course, if I hadn't bought them in the first place, Jim wouldn't be tempted.

I poured myself a cup of Jim's extra-special high-test coffee, stretched (carefully, so as not to throw out my back), and reached for today's newspaper. I'm of the old school, and can't start my day without reading every single page of our daily paper. No online news reporting for me. At least, not first thing in the morning.

The front door slammed, and Jim strolled into the kitchen with a cheeky grin on his face. "You owe me big-time, Carol," he said, bending down to give me a quick smooch.

"I do? Why?"

"First of all, I sat through Phyllis and Bill's travel monologue last night without going to sleep. And second, I found their photo album on the coffee table and returned it to them so you wouldn't have to. I figured that you'd end up being trapped there for an hour, whereas I could make a speedier getaway. Plus, it's icy outside, and I know how petrified you are of falling and breaking something. So, you owe me. Big time." He gave me a loving leer.

"It's a little early in the day for that, Jim," I said, blushing. "And I haven't brushed my teeth yet."

"You're no fun," Jim said. "What happened to spontaneity?"

"I guess I misplaced it," I said defensively. "I'll look for it today, I promise. Maybe I'll find it this afternoon and surprise you." I gave my husband a kiss on the cheek. "I really appreciate your returning the photo album. How did you manage such a quick getaway?"

"I caught them just as they were headed out to do errands," Jim said. "Bill was dropping Phyllis off at the grocery store, and then getting the car serviced. So they were in a hurry. My timing was perfect. Phyllis grabbed the photo album and practically pushed me out the door."

"Well done, Jim," I said. "Although there may have been something in that particular photo album that Phyllis hoped you didn't see."

"Huh? I thought we looked at all their vacation pictures last night. Hundreds of them, in fact."

"That's not what I mean, Jim," I said. "When I picked up the album last night, I accidentally found a very personal note Phyllis had written to Bill tucked inside." I smiled at the memory. "It was lovely. I guess it's never too late to have a romantic getaway, no matter how many years a couple's been married."

Jim humphed. "I don't see why a couple has to go away to have a romantic moment. Or two. Or three. What's wrong with having them at home? Which brings me back to my original topic. In case you've forgotten."

I had to laugh. "I haven't forgotten, Jim. But it must be so special to spend private time with the person you love most in the world. In a different place. Away from home. It's called a vacation. Or, maybe, an anniversary celebration."

I was pushing my luck here, and I knew it. But, what the heck. In for a penny, in for a pound, as my late mother used to say.

"Anniversary celebration?" Jim repeated. "We always celebrate our anniversary. I take you out to dinner. What more do you want?"

I was getting a little miffed. Maybe because I was still feeling defensive that I hadn't immediately responded positively to Jim's earlier romantic suggestion. "Going to a boring chain restaurant with a coupon from the newspaper is not my idea of a romantic anniversary celebration," I snapped.

"We only did that once," Jim said. "And you said the food was great. Besides, the coupon was going to expire."

That did it.

"For your information, dear," I said, "most people choose their restaurants because they love the food. And the really high-end restaurants, like Maria's Trattoria, never offer coupons." I figured I'd throw Maria's into the mix, because Jim knew my three best friends and I had lunch there on a regular basis to support our pal, retired schoolteacher and chef extraordinaire, Maria Lesco. And the fact that Maria's served the yummiest pasta in town was an added bonus. Especially to my waistline.

"Okay, Carol, for our next anniversary, how about if we go to Maria's for dinner?" Jim asked. "You'll remind me, right?"

I congratulated myself silently that I was making some progress in the anniversary celebrations department. If I could convince Jim to dine sans coupon on a special occasion, that was a major victory.

Not that I was going to be satisfied with that, in case you were wondering. No way. Our next wedding anniversary was going to be celebrated in some exotic place, possibly on a luxurious cruise ship, where a variety of handsome crewmembers vied to fulfill our (my) every desire. Within the bounds of decorum, of course. Remember,

I did go to Catholic school.

And since our anniversary was in April, and it was only January, I had a few months to plot my campaign. And lose the ten pounds I planned to re-gain during this vacation.

Chapter 3

I'd rather wine than whine.

Sometimes, I'm subtle. More often, I'm not. Especially when I want something. And I wanted this anniversary celebration trip more than I'd ever wanted anything in my entire life.

Okay, that's a lie. I wanted grandchildren more than anything in my entire life. But that was an area that I had absolutely no control over.

How does that prayer go? Give me the serenity to accept the things I cannot change, the courage to change the things I can, and the wisdom to know the difference. Or something like that.

Nobody would ever describe me as serene. Even when I'm asleep, I toss and turn all over the bed. At least, that's what Jim says. Between his snoring and my tossing and turning, it's a wonder either of us gets any sleep at all. Which may account for his frequent grumpiness, and the increasing size of the bags under my eyes, which are now large enough to accommodate a week's worth of clothes.

Of course, this brings me right back to my hoped-for anniversary celebration trip. (I bet some of you thought I'd never get there.) And my burning desire to make sure it happened before my passport expired.

Oh, wait. I didn't mean to tell you that. Well, since the pup's out of the bag—we don't have cats anymore—here's the other reason why I'm so determined to take an anniversary trip this spring.

My passport expires this June and I have no foreign stamp on it. Zippo. Nada. The closest I've ever come to visiting a foreign land was when the Fairport Merchants Association—of which Jim is a die-hard member—had an international food festival to benefit a local non-profit organization. No passport was required for entry. Merely $50 a person, which Jim took as a tax write-off. Naturally.

Nine and a half years ago, when my current photo was taken, I looked a heck of a lot better than I do now. And I got a real kick out of whipping out my passport whenever I was asked for identification. Not that I was asked for identification that often. Taking the train into NYC on Metro North doesn't require a photo i.d.

But now, well, the thought of having a new passport photo taken for trips to faraway places that would probably never happen seemed like a complete waste of money. And Jim doesn't like me to waste money.

The fact that a new photo of me would be *horrible* has absolutely nothing to do with it. I am not a vain person. I believe it was the late, great Erma Bombeck who was once quoted as saying, "When you start to look like your passport photo, it's time to go home." I say, if you look as bad as your passport photo, you'd better stay home! Since I now looked ten times worse in person these days than my current passport photo showed, I figured that Erma was really telling me I'd better visit exotic ports while the going (and the photo) was good.

Like most men I know, Jim responds best to a well-organized, carefully researched, coherently presented plan of action. While I react emotionally to situations, Jim reacts logically. The old "men are from Mars and women are from Venus" thing.

There are a few exceptions to the Mars-Venus relationship, though. Jim is a real softie when it comes to the dogs. And even more of a softie when it comes to our daughter, Jenny. Don't get me wrong. Jim loves our son, Mike, as much as I do. And he's very proud of how Mike has made such a success of his Miami watering hole, Cosmo's.

But there's something about the father/daughter relationship that defies logic. Jim's been super-protective of Jenny since the day she was born. And subjected most of her beaus to endless third degrees, even when she reached adulthood. Unfortunately, his radar didn't pick up on the most toxic relationship she was involved in. That was left to me (with big-time help from Lucy and Ethel) to figure out. But he gets a pass for that because Jenny was living in California while most of that was going on.

I was sure that if Jenny had married anyone else, Jim would have found a gazillion reasons to dislike her husband. But fortunately, she had the good sense (with a little guidance from me) to marry Mark Anderson, who'd been like another son to Jim and me ever since our kids' grade school days. Jim really liked Mark. And respected him. And the fact that Mark was now a detective on the Fairport police force was the cherry on top of the sundae, from my point of view.

Mark and I had a terrific relationship. Better than most mothers-in-law had with their sons-in-law, not that I'm bragging, mind you. Except for the few times I found myself accidentally involved in one of Mark's police investigations, and Mark didn't appreciate my help as much as I thought he should.

Oh, well. Can't have everything.

I couldn't believe that Jenny and Mark had just celebrated their first wedding anniversary. Where did the time go? I knew they didn't have a big party to celebrate their first official year together. Money is always tight for newlyweds.

But didn't they deserve to have a party? After all, their December wedding on Nantucket was an intimate family affair. Hmm. It was only January. Maybe it wasn't too late to celebrate.

In a split second, I had one of my very brilliant ideas. Jim and I would treat the kids to a trip. Yes, that was it. A cruise, maybe, or a vacation on some exotic island—a belated first anniversary celebration. And if the trip also included Mom and Dad, well… why not? A double date, so to speak. Especially since Jim and I had scrimped (my interpretation) on holiday presents for the family this past Christmas.

I'm sure I don't have to tell you whose idea that was, and this time, to avoid an argument, I went along with him. Besides, part of me agreed that celebrating the holidays wasn't nearly as much fun now that the kids are grown up. Not that I would admit that, of course.

If the way to some men's hearts is through their stomachs, the way to my man's heart was definitely through our daughter. I congratulated myself on my brilliant strategy. Now, all I had to do was convince everyone else.

Chapter 4

If my dog doesn't like you, I probably won't like you, either.

"You can't be serious, Carol," my friend Claire said. "Why in the world do you think Jenny and Mark would want to go with you and Jim on a joint anniversary celebration trip? That's an over the top idea, even for you."

Before I could come up with an appropriate comeback, my BFF Nancy sprang to my defense. "Carol and Jim are very close to Jenny and Mark. It's only natural that Carol wants to do things as a family."

Claire snorted. "Not all things." But she was smiling when she said it.

"Well, I think it's a sweet idea," said Mary Alice, the third member of our close-knit circle. "Assuming Jenny and Mark agree, of course. And Jim."

"Yes," said Claire, "what about Jim? Is he in favor of this idea? I bet you haven't even told him yet. Am I right?"

I started to squirm in my chair. That's the trouble with having friends from pre-puberty days. My group knows me too well.

"I thought we were having a farewell lunch at The Admiral's Table to send Claire off to Florida until the spring," Mary Alice said, turning the conversation into another direction. I flashed her a grateful smile.

"Where exactly is your condo, Claire?" Mary Alice asked. "I don't know much about the state of Florida. Are you anywhere near Orlando? I think that's where Disneyland is."

Claire laughed. "Disneyland is in California, Mary Alice. Walt Disney World is in central Florida. The condo we rent is on the Gulf coast, near Fort Myers."

Our in-house Realtor immediately pounced. "I never knew you and Larry rented a condo," Nancy said. "I thought you owned it. Why don't you buy one? After all, you've been going to Florida for a few years, and real estate prices are still pretty reasonable there. I bet I could help you find something. I'm sure Dream Homes Realty has a reciprocity agreement with a Florida real estate company." She pulled out her Smartphone to send a text.

"Down, girl," Claire said, grabbing the phone away from Nancy. "This is exactly why I never mentioned that we've been renting. I knew you'd react just like this. And we don't want to buy anything. We don't want the responsibility of owning a second place at our time of life. And we don't need to build up equity, either. Renting is the way to go for us. So, back off, Nancy."

Although it was a nice change to have Claire aiming her sharp tongue in someone else's direction for a change, I did feel sorry for Nancy, who looked slightly shell-shocked at Claire's attitude.

"Well," she huffed, prying her phone from Claire's grip and returning it to her Kate Spade purse, "I think I've just been insulted. Are you implying that I am pushy, Claire? I'll have you know that I am one of the most successful Realtors in Fairport. Clients come to me from all over because they know I'm not only good at my job, I'm also very sensitive to each person's needs. At no time have I *ever* been accused of being pushy by anyone."

Nancy stood up and looked directly at Claire. "Unlike some other people at this table I could mention, but won't." Satisfied that her shot had hit home, she turned to Mary Alice. "I'd appreciate your ordering lunch for me. Something light, like a Caesar salad. No croutons or anchovies. And black coffee. I need some fresh air. I'll be outside for a few minutes."

Then, as an afterthought, Nancy said, "Remember, I'm the member of The Admiral's Table. Whatever you order goes on my tab. Some people here don't reimburse me as quickly as others, and I'm not made of money." With that, she grabbed her black suede jacket and marched out the door.

An uncomfortable silence followed.

I looked down at the menu and studied it like I was cramming for a final exam. I shrink from confrontation—the only thing about me that's shrinking these days. Unfortunately. I wasn't going to speak first. Although I wanted to give Claire a good smack for being, well…Claire.

Finally, I heard Mary Alice's voice. "I guess it's my turn now, Claire," she said. "Since you've already managed to insult your other two best friends, go ahead. Give me your best shot. I can take it."

I snuck a look at Claire over the top of my menu. Her face was beet red, and she looked like—wait a minute. Were those tears in her eyes?

"I'm sorry," Claire said in a whisper. Then, louder, "I'm really sorry for what I said to you, Carol. I know how close your family is. I was way out of line."

I wasn't sure I was hearing correctly. Was Claire apologizing for being opinionated and critical? Nah. I must have misheard. So I didn't respond. Instead, I concentrated on the menu, which was rapidly losing its appeal.

"Mary Alice, you know I'd never say anything to hurt your feelings," Claire insisted.

Mary Alice shrugged. "If you say so, Claire. But after what you said to Nancy, you'll have to forgive me if I'm skeptical."

Claire shifted in her chair. "I was way out of line with her, too."

I found my voice. "Well, if she ever comes back to the table, be sure to tell her that."

"I sure hope she comes back," Mary Alice said. "If she doesn't, what'll we do about the lunch bill? I don't want to have to wash dishes in the kitchen to pay it off."

"Maybe they'd give us matching aprons," I said. "Or rubber gloves with the Admiral's Table logo. We could keep them as souvenirs."

I started to giggle. I couldn't help it. The image of us in the kitchen of a fancy private club like The Admiral's Table, up to our arms in soapy suds because we didn't have the money to pay for lunch, struck me as hilarious.

"Better yet, maybe we could sell the aprons and rubber gloves on eBay," Claire countered.

"That's a great idea, Claire," I said. "Jim is always reminding me that we're on a fixed income since he retired. Any way I can earn extra bucks would make him happy."

"Not any way, Carol," Claire corrected me. "I'm sure there are a few ways that are off limits."

That set us all off.

By this time, the three of us were pretty much out of control. To the extent that most of the other diners were staring at us.

A wave of Chanel Number 5 announced the return of our hostess, who was jabbering non-stop into her phone. Nancy slid into her seat and gave us all a huge smile. "I owe you one, Claire. You did me a huge favor."

Say what? Sometimes Nancy's mood swings were a little tough to keep up with.

Even Claire looked confused. "I thought you were mad at me for what I said before. I apologize. I was way out of line. And what huge favor did I do for you? I seem to have missed something."

Nancy's eyes sparkled. "Wait'll I tell you," she said. "You won't believe it." She beamed at the rest of us.

"Come on, Nancy, give," I said. "I'm hungry, and the suspense is making me hungrier."

"Well," Nancy said, clearly drawing out her news for maximum effect, "I had turned my phone to 'mute' when we sat down for lunch. I think using an electronic device is so rude in a public place." She took a deep breath. "After our little tiff, Claire, I walked out to the parking lot and checked my messages. I had one from a buyer who's been on the fence about a very expensive property on Fairport Beach. He'd finally decided to buy it, but only if I could get the seller to agree to the price and sign the contract in one hour. Which, of course, seemed impossible. And, of course, I did."

Nancy paused to take a sip of water, then continued, "So you see, Claire, if we hadn't had our argument, I wouldn't have gotten the message in time. I'm getting a hefty commission on the deal, so lunch is on me. And maybe, by the time we get to dessert, you'll tell us what's really bugging you."

Chapter 5

My husband suggested I donate my mouth to science when I die. I'm not sure if that's a compliment.

"For heaven's sake, Carol, quit wiggling your head. Unless you want one side of your hair cut shorter than the other. That look went out years ago."

"Sorry, Deanna," I said, willing my body to be still so my favorite hairstylist and close friend could work her magic on me. But I couldn't get thoughts of yesterday's lunch out of my mind. I kept replaying it, over and over, the way Lucy or Ethel would gnaw on a favorite chew toy. Something was up with Claire, and I had absolutely no idea what it was. I sighed deeply and shifted my weight in Deanna's chair.

"Okay, Carol," Deanna said, turning my chair around so we were now face to face, "what's on your mind? And don't try to deny it. I know you too well. Is it Jim? Jenny and Mark? Mike? No matter what it is, you know you'll feel better if we talk. So, spill it."

Normally, any trip I took to Crimpers, the Fairport hair salon that Deanna owned and operated, was a guaranteed mood-brightener. (To say nothing of a hair brightener.) But not today.

I sighed again. "It's Claire. Has she been in to have her hair done before she and Larry leave for Florida?"

Deanna nodded. "She came in two days ago. She told me that they're planning on being away until Memorial Day, and asked me for a referral to a Florida hair salon. Why do you ask?"

"Memorial Day!" I said. "That's a lot longer than they usually go for. She didn't tell us that yesterday at lunch." I was lost in thought, a frequent occurrence. "I wonder why."

"I don't do cryptic well, Carol," Deanna said with a trace of impatience. "And I have another client coming in soon. If you have something you want to talk about, I repeat, spill it."

I don't know about the rest of you, but my hairstylist and I have a very close relationship. I know I can tell her pretty much everything and count on her to keep her mouth shut and not betray my confidence. Our bond is even stronger now, since I cleared her of suspicion in the mysterious death of her long-time boyfriend.

Not that I'm bragging about that. I'm just mentioning it in passing to jar your memory. And I didn't clear her all by myself. (Almost, though.)

Deanna glanced at the clock on the wall. "Yikes. It's later than I thought. You can talk, but you have to keep your head still at the same time so I can finish your hair before the next client comes. If you move your head one tiny bit, no more talking allowed. It's up to you."

I gave Deanna a dirty look. "You know that's no choice at all. I can't not talk."

Deanna laughed and picked up her scissors. "That's what I thought. So, what happened yesterday? The abbreviated version, please."

"Well," I began, making an effort to hold still as ordered, "Nancy decided it would be nice to treat Claire to a farewell lunch at The Admiral's Table. We don't go there very often, and you know us. Any excuse to have a meal we didn't cook ourselves."

"Turn a little to your left, Carol," Deanna said. "And lift your chin."

I complied, then continued, "Lunch started out fine. We were getting caught up on each other's lives. And then I happened to mention that Jenny and Mark's first wedding anniversary was last month, and that I thought it would be a great idea for them to have a joint celebration with Jim and me. A family trip for the four of us. Claire jumped down my throat and told me that was the stupidest idea I'd ever had. I was really hurt." My cheeks burned at the memory.

"And then she started talking about the Florida condo, and

mentioned that she and Larry have rented the same one for years. Well, that was all Nancy needed. She suggested that, in her professional opinion as a Realtor, it was time for Claire and Larry to buy a place in Florida, and offered to help them. Claire really let her have it, and Nancy got up and left the table in a huff. It was terrible."

I was silent, waiting for Deanna to comment. But she didn't.

"You know, Deanna, this may be a terrible thing to say about one of my oldest friends, but I'm glad Claire will be in Florida for such a long time. It'll be a relief to get a break from her constant criticism. And she acted yesterday like she couldn't wait to leave town."

The more I thought about our lunch yesterday, the madder I got. "Claire's always been supercritical, even when we were kids. But now that we're older, she's gotten even worse. I don't know how Larry puts up with it."

Without commenting on my ongoing rant, Deanna picked up a hairdryer and prepared to put the finishing touches on my hairdo.

"Before you blast away," I persisted, "don't you agree that Claire was way out of line yesterday? What was wrong with my idea about Jim and I going along with Jenny and Mark on an anniversary celebration? Even Mary Alice called Claire out on her behavior, and you know that she never has a negative word to say about anyone."

I admit it. I'm basically an insecure person. I needed the opinion of someone I trusted—and if a woman can't trust the person who has the power to turn her hair green, who can she trust? Plus, I was sure that Deanna would agree with me.

Which just goes to show that anyone—even me—can be wrong.

"I can't believe you're serious about this idea," Deanna said. "Jenny and Mark are still on their honeymoon, for heaven's sake. It would be a huge mistake for you to horn in on what should be a very special and romantic time. And I can't believe that Jim would go along with it."

I wasn't sure that he would, either. Not that I was prepared to admit that to anyone. I had yet to plan my campaign strategy to convince him that this was one of my best ideas ever.

"Are you siding with Claire?" I asked in a hurt voice.

Ever the diplomat, Deanna replied, "I'm not siding with anyone. Maybe the way Claire phrased her reaction wasn't tactful, and she hurt your feelings. But I agree with her message. All I'm saying is that Jenny and Mark have the right to celebrate their wedding anniversaries on their own."

Humph.

"And as far as Claire is concerned," Deanna continued, "what makes you think that she's so thrilled about being in Florida for such a long time?"

I laughed. "Anyone with half a brain would want to avoid going through another New England winter like the one we had last year. It started with a snowstorm on Thanksgiving and didn't let up until Easter. Jim and I were marooned in our house for days, while Claire and Larry were having the time of their lives in Florida."

"Don't be too sure about that," Deanna said. "Claire told me that Larry spends all his time on the golf course when they're in Florida. And when I asked her what she did, she said she reads a lot of books. Not a very active social life, if you ask me."

Deanna gave my hair a final spritz of hairspray. "I think Claire's bored to death in Florida. And lonely. But she'd never admit it. Especially to her oldest friends. Like you."

Chapter 6

Be careful what you wish for. It may come true
and bite you right in the patootie.

Deanna had given me a lot of food for thought, and since that kind of food is non-fattening, I was tempted to ignore it. After all, as the old saying goes, everything that's fun is usually fattening or a sin.

But by the time I turned onto Old Fairport Turnpike in the direction of our beautiful antique home, I'd come to the conclusion that both Deanna and—I'll admit it—Claire, were right. Jenny and Mark should make their own plans for their anniversary celebrations, with no interference from me.

In an effort to cheer myself up after my double-date anniversary idea had crashed and burned before it even got started, I reminded myself that, with their busy schedules, it was doubtful the kids could have planned a trip without lots of lead time. And Jenny had dropped some hints that they were saving to buy a house, so they wouldn't want to spend money on a lavish celebration.

Of course, that's where Jim and I could be helpful—bankrolling the trip. Oh, well. We'd certainly give the kids some cash toward any potential house purchase. Which would be exciting. And fun. Just not the kind that required flashing my about-to-expire passport.

I sat in my driveway and began to plan a new vacation strategy that would take us to some exotic locale. One that Jim was sure to fall for. I mean, one that Jim was sure to love.

Think, Carol. What does Jim like to do these days? Besides follow you around the house and critique everything you do?

I knew he loved writing his weekly newspaper column, "State of the Town," where he tells the good citizens of Fairport what the town officials are doing (wrongly) with their tax dollars. But that idea led me nowhere. Jim's column was only about what was happening in Fairport itself. That wasn't going to inspire him to get out of town and, even more importantly, go somewhere that would give me a stamp in my passport.

I remembered one friend from high school talking about how she and her husband flew to England, Ireland and Wales to play golf on several famous courses. I pondered that for about a millisecond and discarded it because, before we made a trip like that, we'd have to learn to play golf. Unless we could go as geriatric caddies.

I shook my head. Nah. Too much work carting those heavy golf bags around. I'd end up throwing my back out, and who knows what other body parts that I use on a regular basis.

I continued my musings. Jim did spend a lot of time at the computer these days, and not just writing his column. He'd become totally enthralled with researching his family history.

Hey, that could be the key. Our ancestors came to the United States from somewhere else. All I had to do was feign some interest in Jim's genealogical research, suggest he pick a foreign country to do some in-person investigating, and voila! We'd be on our way to...somewhere.

Okay, it wasn't a perfect plan. It wasn't even one of my best plans. But it was all I could come up with, so I took a deep breath and heaved my body out of my ice-cold car.

Courage, Carol. You can do this. It's going to be great.

I burst into the kitchen, ready to plant a big smooch on Jim and start the wheels turning. But the only ones who greeted me were Lucy and Ethel. Not that I wasn't glad to see them, of course. But seeing to their needs wasn't my primary goal at the moment.

"Where's Jim?" I asked Lucy. I didn't expect her to out-and-out tell me, in case you think I'm really nuts. But, like most canines, she's pretty good at dropping hints. She turned toward our stainless steel refrigerator and stared at it. Then turned, stared at me, and repeated the process.

And there it was, on a bright orange Post-It: *"Got a surprise call from Gibson Gillespie. Mack Whitman wants me to come back to work. I've gone to the city for a meeting. Not sure when I'll be home."*

Now, I'm going to be totally honest with you. And, unlike many politicians, I really mean what I say. A part of me (a large part—being totally honest, remember) wanted to jump in the air, pumping my fist, and yelling, "Wahoo! Yes! Yes! This is fabulous! Jim's going back to work and he's not going to be my shadow anymore! I've got my life back at last!" And I'm betting lots of wives with retired husbands would react in exactly the same way.

Except...the timing couldn't be worse. I was on a crusade for us to take a second honeymoon/anniversary trip to some exotic locale. And if Jim was back at his office, the only trip in his future would be on a commuter train chugging into Grand Central Terminal.

Plus—more of me being totally honest—there were some positive elements to Jim's retirement. Give me a minute. I'm sure I'll think of one.

Oh, yes. The coffee. Jim got up every morning ahead of me and made the coffee. And his coffee tasted better than mine. I'm sure there are a few others. I just can't remember any right now.

I sank into a kitchen chair, and wailed, "Rats, rats, rats. Why does Jim have to go back to work now, of all times?"

It was at that point that I heard Lucy snicker. Of course, I can't swear to it, because she'd turned her head and focused her attention on Ethel. But she uttered a sound that wasn't a bark, and it wasn't a whine. Yep, it was a snicker, all right. One canine companion was laughing at me. And Ethel joined in. Traitors.

Well, I couldn't blame them. They were among the few people (okay, they're dogs, but you get the idea, right?) who knew that I had started a novena two weeks into Jim's retirement that he go back to work. In the future, I'd better be more careful what I pray for.

Chapter 7

I owe, I owe. So off to work I go.

I was a nervous wreck all afternoon, waiting to hear what Jim was up to. I was so upset that I almost vacuumed the entire downstairs just to pass the time. Fortunately, I stopped myself before I went totally crazy.

The house seemed so empty without Jim. After years of his commuting to the city and coming home at all hours, or taking frequent business trips to heaven knew where to do heaven knew what for the varied clients of Gibson Gillespie Public Relations, I'd grown accustomed to his popping home, unannounced, scrounging in the refrigerator for something to snack on, and generally bugging the heck out of me. Like Professor Henry Higgins said about Eliza Doolittle in *My Fair Lady*, I'd grown accustomed to her (his) face.

I didn't even feel like checking my email, which shows how depressed I was. I always think there's an exciting message waiting for me to read. And researching more potential exotic trips was now a complete waste of time. So much for my brilliant strategy for Jim to discover his ancestral roots through international travel.

I did, however, decide to cook an actual meal for that night's dinner, instead of relying on take-out food from local restaurants that I frequently passed off as my own. Don't get too excited about that, though. It wouldn't be a gourmet feast. More like throwing a meal together using whatever leftovers I could find in the refrigerator. I hope you give me points for creativity.

I was just unscrewing the top off a jug of wine (we're on a fixed income, as Jim keeps reminding me, so no corkscrew wine for us anymore) when the newly resurrected breadwinner-in-chief burst into the kitchen, quivering with excitement. Much like the dogs when they've just discovered something really terrific in our back yard.

Jim pulled me toward him and crushed me in a strong embrace. "Put that bottle down and give me a big kiss," he demanded, then proceeded to give me a big smooch. And, as if that wasn't enough, he dipped me backwards the way dancers do, and planted another smooch.

I nearly fell on the floor. Literally.

"Jim," I said, regaining my balance and trying to catch my breath, "what the heck is up with you? Why are you acting this way?"

"Aha, woman," Jim said, "that's for me to know, and you to find out. But not here. Change into something classy. We're going out to dinner. And don't take too long. We don't want to be late." And he waltzed off into the bedroom, whistling. Leaving me speechless.

Hey, there's a first time for everything, right?

Chapter 8

I love dogs. It's people that annoy me.

"All right, Jim," I said, settling myself into our car and wrapping my coat around me for warmth until the heater kicked in. "I'm in my dressiest outfit and my hair looks great, thanks to a trip to Crimpers today. I have no idea what you're up to, or where we're going. Or why. And the suspense is killing me. When are you going to tell me what's going on?"

"Patience, Carol. Patience," said my darling husband. "All in good time."

I gritted my teeth. I have absolutely no patience, and Jim knows it. What a stinker.

He took one hand off the steering wheel and patted mine. "It will all become clear very soon. And I promise that you'll be thrilled. You know how you love surprises."

"I love surprises when I'm the *surpriser*, not the *surprisee*," I said. "If those are real words." Okay, I admit it. I'm a bit of a control freak.

We turned into the driveway of the Westfair Country Club, one of the snootiest places in Fairfield County. We'd only been here a handful of times during the thirty plus years we've lived in Fairport, the most recent time being right before Jenny and Mark's wedding, for a bridal show. Which, in case you don't remember, turned out to be one of the most stressful afternoons I've ever had.

"Jim, why are we here? We're not members."

Jim winked at me. "Patience, my love. Patience."

"If you say that to me one more time, I swear I'm going to let you have it," I said. To my complete surprise, we cruised up to valet parking, rather than self-parking so far away from the entrance that we needed a GPS to find the car again.

Jim hopped out and gave the keys to an attendant, who didn't look old enough to drive. "Here you are, son," he said. "Take extra special care of this car, and there'll be a nice tip for you later."

Then Jim turned and offered me his arm. "Ready, Carol? We're meeting someone inside. Someone you've heard a lot about, but have never met. We're having dinner with my old boss. Mack can't wait to meet you. He has a little proposition he wants to talk to you about."

It's a good thing that I was holding Jim's arm when he gave me that bit of news. Otherwise, I'm sure I would have fallen right on my keister in the lobby of the Westfair Country Club.

"You're kidding, right?" I asked Jim as he led me to the coat check, helped me out of my five-year-old faux fur, and handed it to the attendant for safekeeping. I hoped my faux fur didn't feel inferior nestled among the genuine minks, foxes, and heaven knows what other kind of animals that seemed to be having a private convention in the coatroom. I consoled myself with the fact that, this time, I didn't have to worry about my coat being stolen, or mistaken for someone else's. In this crowd, who'd want it?

"Give me a second to powder my nose," I said. "I need to be sure I look all right."

Jim gave me the long-suffering sigh of a long-married husband. "I'll go inside and find Mack. I don't want to keep him waiting. Don't be too long. And, if it means anything coming from me, I think you look fine."

"I wasn't going for 'fine,' " I snapped back. "I was hoping for 'fabulous' or 'gorgeous.' " Now it was my turn to sigh. "Never mind, Jim. Lead on. There's not enough time in the world for me to make myself look the way I wish I did. Unless someone figures out how to turn back the clock about thirty years."

Jim gave me a puzzled look. I squeezed his arm. "I know you have no idea what I'm talking about." I squared my shoulders and sucked in my stomach. "Let's go."

I started to head toward the ballroom, site of the very few events we'd attended at "the Club" over the years. But Jim stopped me. "We're eating in that room," he said, pointing in the direction of

The Grille Room. "But, Jim," I protested, "the sign at the door says 'Members Only.' Is Mack a member? I thought he lived in Greenwich."

"Mack moved to one of those Fairport mega-mansions north of the Merritt Parkway last year," Jim said. "And, of course, he was immediately invited to join the Westfair Country Club, despite the fact that there was a long waiting list of potential members ahead of him. He made sure to tell me that." For just a second, I caught a glimpse of bitterness on Jim's face. And who could blame him?

Mack Whitman was responsible for easing Jim out of his job at Gibson Gillespie Public Relations because Jim didn't "fit the demographic" of the clients the agency was targeting. In other words, Jim lost his job because he was too old. Not that anyone ever came right out and said that, of course. Age discrimination is grounds for a lawsuit. But there was no doubt, to me at least, that was the reason.

This was going to be some dinner. Although, I was more than a bit curious about Mack's "proposition." Plus, I was hungry. So I was prepared to keep an open mind, at least until dessert.

"There's Mack now," Jim said, gesturing in the direction of a blond man seated at the bar next to an attractive brunette woman who was the object of his undivided attention. "Stop bothering me," she said, and slid off the barstool. She grabbed her mink coat and stalked off.

"Well, I guess that's not his wife," I whispered.

"He's not married," Jim responded. "At least, not at the moment. Come on, Carol. He's seen us."

"Jim Andrews, so good to see you," the blond man said, threading his way through the crowd at the bar and greeting us like we were long-lost royalty. "And twice in one day! What a treat. And you must be Carol. I'm so happy to finally meet you." He gave Jim a hearty handshake and a clap on the back.

I resisted saying that, if Jim hadn't been encouraged to take early retirement, Mack could have seen him every day. At the office.

I gave Mack a phony smile—I know how to play the suck-up game. "Lovely to meet you, Mack," I said. "I've heard so much about you from Jim." I felt Jim stiffen next to me. I knew he was worried about what I'd say next. But I was on my good behavior.

"Our table is ready," Mack said. "I've arranged for a quiet corner so we can talk." He gave us a toothy smile.

After we had settled in our seats, and drink orders were taken, I took a moment to check out our host. I knew my friends would want a complete description, especially Nancy.

According to Jim, Mack Whitman was thirty-eight, but he looked several years younger. He was impeccably dressed in a charcoal grey business suit that probably cost more than I spend on clothing in a year—and that's saying something. A lock of hair dipped over his forehead (which I'm sure took plenty of time to arrange in front of a mirror). The required two days' growth of stubble proclaimed, "Aren't I cool?" His brown eyes, framed by wire-rimmed eyeglasses, frequently darted around the room. I wondered who he was looking for. Or maybe he was just checking out who else was there, looking for another nubile young female to hit on. Or for more important dinner companions than Jim and me.

I know. I'm being mean. But this man had turned our lives upside down a few years back, and I wasn't predisposed to like him, no matter what his supposed business proposition was.

Except that, when I glanced at my husband, Jim was more animated than he'd been in a long time. He was relaxed and clearly enjoying himself as he and Mack traded gossip about agency clients, past and present. It suddenly dawned on me how much Jim missed being part of Gibson Gillespie, even after all this time.

I know. I should have figured that out before. But I'm a little dense, sometimes. I took a sip of my chardonnay and settled back in my chair. I figured the men would get to the point of this dinner meeting eventually; meanwhile, I intended to have a good time.

Then, Mack lifted his own glass and looked directly at me. "To you, Carol. And to new adventures. Welcome aboard."

Huh? Welcome aboard what? Was a train leaving the station that I knew nothing about? I glanced at my husband for clarification, but he had a silly grin on his face, which didn't help me at all.

"I don't mean to appear dense, Mack," I said, "but I have no idea what you're talking about."

"You mean Jim hasn't told you the news?" Mack said. He punched my husband in the shoulder. "Why, you old dog, keeping this as a surprise, were you?"

"I wanted Carol to hear the idea from you, Mack," Jim said. "After all, she may not want to do it." He shot me a little boy, pleading look—the same look the kids used to give me when they really wanted me to let them do something.

"Okay, Carol, here goes," Mack said. "The short version. GG has a brand new client, a television production company. Charles King Productions. Maybe you've heard of it?"

I shook my head "no."

"I guess you don't watch any of the reality television shows, then, Carol," Mack said with a frown. "Oh, well. That doesn't really matter. But the point is that CKP wants to start a series of new shows aimed at an older demographic, like you and Jim." He looked at Jim. "No offense, Jim."

"No offense taken, Mack," Jim said.

I wanted to say, "Speak for yourself, Jim." But Mack was paying for dinner—at least, I hoped he was—so I remained silent. And by now, I was really curious about where this was leading.

"I want to hire you and Jim to be the GG agency reps for CKP. The first show, which is now in the final stages of development, is *The Second Honeymoon Game*. So, what do you say, Carol? Do you want to get into television?"

Chapter 9

My mouth is frequently off and running and my brain never catches up with it.

For the second time in an hour, I was speechless. Hard to believe, but absolutely true. Then, I started to laugh. I figured out in a flash that Jim had put Mack up to this. It was a gag, pure and simple. Payback for all the times over the thirty plus years of our marriage when I'd told Jim I'd gladly switch places with him. Let him be the stay-at-home spouse, trying to be a successful freelance writer/editor while taking care of two kids and an antique house, instead of leading the glamorous life of a NYC public relations guru. I always managed to ignore the fact that Jim left the house to toil in the Big Apple before the sun was up, and usually returned home after it had set. He often complained he'd forgotten what color our house was, because he rarely saw it during daylight hours.

"You almost got me," I said, shaking my finger at Jim. "That's the funniest thing I've ever heard. But I'm not falling for it." I turned my baby blues onto Mack. "I don't know how Jim talked you into this little joke."

Mack started to respond, but, naturally, I didn't let him.

"I'm thrilled, of course, that Jim's coming back to Gibson Gillespie," I said, trying to sound sincere. Because part of me was thrilled. And the other part of me, well…. "He'll be very good at this job. But I'm sure I don't have to tell you that."

Mack turned to Jim, and said, "You're right, Jim. She never lets anyone else get a word in edgewise."

Well! I didn't have to sit here in the swanky Westfair Country Club and be insulted. I felt my face flush. Lemme out of here. I started to push back my chair and stand up, but Jim put a restraining hand on my arm. "Carol, honey, sit down. Listen to what Mack has to say. Please."

He flashed his boss a "What can you do? She's a woman?" look. Jim doesn't dare use that look very often, but I recognized it immediately.

I plopped back down and folded my arms. "Okay, I'm sitting." And I flashed Jim a look of my own.

Mack took a healthy swig of his libation of choice—straight Scotch, no rocks—and then spoke. "We're getting off on the wrong foot here, Carol, if you'll forgive me for using a tired cliché. I apologize for my wisecrack to Jim. I was way out of line. I don't even know you."

I was mollified. A little.

Mack waved away the server who had arrived to take our dinner orders, then said, "I can assure you, Carol, that this is no gag that Jim and I cooked up. This is a serious business proposition, and I need your help. In fact," he cast Jim a sideways glance, "I've got to have it. Yours and Jim's. You two fit the demographic this client is aiming for perfectly."

Mack reached into his briefcase and took out his iPad. In a few seconds, he had pulled up a website. "Take a quick look at this," he said, sliding the device across the table toward me. "It'll give you some background information on the idea behind the show."

I rummaged in my purse for my eyeglasses. Jim is forever telling me I should wear them all the time, but it bothers me if the frames don't match the clothes I happen to be wearing. I'm betting a lot of you agree with me about that, right? Forget about eye-hand coordination. At my age, it's all about coordinating the outfit.

I focused on the iPad screen, then looked at Jim and Mack. "This is about an actual television show," I said.

Jim sighed. "That's what we've both been trying to tell you, Carol. This is on the level."

I swear, at that point I was so excited that I thought I was going to faint. Imagine me, Carol Andrews from Fairport Connecticut, a television star! My friends would freak out when I told them. Even Claire would be impressed. I was lost in a sea of klieg lights and red carpets, signing autographs for my adoring fans.

Jim immediately figured out what I was thinking. (Hey, he hasn't been married to me for over thirty years for nothing.) And—*pop!*—my darling husband burst my bubble. Sort of.

"You're not going to be on television, Carol," Jim clarified.

My face must have mirrored my disappointment. And my confusion.

"GG has been retained to do the promotion for the show," Mack said. "Not to provide the talent." He framed his hands, tilted his head and looked at me. "Although you're very attractive, Carol. You'd look great on television. I can tell you have charisma that would translate well on the tube."

My spirits (ego) soared. Maybe there was still a chance for me to be a star.

Mack sighed. "But, of course, that wouldn't work. We could be accused of nepotism, using our own people as talent on the show." He covered my hand with his own and looked deeply into my eyes. "I hope you understand, Carol."

I leaned back in my chair. "Truthfully, I don't understand any of this," I admitted. "Jim's role is perfectly clear. But what exactly would you want me to do? I'm no public relations expert."

Of course, I'm an expert in so many other areas. But I didn't think it was appropriate to confuse Mack with those. At least, not right now. And I had to admit that I was beginning to warm up to the guy. After all, he immediately recognized that I had "charisma," something Jim has yet to realize.

"It might be simpler if I forwarded you the treatment CKP has come up with for *The Second Honeymoon Game*," Mack said, giving his iPad a few quick taps. "Now you can look at it at your leisure, and you'll have a much better idea about the show and your role in promoting it. I guarantee you, Carol, that it's going to be a once-in-a-lifetime experience for you and Jim."

Mack beamed at us. "Now, who's hungry?"

For once in my life, I refused to be diverted by food. "I really want to understand this, Mack," I persisted. "What exactly is it that you want me to agree to do for the show?"

Mack once again shot a sideways glance at Jim, who appeared to be engrossed in studying his menu. No help there.

"Well, you'd be sort of like, Jim's assistant," Mack said. "You know, provide womanly input when called upon. The position's very flexible. There's really no job description for it."

"Is there financial compensation for this 'flexible' position, Mack?" I asked. "Or is it for love only, like marriage?"

Mack laughed. "That was a good one, Carol. Jim told me you had a terrific sense of humor."

I continued to stare at him, waiting for an answer. "We're still hammering out the details, Carol," Mack finally said. "Isn't that right, Jim?"

Jim nodded. He knew a cue when he heard one.

"But no matter what, you'll have an all-expenses-paid trip to Florida when the show's pilot is shot." Mack focused his huge smile on me. "Sort of like a second honeymoon for you and Jim. How does that sound?"

It sounded like I needed to skip dinner tonight, if I wanted to be presentable in a bathing suit anytime soon. Or, maybe, just skipping dessert would do the trick.

Chapter 10

I never respond to flattery. Since I've been married so long, I'm way out of practice.

"I still don't get it," I said to Jim over breakfast the next morning. "What's the deal? What am I supposed to do—trail around after you all the time, carrying your iPad or laptop?"

Of course, I didn't give the poor man a chance to answer.

"I checked out the information that Mack sent me when we got home last night. I didn't understand one word. What the heck's a logline, anyway? This is like a whole other language."

"Carol, you really are overreacting," Jim said. As I opened my mouth to defend myself, Jim handed me my coffee cup. "Here, drink this. I made it with a touch of cinnamon this morning, just the way you like it. And for Pete's sake, calm down." He ran his fingers through what was left of his hair in a gesture of frustration that I knew all too well.

"Don't ruin this for me, Carol," he said. "This is my big chance at a comeback. To prove to the young geniuses at Gibson Gillespie that the old man's still got what it takes. And I wanted to bring you along for the ride. I thought you'd get a kick out of it. But instead, you spent most of last night's meal interrogating Mack Whitman like he was on the witness stand in a criminal case. Which. Was. Not. Helpful."

"That's not fair, Jim," I said, tears stinging my eyes.

Lucy and Ethel, always attentive to my moods, nuzzled my hand in sympathy. Or maybe they were just reminding me they were still waiting for their breakfast.

I immediately snapped to it and filled both their bowls with kibble. I know who really runs the Andrews house, and hell hath no fury like two hungry English cocker spaniels. By the time I rejoined Jim at the table, I had calmed down. Thankfully, so had he.

"I apologize for what I just said." I started to answer, but Jim held up his hand and stopped me, signaling that I shouldn't interrupt. "Here's the short version of what happened yesterday. Mack called me back into the office to handle the P.R. for a new account the agency had just landed, because I fit the profile of the show's target market. In other words, I'm over fifty. And I thought you'd get a kick out of being involved, too. So I finagled an assistant's position into my contract. Details to be determined as the project went along. I figured you'd jump at the chance. Plus, it's a terrific way to celebrate our anniversary, since the first show will be shot in Florida around that time. I guess I didn't handle it very well. I told Mack you'd love the surprise element, and had him set up the dinner. And...well...."

"And I, of course, did completely misinterpret, overreact, whatever," I finished.

Jim smiled. "No, you were just being yourself," he said. "I'm the one who didn't handle it right. I should have prepared you in advance. I guess I figured that you'd be so starry-eyed about working on a television show that you wouldn't immediately be caught up in the details.

"As a matter of fact," Jim continued, "I'm not too clear on exactly what I'm supposed to do, either. But that's the way Mack operates. He calls himself a 'seat-of-the-pants' thinker. Says planning ahead with too much detail stifles his creative juices. That's one of the reasons why I found working with him so frustrating, in case you've forgotten."

"How can anybody run an important public relations agency like Gibson Gillespie that way?" I asked. "It's nuts."

"I agree," Jim said. "But Mack needs me to make this project a success." He reached over and gave my hand a squeeze. "Correction: He needs *us*. Both of us. We're typical of the audience *The Second Honeymoon Game* is targeting. As a matter of fact," he rose from the kitchen table and headed in the direction of his computer, "I'm betting there's an email from Mack this morning detailing what he wants us to do for the next few days."

In less time than it took me to clear away the remains of our breakfast, Jim was back. "No time for that now, Carol. We've got to get a move on. Mack wants us in New York in three hours to meet the show's production staff, some possible contestants, and the host of the show."

"But Jim," I protested, "I can't possibly be *ready* in three hours, much less get to New York by then."

I had already planned a leisurely morning, beginning with texts to Jenny and Mike to bring them up to date on the unexpected turn their fuddy-duddy parents' lives had taken. These texts would be immediately followed by calls to Nancy, Mary Alice and Claire to tell them about our (my) foray into the field of television. I was sure that each call I made would be met with a combination of squeals of excitement tinged with a pinch of envy.

Finally, a quick call to Deanna, to plan a hair appointment calendar so my locks would be lovely all throughout this adventure. Which brought up an interesting idea: Maybe Deanna could become the official hair stylist for the show, and travel to Florida when we did the show's pilot episode. Wow. That would be so cool.

If my role in promoting *The Second Honeymoon Game* was nebulous, I could certainly carve out a job description all by myself. In fact, that'd be preferable. Not that I'd admit that to Jim, of course. Or, heaven forbid, Mack Whitman.

And now, in a flash, my day was completely turned upside down. Oh, well. I guess that's show biz, and I'd better get used to it.

I had dithered for too long in front of my closet, trying to find a perfect outfit that screamed "New York Public Relations Expert," but the best I could do was a woolen, below-the-knee skirt and cashmere turtleneck sweater. Black, of course. I did have time to send a quick S.O.S. to Nancy asking to borrow appropriate footwear for a quick trip into Manhattan. I didn't tell her why. Pal that she was, she met me and a fuming Jim at the Fairport train station with a Coach tote bag, which she thrust into my hands just as we were about to board.

"Here," she said. "Be careful when you walk in these so you don't trip. I want them back in the exact condition I loaned them to you. They cost a fortune, but they're bound to impress. And don't lose the tote bag. Have fun." And she was gone.

"I still don't see why we have to walk," I said, puffing as I tried to keep up with my sprinter husband. "Wait up, will you? You know I can't walk as fast as you do." I looked down at my feet. "Especially since I'm wearing Nancy's shoes. I should have left my sneakers on instead of changing shoes on the train. But I figured we'd take a cab."

Of course, there are no coupons for New York City taxis, I reminded myself, which was probably why we were hoofing it.

Jim stopped, turned around, and gave me a look. "We could have taken a cross-town bus, and then the subway, Carol. But you didn't want to."

He had me there. I'm extremely claustrophobic, and being underground in a tin can that could stop at any minute and leave me trapped for…well, I think you get the idea. I have the same problem with self-service elevators. I was trapped in one of those for hours in my younger days, and haven't gotten over it yet.

Sue me.

Jim grabbed my hand. "We've only got a few more blocks to go. You can do it. Come on."

"It better be only a few more blocks," I grumbled, trying to ignore a persistent stitch in my side. "We're so far on the West Side now that we might as well be in New Jersey."

"The West Side is where all the television studios are," my husband, the Manhattan expert, informed me as he hurried us along, making me feel like a hick from the sticks. "And at least the sidewalks aren't icy." He glanced at my choice of footwear. "Those shoes are killer, though," he said. "In a good way."

"Well, they're sure killing me," I said. "And I don't understand the red soles, either. I feel like I've stepped in something. Ketchup, maybe. Or something even worse."

We continued on West 69th Street and sprinted across 11th Avenue when there was a small break in the traffic. Well, Jim sprinted. I merely hobbled, hanging onto his arm for dear life.

"Doesn't anybody wait for the 'walk' light in New York?" I asked, once we'd found safe landing on the opposite side of the street.

"Only the out-of-towners," Jim informed me. He checked his phone. "Charles King Productions is on the next block, according to Mack. He's going to meet us there."

"I hope one of Charles King's productions is a place to sit down," I said. "Or, better yet, lie down. After this walk, I'm pooped."

"Funny, Carol," Jim said, stopping in front of a non-descript brownstone building with "C.K.P." etched on the door. "I think this is it."

I leaned against a friendly light pole and massaged the stitch in my side, not easy to reach when you're wearing a faux fur winter coat. Jim, meanwhile, was searching for a buzzer or doorbell or intercom to announce our arrival.

"Charles King isn't very welcoming," I said. "Are you sure this is the right place? And where's Mack?" Jim ignored me. Something he often does when he suspects that I'm right.

And then we heard a disembodied voice. "Welcome to Charles King Productions. Please enter the access code, then wait for the green light."

"We don't have an access code," Jim yelled in the direction of the doorknob. "My name's Jim Andrews. I'm from Gibson Gillespie Public Relations."

I tugged at Jim's sleeve. "*We're* from Gibson Gillespie," I reminded my husband."

Jim glared at me, then continued, "Carol Andrews and I have a meeting here with Mack Whitman and the production staff of *The Second Honeymoon Game.*"

Magically, the front door clicked open, and we stepped into a richly appointed vestibule. Normally, I take a lot of time checking out my surroundings so I can report back to Nancy and the gang, but not this time. All I cared about was that the place was warm and had plenty of chairs. I plopped myself down in the nearest one. Ah, heaven. "Stay put, Carol," Jim said. "I'm going to find out where the meeting's supposed to be."

I nodded and hugged my coat around me. I was exhausted. I checked myself out in my mirror; I looked as bad as I felt. Worse, even. Maybe I had time for a quick power nap before the meeting. I leaned back, rested my head against the chair, and closed my eyes. But not for long.

In a flash, Jim was back, accompanied by a tall, silver-haired man with movie star looks. Not exactly Swoon City, but close enough. And he exuded power from every pore, which is a potent aphrodisiac, or so Nancy claims.

Rats. I hadn't taken the time to freshen my makeup or comb my hair.

"Carol," Jim said, "this is Charles King. Mack had an emergency with another client, so we're starting the meeting without him." *So watch what you say*, Jim telegraphed to me. *Be professional. No wise cracks.*

I struggled to my feet and held out my hand. "I'm so happy to meet you, Mr. King."

Charles King had the strangest expression on his face. Then he took both my hands and squeezed them tight. "No need to introduce yourself, Carol. I'd know you anywhere."

Huh?

King smiled broadly. "You don't recognize me, do you, Carol?" He paused for a millisecond and, ignoring Jim completely, said, "May I have this dance, Carol? I'm a little taller than the last time I asked you that."

The light bulb went off in my brain. "Chuckie? Chuckie Krumpelbeck? Is that you?"

Charles King flashed a thousand watt smile and crushed me, coat and all, into a bear hug, while Jim looked on, perplexed and slightly miffed to be immediately upstaged in this Very Important, Professional Meeting, by his lowly assistant (a.k.a., his lovely wife).

Chapter 11

Hair today, gone tomorrow.

"My gosh, Chuckie, you certainly have changed since grammar school," I said, releasing myself from his grasp with some difficulty. Then I realized how stupid that sounded. It had been a long time (and don't bother asking me *exactly* how long because I'm not going to tell you) since we'd seen each other. Of course he'd changed.

"You haven't changed at all, Carol," Charles King said, gazing at me with such fondness that I wanted to melt into a warm puddle right there on the floor. "I'd know you anywhere. You're just as pretty now as you were then. And you're the only person in the world I'd allow to call me Chuckie."

King turned to Jim. "I hope you know how lucky you are, to land a prize like Carol for your wife."

Poor Jim. This business meeting wasn't going at all the way he'd expected. Or planned. Or hoped for. I, of course, was in my glory. But wifely duties came first. I'd preen and brag later, when I shared the story with Nancy, Mary Alice and Claire. Especially Claire.

"I'm the lucky one," I said, taking my husband's hand. "Jim and I have been married for over thirty years, and we have two great children, Jenny and Mike. We're still in Fairport, too, in a beautiful antique house on Old Fairport Turnpike."

Jim found his voice at last. "This is certainly a surprise," he said. Well, it wasn't brilliant, but I was glad he figured out something to say.

King reached out his hand to Jim. "It's a pleasure to meet you, Jim. I'm looking forward to working with you…" he turned and locked eyes with me…"both of you on this television show for Boomers. I've heard great things about your work from Mack Whitman, Jim. In fact, you're the main reason why our company decided to sign with Gibson Gillespie. You have an impressive track record, and I'm delighted that Mack was able to entice you to come out of retirement to handle our account."

King smiled. "I didn't want some young kid working on promoting *The Second Honeymoon Game.* I told Whitman that, if he wanted our business, he had to hire a grown-up. Someone who really understand the boomer market." He clapped Jim on the back. "And you're absolutely the right man for the job. I can tell right away we're going to have a great working partnership."

How King would tell that so quickly was a mystery to me, since Jim had only spoken five words so far, but what the heck. Points to him for being such a quick judge of good character.

"I'm looking forward to the challenge, Mr. King," Jim said.

"Not Mr. King, please. And," with a quick glance at me, "definitely not Chuckie Krumpelbeck. I left him behind years ago. I'm Charlie now, at least to my friends and business associates. Speaking of which," King gave his Rolex a quick glance, "I think it's time you both met the other key members of our team. They're waiting to start the meeting in Studio A. Follow me."

We trudged behind King down a long hallway decorated with photos of television shows I figured his company had produced over the years. I'll admit this to you, but no one else—I never heard of any of them. I'm more of a PBS kind of person than a reality or game show fan. Except for *Jeopardy!* and *Say Yes to the Dress,* of course. I never miss those shows if I can help it. Oh, and *Dancing with the Stars.* I love that one. I have a favorite fantasy where I get to compete on that show and bring home the Mirror Ball Trophy. Much to the surprise of my family and friends.

I took a quick detour to the women's room—it had been a long train ride and I'm only human, after all. So by the time I got to Studio A, all the seats around the square conference table in the center of the room were taken, except for the one to Charlie's immediate right. I was quick to note that Jim was at the opposite end of the table.

I tried to act nonchalant, but inside, I was screaming, "I'm actually inside an honest-to-goodness television studio!" I was dying to ask someone to take a picture of me beside one of the cameras that I spotted lined up at the rear of the studio, but I figured that'd mark me as an amateur right away. (Although I was more than ready for my close-up.)

Charlie immediately rose and gestured for me to take the seat next to him. I couldn't help but notice that my chair had seen better days, as had the conference room table. Truth to tell, the furniture in the room looked like it had been purchased from a low-end thrift shop. Not that I was being critical, understand. No siree. I figured Charlie saved the big bucks to spend on his shows. He always was good in arithmetic when we were in school.

"Everyone, this is Carol Andrews, also from Gibson Gillespie Public Relations," Charlie said. "She and Jim will be working as a team on *The Second Honeymoon Game*." He flashed me a thousand watt smile. "Carol and I go way back, and I can't tell you how delighted I am that she's here."

I wasn't sure how to respond to my sudden role in the spotlight. A royal wave? A smile? A humble look? No, that last one would be too tough for me to carry out.

I noticed that Jim was shifting in his chair, a sure sign that he was uncomfortable. And shooting me a look that reminded me to "Be Professional." So I settled for a brief smile at my subjects. I mean, the members of the production team.

"Now, people, we can all get acquainted after this meeting," Charlie said, effectively putting a stop to my woolgathering. "For now, let's get down to the business of putting together this television show. Please introduce yourselves to Carol and Jim so they'll know what your role is." He flicked his eyes to a young brunette woman, seated directly across the conference table. "Carol Ann, why don't you begin?"

"I prefer to be called Carrie," she said, locking eyes with him. "As you very well know."

Jeez. This girl, whoever she was, was looking to get fired. Nobody should talk to a boss like that.

Charlie, to his credit, ignored her rudeness. "Of course," he said. "You're absolutely right. Old habits die hard." He laughed. "A little Catholic school humor for my old friend, Carol."

Carrie cleared her throat and sat up straight in her chair. "I'm the assistant producer for *The Second Honeymoon Game*," she said.

"I guess you could say that I go back a long way with Charlie King, too. I'm his daughter. And if you're the Carol I think you are, I was named after you." She flashed me a huge smile. "I can't tell you how thrilled I am to meet you after all these years."

Chapter 12

My best ideas seem to come when I have no clue what I'm talking about.

Wow. I mean, WOW! Talk about a shock. It was like being told I had another child, and Jim wasn't the father. I was at a loss for words, something that doesn't happen to me very often. Like, never. I searched my memory for an appropriate comeback and came up empty. I was sure my face was beet red.

"My goodness," I said. Well, it was lame, but I had to say something.

Uncomfortable silence followed.

"Did I miss anything?" Mack said, breezing into the studio and searching for a place to sit. "Sorry I'm late, people, but another client had a crisis and just had to talk to the big boss at the agency. No one else would do."

Talk about great timing. The atmosphere in Studio A changed immediately as everyone (except Charlie King) shifted positions to allow for an additional chair, which had magically appeared at the opposite end of the table, next to Jim.

I could tell that Charlie wasn't pleased that Mack was late. As for me, I wanted to throw my arms around Mack's neck and whisper my thanks into his ear. Don't worry. I restrained myself.

Instead, I jumped up and gestured for Mack to take my place at Charlie's side, then scurried to the safety of the other end of the table and plopped myself down beside the comforting presence of my husband. I reached under the table and gave his knee a reassuring pat. (At least, I thought/hoped it was Jim's knee and not one belonging to a complete stranger.)

Carrie cleared her throat. "Yes, well, as I was saying just before you arrived, Mack, I'm the assistant producer for this show. That means I do all the nuts and bolts work that putting together a game show like this requires. And other duties as assigned. I'm looking forward to working with everyone. I'm sure we're going to have a great time and produce a great show." She sat back in her chair and looked at her father. "Right?"

Charlie nodded his head. "Absolutely right. This one's going to be a ratings blockbuster with all those Boomers as a potential audience."

"Perhaps it would be a good idea," Mack said, opening his laptop and powering it up, "since Jim and Carol are new to the team, to give a little background information on the who, what and why of our audience. In fact," with a nod to the other people at the table, none of whom had spoken yet, "it might be beneficial to everyone here. I've put together a knock-your-socks-off presentation for us to eyeball."

I confess that I zoned out of Mack's presentation, even though it was punctuated by flashing lights, loud music, and short clips of impossibly happy people enjoying themselves in a variety of activities that made me tired. I already knew how many Boomers there were in the United States (78.2 million, in case you were wondering), what their average household income was (way more than Jim's and mine), and what percentage of the buying market they were (the 55+ age group currently controls more than ¾ of America's wealth). I had other things on my mind.

"An American turns fifty every seven seconds," Mack intoned, "and by the end of this year, adults aged fifty and over will represent forty-five percent of the U.S. population according to AARP. And Baby Boomer women spend $21 billion annually on clothing."

I snapped to attention with that statistic. I guess a lot of Boomer women don't shop in consignment and thrift shops, the way I do. I gave Jim a sideways glance, but he had his poker face on and didn't acknowledge me.

King turned to an as yet unidentified person, and said, "Make a note that we need to go after a women's clothing line for show sponsorship. Maybe Chico's. It's the right demographic."

Mack opened his mouth to continue his presentation, but King ignored him. "We all know who our market is, and why we're targeting them," he said, effectively bringing Mack's presentation to a grinding halt and taking back control of the meeting. "As a matter of fact, our research shows that Boomers will control 70% of U.S. disposable income by 2017. That equals $3.4 trillion in buying power."

Note to self: Take extra good care of yourself to be sure you reach 2017. It would be a shame to miss that spending opportunity.

"We've prepared a brief presentation about the show itself for you," King said, looking directly at Jim and me. "Perhaps now would be a good time to show it."

Carrie jumped to her feet and positioned herself behind her father. "I'll take this part," she said. "After all, I put the presentation together in the first place. Although it's pretty sketchy right now. I hope you can help fill in the blanks soon, Carol, since you're typical of our target audience. Jim, too, of course."

Of course. Piece of cake. Especially since I had absolutely no idea what we were talking about.

In a flash she'd cued up a presentation titled "TV Show Treatment: *The Second Honeymoon Game.*" I was so fascinated to find out how a show is put together that I actually put my glasses on.

"Title," Carrie said. "Well, we all know why we came up with the name. We're aiming at the Boomer market, and most of them who are in committed relationships have already had a first honeymoon. Moving on."

Click.

"Logline. This is a one or more sentence description of the show to sell sponsors and possible additional producers on the idea. Of course, we won't have any additional producers," she added, throwing a glance at her father.

I heard someone whisper, "What a lame presentation."

Carrie flushed. I felt sorry for her. So, of course, I spoke up. "I think this is so interesting," I said, giving Carrie an encouraging smile.

"The logline is one of the things we'll count on Gibson Gillespie to put together for us," King said. Mack started to speak, but King steamrolled forward. "It takes Boomers to know how to appeal to Boomers," he said, again looking directly at Jim and me. "That's why I wanted you two on board. We need a logline that's short and punchy, that will attract sponsors."

Short and punchy, that's me. Or, maybe short and paunchy.

"We'll film the pilot episode in Florida," Carrie said. "But now we're putting together a short promo video about the show to attract sponsors. In fact," Carrie checked her Smartphone, "we have two of the actors waiting in Studio B right now to shoot some preliminary footage."

Actors? Why not use real people who are also Boomers? I made a note to ask that question if time permitted. And I remembered it.

Click.

"Synopsis," Carrie continued. "Proposed Contestants and Host."

"I'll jump in here," said a man who looked like he was barely old enough to shave. "I'm Kurt Armitage," with a nod to Jim and me, "and I'll be handling the talent portion of the show. In fact," with a nod to King, "I also handled the talent for CKP's last reality show, *Gold Coast Confidential*. I'm sure you saw it, right?"

I started to answer, but Jim beat me to it. "I'm afraid Carol and I aren't fans of reality shows," he said. Of course, I am, but I didn't dare correct Jim in front of everyone else. Especially my grammar school classmate.

"Well, you don't know what you're missing," Kurt said. "It was a great show. In fact, there was some talk of making *The Second Honeymoon Game* a reality show. But we discarded that idea."

"You mean like *Jersey Shore*, except for geriatrics?" I quipped. I couldn't help myself. Jim gave my knee a warning squeeze and I shut up.

Charlie, however, laughed at my feeble joke and, pretty soon, everyone else was laughing, too. "You always did have a good sense of humor, Carol," he said. "And a tart tongue."

"You mean a big mouth, don't you?" I said, smiling back at him.

Well, now that I had the floor (sort of) and the implied blessing of the Big Boss to speak my mind, I had a few questions to ask. "I may not know much about putting together a television show," I said, looking directly at Charlie, "but I wonder why actors are being used for the promo instead of real people? Not that actors aren't real people. But you know what I mean, don't you?"

Kurt bristled at my intrusion into his territory. "Real people, as you call them, Carol, just can't be depended upon to do the job for this promo," he said. "Professional actors will learn their lines so they can play the game and deliver the performance we're looking for. Kim and Tim already know the questions they'll be asked, and they have their answers down pat. They're in makeup now, to make them look like they're really Baby Boomers." He shook his head at my obvious lack of knowledge. "Using amateurs for a promo. What a ridiculous idea."

"They're in makeup?" I repeated. "You mean, to age them? How old are Tim and Kim, anyway?"

Notice that I didn't make a crack about the actors' similar first names. I hope I get points for that, because it took a lot of self-control on my part. Jim gave my knee another warning squeeze. This one was a little stronger.

"Tim's twenty-eight and Kim's thirty-one," Kurt responded, shifting a little in his chair. "What's your point?"

Now that really frosted my cupcakes. Hiring young people and making them look like they were in a more...mature...age bracket was just plain wrong.

I cleared my throat. By this time, Jim was gripping my knee so hard that I was beginning to lose feeling in it. But I plowed ahead, anyway. I had a point to make. A very important point, on behalf of the millions of people over fifty who weren't at the meeting to speak up for themselves. And, by golly, I was going to make it.

Chapter 13

I'm not disagreeing with you. I'm just saying
that you're wrong.

"My point, Kurt," I said, choosing my words with care, "is that, when people reach a certain age, they become invisible to the younger generation. Furthermore, that generation also assumes most people over fifty no longer have anything worthwhile to contribute to the world.

"Fortunately, Charlie," I continued, with a nod to my grammar school classmate, "being of the Boomer generation himself, realizes how unfair that is. Please, let's not perpetuate that stereotype on the show. It sends entirely the wrong message. And if you don't think the audience and potential sponsors will figure out what's going on, you're mistaken. We're a very smart bunch of folks." I took a deep breath. My Joan of Arc speech was done.

Charlie leaned back in his chair and looked pensive. Finally, he said, "Using real Boomers for a promo video may not be such a ridiculous idea. It certainly is unusual, though. And we'd be going out on a limb to use non-professionals." He gave me a piercing stare that I bet brought his employees to their knees. "Convince me, Carol. If you can."

Sometimes my greatest accomplishment is keeping my mouth shut. But this was not one of those times. Especially since I figured that Charlie was already on my side. And he was the boss, after all. All he had to say was that the show's promo video would use real

Boomers and that would be that.

But for some unknown reason Charlie wanted me to convince the rest of the folks. Go figure. Maybe he wanted to see if I still was the champion debater I was back in grammar school.

"Well…" I began. *Brilliant, Carol. Just brilliant.*

I looked around at the other five people at the table, all of whom knew far more about public relations, marketing, and television production than I did. In their eyes, I was just a suburban wife and mother with a flair for writing and an extra big mouth.

Mack looked like he was about to have a coronary. And as for Jim, well…I didn't have to look at him to know the expression on his face. I'd seen it many times before, when I "acted up," as he so quaintly put it. It was a cross between apoplexy and disbelief.

I started again. "I'm sure it's difficult for some of you to identify with, but as I said before, being in the over-fifty category can be a mixed blessing. Our life expectancy is much longer than our parents', but what do we do with all the extra years we've been given? Many of the younger generation think that we are no longer useful. And, dare I say it, unemployable. That we have nothing more to contribute, but instead should sit at home, rocking on the front porch and waiting for the grandchildren to arrive."

I took a deep breath. That part about waiting for the grandchildren was a particularly sore spot with me, but I wasn't about to air my personal gripes with this crowd.

"This television show is an opportunity to show the world how important and intelligent the Boomer generation is. I suggest using real Boomers, not just for the promo but for the show itself, and give them the chance to show what they've accomplished in their lives."

"We were always going to use real Boomers on the show," Kurt interrupted. "We just hired the actors for the promo."

"And we've signed a contract with Gene Richmond to be the show's host," Carrie added. "He's definitely in the right age category." She looked at me. "You know who he is, right?"

"Of course I do," I said. "I loved him when he hosted *Funtastic Trivia.* That was an intelligent game show. Too bad it was cancelled so quickly."

Charlie beamed at me. "We produced that show, Carol. Unfortunately, it only lasted one season. Everyone thought we were only doing another version of *Jeopardy!,* and the show never really found an audience. We're going to do a lot better with *The*

Second Honeymoon Game."

"Well, I can tell you that Jim and I watched every episode of *Funtastic Trivia*," I said, with a quick glance at my husband who nodded in agreement, for once.

"In fact," Jim added with a grin, "if I caught a late train to Connecticut and ended up arriving home in the middle of the show, Carol made me wait for my dinner until it was over."

Everyone had a good laugh about that, even me.

"And I bet that she's thrilled about the chance to meet Gene Richmond at last," Jim added. "Aren't you, Carol? I always thought you had a little crush on him."

I blushed. Busted! Truth to tell, I had more than a little crush on the television game host back in the Eighties. Not that I ever actually wrote him a fan letter or anything, mind you. I just admired him from afar. And, every now and then, allowed an innocent fantasy or two to bubble up in my mind.

A man who, up to now, had remained so quiet that I hadn't even noticed him, stood and took a mock bow. "It's always nice to meet a fan," he said to me.

"A fan?" I repeated, not quite getting his meaning.

"Why, yes," he said. "I'm Gene Richmond." He twinkled at me, then said, "I bet you don't recognize me without my hair." He brushed his hand over his head, which was almost completely bald. "I used to get loads of fan mail asking me who my barber was. It was a closely guarded secret that I was wearing a hairpiece."

For the second time in less than ten minutes, I blushed. One of the things that I'd found most attractive about Gene Richmond back in the day was his lush locks, which always looked perfect. Unlike Jim's locks which, even then, were waging a battle with his forehead. And losing. It never dawned on me that Richmond was wearing a wig. Excuse me, a hairpiece.

"I'm looking forward to working with you, Carol," Gene said. "Jim, too, of course."

"Yes, well, moving along," Carrie said, "let's get back to the presentation, okay?"

I was still trying to process the fact that I had met the object of one of my long-time crushes. This day was turning out to be filled with more surprises than Christmas.

"One of the secrets of a successful game show is identifying unique contestants or lifestyles," Carrie said in a loud voice, sensing that she was losing her audience. "That could be an opportunity to publicize what each of the Boomer contestants have so far accomplished in their lives. As Carol has suggested," with a nod to me.

"And what they hope to accomplish in the future," Kurt threw in, finally getting into the proposed spirit of the show. "I like it."

"I have another question," I said, snapping back from fantasyland and ignoring the all-too-familiar groan emanating from the direction of my husband. "How are the contestants going to be chosen?"

"I was getting to that part in my presentation," Carrie said, now clearly annoyed. "We're going to have online auditions for potential contestants, with a registration form, and ask them to submit a short video about themselves. That way, we can see how articulate they are, and how they'd look on camera."

I nodded. "That sounds like a great idea."

"I'm relieved that you approve, Carol," Kurt said with just a touch of sarcasm, which I chose to ignore. I hope you're all proud of me."

"But what's the criteria for applying to be a contestant?" I asked. "Have you set one?" I know, at this point I should have zipped my lip. But I couldn't seem to stop myself.

"Well, of course, they have to be the right demographic," Kurt said, clearly uncomfortable. "What more do you want? We're looking for variety here, not cookie cutter contestants."

"Well, if the show is going to be called *The Second Honeymoon Game*, I would think that the ideal contestants would be married or be in a long-time committed relationship. Doesn't that make sense?" I asked, with a quick glance at Charlie.

"Why don't we just re-name it *The Carol Andrews Show* and be done with it?" I heard someone mutter. Kurt? Or, horrors, Mack?

Oops. Better be careful, Carol. You don't want to lose this job. Mack's your boss on this project. And, more important, he's Jim's boss.

"I know I'm asking too many questions," I said. "It's one of my worst faults. Jim adds that to my 'Honey Don't' list every week."

" 'Honey Don't' list?" Charlie repeated. "I've never heard of that. I know what a 'Honey Do' list is, of course."

Jim rushed in to explain, upstaging me before I could open my mouth again. "Carol and I have been married for more than thirty-five years," he said. I couldn't tell from his tone of voice if he was bragging about the longevity of our marriage or nominating himself for a medal for putting up with me for so long.

"That's longer than I've been on this earth!" Kurt exclaimed.

"Exactly my point," I said, not wanting Jim to completely take over the floor from me.

"One of Carol's most annoying traits," Jim said, glaring at me, "is that she interrupts. All. The. Time. Just like she's doing right now."

Humph.

"We came up with the idea of the 'Honey Don't' list few years ago," Jim continued. "It's a pretty simple concept. We make a list of the personality traits the other person has that really get on our nerves."

"The list of my own faults is very short," I put in. Well, you didn't think I was just going to sit back and let Jim talk, did you? And the 'Honey Don't' list was entirely my idea, but in the interests of long-time family harmony and wedded bliss, I didn't correct him... on that point.

"It's funny how some of the traits that attract one person to another in the beginning of a relationship can start to grate on a person after a while," I said. "Even my own."

"Carrie's mother and I never had the chance to have that happen to us," Charlie said with a glance at his daughter. "Hope and I were only married two years before she died."

"I had no idea," I said. "I'm so sorry." Poor Charlie. He looked so vulnerable and sad.

"Maybe we should take a break," Carrie suggested, realizing her father was getting too emotional. "Kurt, those actors are still waiting in Studio B. What should we do about them?"

"Dismiss them," Charlie said, snapping back into professional mode. "We're going in a whole new direction, thanks to Carol's input." He flashed me a big grin.

"We have to pay them, anyway," Kurt objected. "Since they're here already, why don't we shoot the scene as originally planned and then we'll have it in case things don't work out with Carol's idea? Which will probably happen, since she has absolutely no experience putting together a television show. No offense, Carol."

"None taken, Kurt," I lied.

"I said to dismiss the actors, Kurt," Charlie said. "What part of that sentence don't you understand? Pay them for one day's work, so we don't have any trouble with the actors' union, and dismiss them. Is that crystal clear?"

Kurt flushed. He obviously didn't like being told what to do by his boss in public. Not that I blamed him. Then, he nodded. Well, what else could the poor guy do?

I immediately felt guilty, because my big mouth was the cause of Kurt's embarrassment. And he was right. I had absolutely no experience putting together a television show.

Sometimes, I'm much too opinionated.

Okay, often I'm much too opinionated.

"Carol may have no television experience," Charlie said, "but she has years of life experiences to draw on. And, let me emphasize, she's a perfect example of the demographic we're targeting for our audience. So her opinion counts. I hope everyone here understands that." He looked around the table, daring anyone to disagree. Of course, nobody did.

Much later, it dawned on me that I had met a powerful enemy at that meeting. But I was too stupid, and too vain, to realize it in time to save an innocent person's life.

Chapter 14

A recent study has found that women who carry a little extra weight live longer than the men who mention it.

"Well, this day has certainly been full of surprises," I said to Jim, who was doing his best to ignore me.

Oh, dear. Jim was pouting. Not good. But it wasn't my fault that the producer of *The Second Honeymoon Game* turned out to be my grammar school classmate. No, not just a classmate. The former Chuckie Krumpelbeck, now Charlie King, had been my regular partner during all those after-school dancing lessons we were required to take in eighth grade. Way back when, I figured he always asked me to dance because I was the only girl in class who was shorter than he was. But today, I found out that wasn't the reason at all. Well, not the entire reason, anyway.

Charlie apparently had a major crush on me. A crush he'd never got over. So much so that he and his late wife named their daughter after me. And I had no idea. Go figure.

I pondered how strange life can be all the way back to Fairport, the return journey made much more pleasant because, instead of riding on a crowded train with the hordes of commuters who regularly toil in the Big Apple, Jim and I were sent home in style in Charlie's chauffeured limousine. Hey, not my idea, but when the offer was made, it would have been rude to refuse, right?

Jim maintained a stony silence throughout the entire ride, even when we got stuck in traffic on the Merritt Parkway and sat for half an hour because a truck driver, ignoring the "No Trucks Allowed" sign, had driven onto the highway and gotten stuck under one of the overpasses. Normally, my husband would have come up with several alternate route suggestions for our driver, as he hates sitting in traffic. But not this time. Nada. Zip. Zilch.

Instead, Jim concentrated on sending and receiving a constant series of texts until the *ping* noise started to drive me crazy. Part of me really wanted to know what the texts were about. But another part of me was scared silly that they were from Mack, and he and Jim were plotting a damage control strategy after my poor performance at the television production meeting.

I knew that I had some major bridge repair work of my own to do when we got home. Although, of course, I was absolutely dying to get on the phone ASAP to Nancy, Mary Alice, and Claire, and fill them all in on what had happened to me today. I knew they'd remember Chuckie from our grammar school days. And I was still wearing Nancy's expensive shoes, which now were pinching my tootsies like crazy. I figured the pain must be a tradeoff for fashion, but I couldn't wait to reward my feet for brave behavior by easing them into a pair of well-loved bedroom slippers.

When the limo had finally cruised to a stop in front of our house, I was hoping that Phyllis Stevens would just happen to be glancing out her front window and catch a glimpse of our mode of transportation. I knew that Phyllis thought of that window as her own private viewing area on the comings, goings, and everything in between of everyone on our block. And didn't hesitate to blast news bulletins around the neighborhood whenever she felt the urge. But today—wouldn't you just know it?—she wasn't at her usual post. Darn it.

I wanted to have the driver, whose name was Nick, take a picture of Jim and me exiting the limo, but when I started to suggest it, Jim silenced me with a look. Oh, boy.

Once inside the privacy of our own home, after Lucy and Ethel had been tended to, Jim headed toward the home office, still without uttering a word. I stood stock still in the middle of the kitchen and ran through a list of possible response options. I finally decided that none of this was my fault, and if he wanted to behave like an infant, that was his privilege.

Meanwhile, I would behave in my most adult manner and,

instead of slamming pots and pans around the kitchen—which was what I really felt like doing—I would prepare a meal from whatever I could find in the refrigerator. I do like to give Lucy and Ethel examples of proper behavior whenever possible, so that if they're faced with difficult situations on their walks around Fairport—that German Shepard, Jake, who lives around the corner from us, always gave them a little trouble—they'd know how to act appropriately.

Fortunately, I found small containers of chili hidden in the dark recesses of the freezer. Jim always believes chili tastes better as leftovers. I was about to test that theory, because only the Good Lord Himself knew how long ago the chili had been originally made. I scraped off any excess freezer burn and defrosted our dinner in the microwave.

By the way, I have a little trick about leftovers that I figured out years ago. Like most husbands, Jim can't stand seeing anything go to waste. Especially food. So if there's a helping (or two) left in the pot, or on the serving platter, he feels obligated to finish it. Waste not, want not.

What's my trick? Why, I just portion out what I think is a fair amount for one meal for two adults who should be watching their caloric intake, and put the rest in another pot that I hide way back in the refrigerator behind my diet cranberry juice so Jim won't see it. Presto—instant leftovers for another meal. Works every time! And if I've made Jim's all-time favorite meal, meatballs and tomato sauce, I portion out part of what I've hidden and freeze it when the coast is clear. It may not be an idea original to me, but give me a break and let me think it is, okay?

Jim wandered back into the kitchen while I was heating the chili in the microwave. He had a big grin on his face. "Lucia Pellogrini," Jim announced. "That was her name." He sighed. "We used to call her Luscious Lucia," he said. "She sure was something."

"I don't recognize the name," I said, waving off Lucy and Ethel who were now circling around me with plaintive "feed me" looks on their faces. "But she's put you in a much better mood, so I'll bite. Who's Lucia Pellogrini?"

The microwave dinged, and I handed Jim a pair of oven mitts. "Wear these so you don't burn your hands. The dish will be extra hot."

Jim waved me off exactly like I'd waved off the dogs. "I don't need them, Carol. Why do you make such a big deal out of everything?"

Go ahead and burn your hands. See if I care. I didn't really say that out loud, of course.

"So, who's Lucia Pellogrini?" I repeated, handing Jim a box of red wine to open.

Jim got a dreamy look on his face. "She was our grammar school class sex symbol," he said. "Not that we ever actually called her that. But all the guys in my class had super crushes on her. Including me. She was an…early developer, if you get my meaning." He sighed. "I wonder what she looks like now. I bet she's still a hot number." The man was practically drooling, lost in his overactive fantasy world.

Honest to goodness, the only major difference between a boy and a man is that a man is usually taller. Other than that, they are exactly the same. So childish.

"Why don't you google her and find out?" I suggested like the good sport I was on rare occasions, sliding into my chair at the kitchen table and preparing to take my first forkful of food. It suddenly dawned on me that we had completely missed lunch today. No wonder Jim was crabby on the way home. He was probably starving.

"What, and ruin the fantasy?" Jim asked. "No way. If she's gotten fat and matronly, I don't want to know about it. In my mind, she's still my grammar school hottie. Which, of course, brings us back to your grammar school boyfriend. And what happened at the meeting today."

I started to respond, even though my brain hadn't come up with any sort of strategy yet, but my phone pinged, indicating an incoming text. "I'm sorry, Jim," I said. "I know we agreed to turn off our phones while we're having dinner, but I forgot. Besides, it might be important."

Jim didn't answer me. I gathered from the faraway look on his face that he was back in grammar school again, perhaps passing a love note to Luscious Lucia.

Of course, the text was from Nancy.

Nancy: *How r my shoes? Can u still walk?*
Me: *Huge news. 2 much to text. Coffee 2morrow morning at 9.*
Nancy: *Okay. Fairport Diner. Bring shoes.*
Me: *Okay! M.A., C 2. U text them.*
Nancy: *C and L left 4 FL 2day. Will text M.A. C u 2morrow at 9.*
Me: *Okay.*

Darn it. I'd completely forgotten that Claire and Larry had

started their southern trek. They were probably already on the auto train. I wondered if I could still text Claire. I still didn't understand how the various cyber connections worked, and I was dying to tell her about my adventure in Manhattan today. And how I was morphing into a key player for a major television show, thanks to someone we went to grammar school with.

Oh, all right. I was dying to brag about it to her. So, sue me. Sometimes I think I haven't progressed much beyond childish behavior, myself. I toyed with my chili, imagining the look of surprise—and envy—on her face. And smiled. For once, I'd have the last word with her. I could hardly wait.

Under normal circumstances, once I'd cleaned up the kitchen and given Lucy and Ethel their last stroll of the evening, I'd hop on the computer and catch up on all those important emails I knew were begging to be answered. And, just for the heck of it, I'd probably do some googling about Charlie King, too. After all, if I was going to be working with the guy, it would behoove me to find out how he morphed from a little squirt of a kid into a corporate mogul and television producer. That would mean finding out all I could about his family—including his late wife.

But tonight I was too beat to stay up past 9:00, no matter how much the computer beckoned me. Plus, my feet were killing me from wearing Nancy's admittedly gorgeous but way-too-tight (there, I finally admitted it) shoes all day. I know you're all thinking I should have changed back into my sneakers for the ride home, but I wanted to impress the limo driver. Soaking my weary bones in a steaming hot tub held much more appeal for me than cruising down the Internet superhighway, even if I could do it while sitting down.

And, truthfully, I knew I had some repair work to do in the marriage department, which took precedence over everything else. Sometimes, a good meal just doesn't do it. I'm sure you know what I'm talking about. And I'm not going to tell you any more about that. Except to say that Jim not only made the coffee the following morning, but he also served me breakfast in bed. With a big smile on his face.

Chapter 15

The best thing about having friends the exact same age is that they remember the same things you do. Unfortunately, they forget the same things you do, too.

"Why are we meeting here?" I asked, sliding into a booth at the Fairport Diner next to Mary Alice. "What happened to the Paperback Café? That's been our favorite coffee hangout for years."

"Gone," Nancy announced with a wave of her hand. "Out of business." She pursed her lips. "Really, Carol, you need to keep up with what's happening in town."

"Gone?" I repeated. "How could it be gone? I just walked by it two days ago."

"I don't mean the building is gone," Nancy clarified. "It's still there. But it's been sold. Nobody's sure what's going to happen to it. Meanwhile," she gestured around the Fairport Diner, "I thought this would be a perfect place for us to meet for coffee this morning and catch up. Can either of you guess why?"

"Neither of us is privy to your insider real estate news," Mary Alice said with a rare trace of annoyance. It didn't take a major leap of intuition to figure out that she had worked the night shift at the hospital and wanted nothing more than to go home and climb into bed. Especially since she insisted on decaf coffee. Mary Alice doesn't drink a lot of coffee—she's usually a tea kind of person—but when she does, it's always high-test.

"I guess you pulled an all-nighter last night, Mary Alice," I said. "I thought that when you retired, you didn't have to do that anymore. Oh, thank you." This last comment was directed toward a server who placed cups of steaming hot coffee in front of us.

Nancy waved away the menus he offered. "We'll just have coffee." As an afterthought, she added, "Thank you."

"Honestly, Nancy," Mary Alice said, "where are your manners? You practically bit that poor guy's head off."

"Sorry," Nancy said. "I've got a really full day today. And Her Nibs here," gesturing across the table at me, "seems to have something vitally important to tell us. The reason I suggested meeting here, Carol," she said, "was because I thought you'd love the location. And the other customers. Don't you get it?"

I looked at my BFF for a hint, and got none. "I give up, Nancy. Why? What?"

Nancy gestured around the diner. "Look at the other customers, doofus. They're mostly on the Fairport police force. I figured you might be able to pick up some good gossip here, in case you want to eavesdrop." She laughed, and I couldn't help it; I laughed, too. But first, I swatted her across the table. Just because I could. And because she knew me far too well.

"This is all very interesting," Mary Alice said, her tone conveying the opposite. "But why are we here at all? I mean, why are we getting together for coffee?" She yawned, then covered her mouth. "I'm sorry. Can't help it. I'm exhausted. I want to go home and go to bed."

"Then I'll make this quick," I said. "Chuckie Krumpelbeck. Ring any bells?"

Nancy furrowed her brow in concentration. Then, when she realized what she was doing, immediately relaxed her face. Of all of us, she's the most concerned with keeping herself as young-looking as possible for as long as possible, no matter what it takes.

"I remember him," Mary Alice said. "We went to grammar school with him. Wasn't he the shortest boy in our class? And I think he had terrible acne, too." She blushed. "Not that I mean to criticize him. We all had complexion issues in those days."

"Mary Alice," I said, "you've never said a critical thing about a single person in your whole life. At least, not something that wasn't true. And you're right. Chuckie did have bad skin. But just wait till

I tell you…"

"That's right," Nancy interrupted. "He was a real loser. And if I'm remembering correctly," she said, zeroing in on me from across the table, "you always got stuck dancing with him at those horrible classes we had to take after school in eighth grade."

I took a sip of my coffee. "Well, guess what? I saw him yesterday. Actually," I clarified, "Jim and I had a meeting with him in New York. That's where I wore the shoes you lent me, Nancy," I said, handing her back the Coach bag. "Here they are, safe and sound. Thanks for loaning them to me. They were a big hit, although they did pinch my feet."

Nancy took the bag, peeked inside to be sure her precious shoes were still in good shape and, satisfied that I hadn't wrecked them, tucked the bag under the table. I tried to pretend I hadn't noticed her checking the shoes for damage. As if I wouldn't take good care of them. The idea!

"Okay, Carol," Nancy said, "what's up with you? You saw Chuckie? How? Why? Is that the reason why you insisted we get together this morning?"

I took another sip of my coffee and savored it. Slowly. I was enjoying myself, and didn't want to drop my bombshell too quickly. More than anything, I wished that Claire was present to hear what I had to share.

I know. I am a very bad person.

"Well, Chuckie's all grown up," I said.

"Of course he is, Carol," Mary Alice said. "All of us are grown up. Can you get to the point? I'm sorry to be impatient, but I need to go home and get some sleep."

I took pity on my friends. "Believe it or not, Chuckie Krumpelbeck has changed his name and morphed into a hotshot television show producer. He's Charlie King now," I said. "Maybe you've heard of him. He's pretty famous."

Nancy gaped at me. "Chuckie Krumpelbeck is Charlie King? You're kidding. Of course I've heard of him." She gestured around the diner. "I bet everyone in this place has watched at least one of his television shows, even if they wouldn't admit it."

"Why did you and Jim meet him?" Mary Alice asked. "Did Chuckie contact you on Facebook?"

I smiled. "No, that's not how it happened at all. Jim got a call from Mack Whitman, his old boss, about coming out of retirement

to consult on a new television show, *The Second Honeymoon Game.*
And Mack wanted me to be part of the team." I laughed. "Actually,
he insisted," I said, and tried to look modest.

I paused for a beat and hoped the magnitude of what I'd said
registered with Nancy and Mary Alice. "That's why I borrowed your
shoes, Nancy. I didn't want to look like a suburban hick when we
went into the city for the initial meeting. And it turned out that
the executive producer for the show is Chuckie. I mean, Charlie.
So, I guess you could say that I'm in show business!"

"I can tell this is going to be some story," Mary Alice said. "And
I know that sometimes, it takes you a while to get to the point,
Carol. Maybe I should switch from decaf to the real stuff. I don't
want to nod off and miss a word. Even if I can't get to sleep right
away when I get home."

"Well, I don't want to brag," I said, "but I have to say that, once
I got over the shock of seeing Chuckie Krumpelbeck after all these
years...I didn't recognize him at all, by the way, but he knew me
immediately...."

Nancy waved her hand. "And then..."

"He was thrilled to see me," I said. "It was almost embarrassing,
especially in front of Jim."

"Did he ask about me?" Nancy said. "We sat next to each other
in seventh grade. Sometimes I let him copy off my tests."

"Nancy, you cheated on tests? I'm shocked at you," Mary Alice
said.

"Mary Alice, it was more than forty years ago," I said. "I think
the statute of limitations has expired."

"You think you know someone," Mary Alice muttered.

"Anyway," I said, "I met Chuckie's daughter, Carrie, too. She's
a member of the production team." I decided to omit the fact that
she'd been named after me. No sense overwhelming my friends
with too much information at one time.

"Well, this is all very interesting," Nancy said. "And if you're
trying to make us jealous, consider yourself successful. But what
exactly do you mean, you're in show business now? Are you really
going to be helping Jim with this job? Wait a minute. Is Jim going
back to work? Oh, Carol, that's your dream come true!"

"He is going back to work," I said. "At least, for *The Second
Honeymoon Game.* Jim was called back to Gibson Gillespie because
he's the 'right demographic' for the audience the show is aimed

at, according to his boss, Mack Whitman."

"You mean, because Jim's old?" Nancy asked, getting right to the point as usual, even if it hurt.

"Well, if Jim's old, that means the rest of us are, too," Mary Alice pointed out. "Since we're all pretty much the same vintage."

"I am not old!" Nancy said. "As a matter of fact, most people think I'm at least ten years younger than I really am. Just in case you've both forgotten, I was the youngest member of our class." She huffed and took a sip of her coffee.

"So, what about Chuckie?" Mary Alice asked. "How did he become so successful? And why did he change his name?"

"That's an easy one," Nancy said without giving me a chance to respond. "If Chuckie Krumpelbeck was your name, wouldn't you want to change it, too?"

"Charlie King certainly is an improvement," Mary Alice agreed with a smile. "I hate to admit this, but I'm hungry. I may have to order some food to go along with this coffee."

"You know how you always lecture us about how bad it is to eat and then go to bed on a full stomach," I said to my friend the nurse. "You have to make a choice. Eat and stay up for a while longer, or stick to your coffee."

"So what's up with this television show?" Nancy asked, saving Mary Alice from responding. "And what do you mean about being in show business? You never did answer my question."

"We were all in this meeting at Charlie's office in New York," I said.

"Yes, Carol, we already know that," Nancy said and rolled her eyes at Mary Alice. "So...?"

"Well, Charlie kept deferring to me in the meeting. No, that's not true." I colored a little. "I guess I started to ask some questions first about the way the show was going to be designed. It's a game show aimed at and for Baby Boomers, so I figured that all the contestants would be Boomers themselves. Then I found out that Charlie was hiring young actors for the promo video and aging them to look like Boomers."

"That's ridiculous," Nancy said.

"That's exactly what I told Charlie," I said. "The promo video should use real Boomers, not actors. And one thing sort of led to another."

"Jim must have loved that," Nancy said. "He's pulled out of

retirement to be a public relations consultant on a television show, and the first thing he finds out is that the hot shot producer is his wife's grammar school boyfriend. And to top that, he's immediately upstaged by his outspoken wife."

"Jim wasn't happy," I admitted. "In fact, he kept squeezing my knee. I knew he wanted me to shut up. But what was I supposed to do when Charlie kept asking my opinion about everything? Not answer him?"

"What happened with the actors?" Mary Alice asked. "And what do you mean by a promo video?"

"A promo is a short video meant to attract sponsors for a television show," I explained. "They were going to shoot part of it yesterday in the New York studio until I opened my big mouth. I'm not sure exactly what will happen now."

And how much trouble I've caused, particularly to Jim, by voicing my opinion over and over, even when it wasn't asked for. I sure hoped Charlie and his staff weren't mad at me for being so outspoken. Not that I intended to share my concerns with Nancy and Mary Alice right now. I wanted to bask in my friends' admiration (and envy) for a little while longer.

"There's something else I forgot to tell you," I said. "The pilot of *The Second Honeymoon Game* is going to be shot in Florida this winter. And the show's going to use real Boomer couples as contestants."

Nancy's eyes lit up. "Carol, that's great! And I have a perfect Boomer couple for the show. Bob and me."

Chapter 16

If men are from Mars, can we send a few of them back home?

I choked on my coffee. "What? Are you crazy? You and Bob aren't really married anymore. You've been separated for over a year."

"Oh, pish," Nancy said, waving aside my objections with her perfectly manicured fingers. "That's a minor detail. Legally, we're still married. We just don't live together. We still see each other all the time. We're the poster couple for a modern Boomer marriage. Oh, this is going to be such fun. I can't wait to tell Bob, and go shopping for the right clothes for a trip to Florida." She pulled her tablet out of her voluminous Dooney & Bourke purse and started making a list.

"Hold it," I said, gripping her wrist. "There is no way that this is going to happen, Nancy. What are you drinking, anyway? It sure isn't just coffee."

"You can make it happen, Carol," Nancy said, still typing furiously. "I have faith in you. I'm sure Chuckie will remember me from grammar school. And when he hears my idea, he'll jump at it. You'll see. He always admired my creativity."

"He's not Chuckie anymore, Nancy," I said. "He's Charlie now. And you are delusional. What about your so-called 'creativity' did Charlie admire? Helping him cheat on tests?"

"That's not what I meant at all," Nancy shot back. "You're just being selfish. You don't want to share the spotlight with anybody else. You've always been a selfish only child."

Whoa. Them's fighting words. True, I'm an only child. And due to the long ago demise of both my parents, I was doomed to remain that way. But selfish? No way. There is not a selfish bone in my entire body. Maybe a touch of self-centeredness on occasion. But only when completely, totally justified.

Before I had the chance to give in to my urge to slug my BFF—or say something that I'd bitterly regret later—Mary Alice intervened.

"Hold it, you two. You'd better calm down," she said, giving us the same kind of look I used over the years to make Jenny and Mike behave. It never had the same effect on Jim, though. Much to my disappointment.

"Why, Mary Alice," I said, "I never realized you could be so forceful. That look always worked on Jenny and Mike when they were kids."

"Good," Mary Alice said. "Because you're both acting like children. Although I can't say I'm surprised. It's the way you always behave. And, quite frankly, I'm sick and tired of it. It's even worse, now that Claire's gone. She used to be able to knock some sense into you two. I'm afraid I don't have her no-nonsense style. Yet. But if you keep this up, I'll have to learn. It's either that, or only get together with one of you at a time. Which, now that I think about it, might be quieter. But not nearly as much fun."

Properly chastised, Nancy spoke first. "You're right, Mary Alice. I'll play nice if Carol will."

I nodded. After all, what else could I do? Although none of this was my fault. It was just another example of Nancy going off on one of her frequent hair-brained tangents.

"I'm glad we're all behaving like adults now," Mary Alice said. "Although I know it's harder for one of you than the other." She grinned and continued, "No way am I saying which one of you I'm talking about, so don't bother asking. Moving along, I just thought of the perfect Boomer couple to be contestants in the pilot of *The Second Honeymoon Game*." She beamed at me. "Can you guess? I'm surprised you didn't think of them yourself, Carol. And the beauty of my idea is that the couple is already on their way to Florida."

I shook my head. "I'm afraid you lost me," I admitted.

"Carol, how can you be so dense?" Nancy asked. "It's a brilliant idea, Mary Alice. Although they're such a traditional choice. Bob and I would be much better. Edgier. More modern. I'm sure we'd attract many more viewers." She paused for a second, then said, "Maybe we could all be contestants. After all, the show will need a least two couples, right?"

"Don't start that again," Mary Alice warned her.

All of a sudden, the light bulb went off in my brain. I tried my best to hide my negative reaction, but Mary Alice and Nancy know me far too well.

"What? You don't like the idea, Carol? Claire and Larry are the perfect choice. Larry's a lawyer, so he's used to public speaking. And Claire, well...Claire is used to speaking. As we well know." Nancy laughed.

"I'm not so sure how much input I'll have on the show," I protested, trying my darndest to wiggle out of this unexpected development. "Charlie may not want any more suggestions from me. And I'm sure Mack Whitman doesn't, judging by the looks he was directing at me in yesterday's meeting."

Besides, Larry's so boring, and Claire's so critical and controlling.

I didn't really say that, of course. But if you knew Claire and Larry as well as I do, I'm sure you'd agree with me.

"Well, at least promise me you'll think about suggesting them," Mary Alice said.

What else could I do but agree? After all, thinking about doing something and actually doing it are two completely different things, right? Of course, right.

"What did the kids say about this new adventure in your life?" Mary Alice asked. "I bet Mike is thrilled about you and Jim coming to Florida."

"Will the pilot episode be filmed in Miami?" Nancy asked. "I've always wanted to visit South Beach. I've heard it's the 'in' place to go. All the celebrities hang out there."

"I'm embarrassed to admit this," I said, "but I haven't contacted Jenny or Mike about the television show yet. We got home late from the city, one thing led to another, and..."

"No time like the present," Nancy said, reaching into my purse and fishing around for my cell phone, which was easy to find thanks to its pink and green Lilly Pulitzer phone case. "Go for it. They're going to be so excited for you and Jim." She took a quick look at the phone, and said, "For Pete's sake, Carol, how long has your phone been off? What if someone was trying to reach you?"

I looked at my phone and realized Nancy was right. "I guess I turned it off after you and I texted last night," I said, pushing the power button to "on." "But I'm sure nobody tried to...holy cow!"

There were ten texts from Jenny, and three from Jim. The latest one, from Jim, had arrived ten minutes ago.

Carol, where are you? Mark's in Fairport Hospital. Get over here right away.

Chapter 17

Every morning is the dawn of a new error.

"I'm really fine," my son-in-law protested as Jenny fluffed the pillows behind his head, being careful not to touch the bandage on his left temple or dislodge the intravenous line attached to his hand. "It's just a scratch. I don't know what everyone is making such a big deal about."

"You don't look fine," said my daughter, her brow wrinkled in concern. "And it's more than just a scratch, or you wouldn't be kept in the hospital for observation. They want to be sure you don't have a concussion. You're weak and you've lost some blood. For heaven's sake, lie still and try to get some rest."

"You'd better do what Jenny says," I echoed from the doorway. "You know how bossy she can be."

"Mom, you're finally here! Thank God," Jenny said, her blue eyes (so like mine!) filled with tears. She gave me a quick hug, burrowing her face in my shoulder the way she did when she was a little girl.

"It's about time, Carol," Jim said from the far corner of the room. "Where the heck have you been? We've been trying to reach you for hours."

I ignored his accusatory tone and focused on Mark, hooked up to several machines and looking so pale and weak in his hospital bed that it scared me. "Hey, how's my favorite son-in-law?" I said, giving his cheek a gentle kiss. "I haven't seen you like this since you fell off your bike in sixth grade. As I recall, you were doing wheelies in our driveway to impress Jenny. So, what trouble did you get into this time?"

Mark moved slightly, then winced in pain. Jenny was by his side in a flash. "Do you hurt, honey? Do you want me to call for a nurse?"

"I'm okay," Mark insisted. "I just moved the wrong way." He reached out, grabbed Jenny's hand and squeezed it. "Don't worry. And to answer your question, Carol, I wasn't doing any wheelies this time." He flashed me a weak grin. "I remember that incident very well. I always tried to show off to impress Jenny."

"You always impressed me, honey," Jenny said. "Even if I didn't tell you so." Mark nodded and closed his eyes.

"Let's give the poor guy a chance to sleep," said Jim, propelling Jenny and me out of the room. "We can stop at the nurses' station and tell them we'll be in the cafeteria, so they'll keep an extra careful eye on Mark. I think a little sustenance will do us all some good."

For once, I went along with Jim without comment. Or question. But I still had no idea why our poor son-in-law was in the hospital. When I opened my mouth to ask, my dear husband silenced me with a warning shake of his head. Not as effective as the "Look," but I still got the message and zipped my lips.

"I'll get us all some coffee," Jim said. "You two find a table." He gave Jenny a fatherly hug. "Don't worry, honey. Mark is going to be just fine."

Jenny nodded. "I know, Dad. Thanks for being there for me." She headed toward the opposite side of the cafeteria, threading her way around tables filled with hospital employees on break.

I grabbed some sugar packets and napkins from the condiment station and prepared to follow Jenny. (Although I usually take my coffee black, I knew from Mary Alice that the Fairport Hospital coffee was terrible and figured I'd need the sugar to make it drinkable.) That's when I saw a familiar figure—head down, face in his hands, sitting at a nearby table. It was Mark's partner, and my nemesis, Detective Paul Wheeler.

For those of you who've not had the pleasure of meeting Paul before, let me explain that Paul is easy to miss, since he barely makes the minimum police height requirement. He also barely makes the minimum police intelligence requirement, in my opinion. In other words, he's not the shiniest badge on the force.

Paul and I have crossed paths in the past, when I found myself involved in a few situations that also involved some of my nearest and dearest and the Fairport police. When the aforementioned nearest and dearest reached out to me for help, well…I couldn't exactly say no, could I? And I was the one (well, with some help) who ended up solving the case, each time. Or, at least, uncovering the key evidence that led to the solution of each case. I am modest to a fault, despite what others may have told you about me.

Unfortunately, Paul Wheeler saw me as an interfering busybody, not a concerned public citizen trying to help her friends and family. I'll give you a beat or two to process his totally unfair opinion of me.

There isn't a doubt in my mind that Small Paul (my own term of endearment for the little twerp, not that I ever voiced it) is threatened by a person of my superior intelligence and intuition. However, since Paul is also the partner of my son-in-law, I have to be nice to him.

It would have been so easy to pretend I hadn't noticed him, but he looked so miserable sitting there, my maternal instinct kicked in. Sometimes, I swear, it's on automatic pilot. So I touched him on the shoulder, and said, "Are you all right? Can I do anything for you?"

Paul looked up in surprise. When he realized it was me, instead of reverting to his usual odious personality, he asked, "How's Mark? I tried to see him, but the doctors said that only immediate family would be allowed in."

I pulled out a chair and plopped my derriere onto it. "We just came from his room," I said. "Jenny and Jim are here, too. Why don't you come sit with us?"

"I'm the last person Jenny would want to see right now," Paul said. "This whole thing, Mark getting hurt, it's all my fault."

"I'm sure that's not true," I said. "Although, I have absolutely no idea what happened."

"He's my partner," Paul said. "We're supposed to protect each other. Be sure we get the job done, of course, but also have each other's backs all the time. I really screwed up."

I waited in silence for him to continue. I've finally figured out that, if I just keep my big mouth shut instead of asking a lot of questions, people will eventually tell me what I want to know. A late life lesson, but better late than never, right?

This time I wanted to grab Paul by the shoulders and shake the story out of him, but since he'd probably have me busted for beating up a policeman, I sat on my hands instead.

"We were sent out to take a routine follow-up statement from a domestic violence victim," Paul said. "But we didn't know that the abuser was still in the house. When we knocked on the front door and announced we were from the Fairport Police, the guy came out waving a kitchen knife. I was in front of Mark, and I immediately stepped back and went for my gun. I slammed right into Mark. He fell and his head hit the pavement. I'll never forget that sound. The perp jumped over Mark and got away. I really screwed up, didn't I, Carol?"

The rational part of me (the part I *never* listen to) told me that this whole thing had been an accident, pure and simple. Paul's initial reaction was instinctive, and he had no idea that Mark was standing so close behind him.

The other part of me suggested that this could be my only chance, *ever*, to get back at Paul a little for all the angst he'd put me through at every opportunity. I don't need to tell you which part won, do I?

Well, if you're thinking my evil side, you'd be wrong. I decided to find some middle ground—to make Paul sweat, just a little, while offering him some emotional support at the same time. Not an easy decision. But with my inadvertent forays into crime-solving SJR (that would be, Since Jim's Retirement) in the fair town of Fairport, I figured I'd better stay on Paul's good side, assuming I could find it.

"Please don't blame yourself, Paul," I said. "You certainly didn't mean for Mark to fall. It's not like you pushed him deliberately, after all."

I thought for a minute, then added, "I don't know anything about police procedures, but I don't understand why you didn't try to disarm the perp. Is that what you called him? Instead of backing up and going for your gun, I mean."

No kidding. I didn't understand that. Although, if I were ever faced with a similar situation (please God, don't ever let me be), I'd probably turn around and run away as fast as I could. At least, Paul hadn't done that.

Paul looked even more miserable. "I acted instinctively. Not professionally. I could have taken him down easily. And you want to know the worst part of all?"

"Only if you want to tell me, Paul. I'm not using rubber hoses to make you talk." Then, I clapped my hands over my mouth. Paul and I were bonding, and I had ruined it by my smart aleck remark.

Paul smiled a little. "I know you're not, Carol. And for the record, we don't use rubber hoses anymore. Our budget's been cut."

I smiled back. Who knew that underneath that height-challenged exterior lurked a sense of humor just waiting for the right moment to show itself?

"The worst part is," Paul said, "the guy didn't have a real knife at all. I was wrong. It was a kid's toy."

As I started to respond, Paul's phone sprang to life. He took one look at the screen and jumped to his feet. "I have to leave. Tell Mark I'm pulling for him. And, Carol, one more thing." He fixed me with the beady stare I'd come to know far too well.

"Yes?"

"Don't you dare repeat what I told you to anyone else. I know what a blabbermouth you are." And he stalked away.

Well, the idea! Any shred of compassion I had previously felt for Paul vanished in a flash of anger and humiliation. It was time to join my family. Jenny needed the strength and support that only her mother could give to her. But when I looked around the hospital cafeteria, I realized that Jenny and Jim had left without me.

So much for family solidarity.

Chapter 18

I try to take one day at a time, but sometimes several days attack me all at once.

If you know me well, you know that I never, *ever*, feel sorry for myself. Even if a loved one (not mentioning anyone by name, understand) should hurt my feelings, make fun of me, or criticize me in any way. I just let that behavior roll right off my back. I never hold a grudge, either. Forgive and forget, that's what I always say. And the older I get, the easier the forgetting part seems to be.

So you'll be surprised when I admit to you that I was a little miffed (well, a lot miffed) that Jim and Jenny had chosen to abandon me in the hospital cafeteria without a word. As a matter of fact, it seemed more and more like Jim was becoming Jenny's go-to parent of choice in this situation. Not that this was a competition. No way. But, still….

Good sport and model parent that I am (remember the part about how I never carry a grudge), I rummaged in my purse for my glasses and phone, and sent Jenny a quick text.

Me: *R u back in Mark's room? All okay?*

Jenny: *Docs releasing him now. Going home!*

Me: *Yay! Is Dad there?*

Jenny: *Yup. Driving us home.*

Me: *Will be there soon. Love u.*

Jenny: *Love u 2.*

Well, that explained a lot. Jenny must have gotten a text from the doctor and rushed off to her husband's side, with her father trailing behind her. They probably didn't take the time to look for me, which was perfectly understandable under the circumstances. Except, I couldn't help but wonder if Jim was trying, in his own subtle way, to one-up me for my valuable input at yesterday's television show planning meeting.

Nah. He'd never be that devious. He'd just come straight out and yell at me, and after we made up last night, that seemed like a stretch. Even for me.

I sat in the cafeteria and considered my options as I nursed my now-cold coffee. (I figured that was an appropriate activity—my being in a hospital, after all.)

It looked like all was calm on the home front, thank God. In my son-in-law's chosen profession, the possibility of being hurt was always part of the job, so, thank goodness Mark hadn't been seriously hurt. I wondered if I could steer him into another career. Not that I *ever* interfere in the lives of my children. Or my child-in-law. In fact, I was betting that if there was an award for "Mother-In-Law of the Year," I'd win it for sure.

My cell phone pinged again. I rummaged for my glasses one more time, praying it wasn't bad news about Mark. I'd read somewhere that head wounds are tricky, and unexpected complications are always possible.

OMG. This text was from my husband.

Jim: *All okay here. Don't panic.*

Me: *???*

Jim: *Mark's resting. Jenny's keeping a close eye on him. No need for u to come.*

Me: *Good news, but r u sure I shouldn't stop in?!*

Jim: *No need. I'm leaving now. Headed to NYC for tv show meeting with Mack.*

Me: *When? Me, too?*

Jim: *No. Just me.*

Me: *Why not me?*

Jim: *Not sure. C u later.*

And the screen went black. Just like that. Not only were my services as a mother not needed, I guess my brief foray into television was over, too. It looked like I'd been fired from my new job before I even started it.

Chapter 19

I'm a real team player. Just as long as I'm the captain.

"Well, what exactly did you expect?" I asked myself on the ride home from the hospital. "You were way out of line at the production meeting yesterday. I bet you ticked off the entire staff of Charles King Productions with your high-handed suggestions. If you're really fired, you have nothing but your own big, unfiltered mouth to blame." My vision was briefly obstructed by a flood of tears. Yes, I'd decided to throw myself a full-blown pity party, and there was no time like the present to get the party started.

"And then, to make matters even worse, you weren't there for your very own daughter when she needed you. You really are a jerk!"

I screamed the last sentence so loud that the driver who was idling at the traffic light in the next lane looked over at me with alarm. "Sorry," I mouthed to him. "Got a little carried away." He nodded and sped off. I'm sure he couldn't wait to get away from me. Just like everybody else in my life.

Except for Lucy and Ethel, of course. "They're always there for you," I reassured myself. "They love you unconditionally, and are completely non-judgmental. Especially when you give them extra biscuits. I bet they'll both be thrilled to hear that Jim and I aren't going to Florida, after all. Well, maybe Jim is, but I'm sure not. We couldn't have taken them with us, and it's not fair to put them in a kennel.

"This really is for the best," I lied to myself as I neared Old Fairport Turnpike. "Jim can go to Florida, and I can stay here and take care of my family. Maybe even give Jenny and Mark a gentle nudge into the baby-production process, without Jim telling me to mind my own business."

I nodded in satisfaction. That was a perfect plan.

"But it would have been wonderful to see Mike," I countered. Sometimes I hate talking to myself. I always see too many sides to the same issue, which confuses me to no end.

"Your television career was fun while it lasted," I insisted. "Even if it was only for twenty-four hours. Wasn't it Andy Warhol who said everyone was entitled to fifteen minutes of fame?" I frowned. "Or maybe that was Andy Rooney. Anyhow, you had way more than that, and reconnecting with Charlie was a bonus. Except he probably thinks you're a doofus, too. After all, he's the chief honcho of *The Second Honeymoon Game*. If you're really fired, it must have been his decision."

I shook my head. "It doesn't matter. None of this matters. What's important is that Mark's going to be okay, Jim's going back to work, and I'll have my freedom back, even if it's only for a little while. Just like the good old days."

I turned the corner onto Old Fairport Turnpike and was shocked to see a Silver Cloud Rolls Royce in front of my house, blocking my driveway. Nancy's BMW was parked right behind it.

I pulled over to the curb and beeped the horn. That Nancy, honestly. She never thinks about anyone but herself. And the nerve of her, to arrange a meeting with a big bucks real estate client in front of my house. Why didn't she use her own office, for heaven's sake? That's what offices are for!

In a flash, the driver was out of the Rolls Royce and opened the passenger door. Who should emerge, looking like the proverbial cat who swallowed the canary, but my BFF Nancy? The driver was none other than our grade school classmate and media mogul, Charlie King.

Resisting the urge to rear-end Nancy's BMW took some restraint, let me tell you. But I managed. Points for me, right? But I was seething. How the heck had Nancy managed to contact Charlie and arrange a meeting with him so fast? We'd only had coffee together a few hours ago. Although, with all that had transpired since then, it felt like years.

I stuck my head out my car window and said, in my sweetest voice, "What a lovely surprise, finding you two here. But would you mind moving your cars up just a teeny bit? I can't get into my driveway."

Charlie flashed me an apologetic grin. "Sorry, Carol. I should have been more careful. I'm not used to driving a car myself. I usually have someone else do it. But I just got this new beauty, and decided to take it for a spin. Just give me a minute." He hopped back into the Rolls.

Nancy gave me a bright smile. "Are you surprised?"

"That's one word for it," I said. "What the heck are you up to?"

"Why do you assume I'm up to something?" Nancy said, widening her eyes in a pretense of innocence.

"Maybe because I know you so well," I said. "What are you trying to do? Sell Charlie a house? How did you find him so fast?"

"I Googled him, of course," said Nancy. "And when I reached him, he was already on his way here to see you. So I said I'd meet him here, too. What's your problem with that?"

Put like that, I guess I didn't have a problem. At least, not one that if I said it out loud, wouldn't make me look like a spoiled two-year-old who was whining because she didn't want to share her toys.

"Well, the house isn't clean," I said, "and there are probably breakfast dishes in the sink. I wasn't expecting company. I know you're not really company," I said as Nancy started to object, "but Charlie certainly is. And you know I like everything to be perfect when I'm entertaining."

Nancy raised a perfectly sculpted eyebrow at that ridiculous statement, and I burst out laughing. It was impossible for me to stay mad at her. "At least let me go into the house first," I said. "Just in case Lucy and Ethel have been up to some mischief while I was gone. Follow me into the driveway. I don't want your BMW to distract any neighbors, especially Phyllis Stevens, from drooling over the Rolls Royce while trying to figure out why it's parked in front of my house."

In a flash, I was in the kitchen. I gathered up Jim's dirty coffee cup and plate (the man simply will not clean up after himself) and hid them in the dishwasher without rinsing them first. I was breaking one of my cardinal rules, but I was in a time crunch.

"Now, you two behave," I said to the dogs, tossing each one of them a biscuit. "No growling because a strange man is here. I don't need any protection, thank you. He's an old friend."

Lucy gave me a suspicious look. Ethel merely yawned.

"No, really, he is," I insisted to Lucy. "Your pal Nancy is here, too. It's all good." *At least, I hope it is.* Lucy wagged her stubby tail in approval at the female name, while Ethel yawned again.

The front doorbell rang, which threw me off. For a second, I thought I had even more company, but then I realized that Nancy wanted to usher Charlie into my house the "official" way, as opposed to using the kitchen door—the way she always does. For a second, I worried that she was going to try and sell Charlie my house, then told myself I was really being stupid.

Lucy and Ethel raced ahead of me and got to the door first. It's hard to stop two enthusiastic English cocker spaniels from running outside and still appear to be a gracious hostess, but I did my best. Fortunately, Nancy's wise to the dogs' escape tactics and helped me block the door.

Charlie bent down and embraced them both. "Aren't you two beauties? Yes, you are." He ruffled their ears.

Lucy checked out Charlie and, I swear, it was love at first sniff. In fact, it was almost embarrassing the way she flung herself at him. Ethel rolled over on her back, begging for a tummy rub. Lord, this was way over the top. I'd never seen the dogs react this way to anyone else before. Even Jim.

I grabbed them by their collars. "You'll have to excuse them," I said. "They've forgotten their manners. That's enough, girls."

I heard Nancy snicker. She knows who really runs the Andrews house, and that they have four legs each, not two.

"I don't mind at all, Carol," Charlie said. "I love dogs. My wife and I had two Springer Spaniels. These two look a lot like them. What breed are they?"

"They're English cocker spaniels," I said. "Emphasis on the word English. They're very different from the American cockers. Just look at their heads. They're not square, like the Americans."

"They really look like smaller Springers," Charlie said, "and they're much more handsome than the Americans. I never knew there were two different types of cocker breeds."

I beamed. I couldn't help it. I just love my dogs. And Charlie was right; English cockers are much more handsome. Or, in the case of Lucy and Ethel, more beautiful. Both my dogs are very sensitive to gender classification.

I'd been so fixated on Nancy's showing up with Charlie that it didn't hit me right away to wonder why he was here, even though Nancy's powers of persuasion are impressive. After all, if he was going to fire me, he wouldn't have to do it in person, right? An email or text would have done the job. Maybe his being here was good news for me after all.

I immediately switched into gracious hostess mode. Imagine *Leave It to Beaver*'s mom, June Cleaver, in sweat pants with an elastic waistband instead of a frilly apron and pearls, and you'll get the picture. "Let's all go into the kitchen," I said, heading toward the rear of the house behind the two dogs. "I'll make a pot of fresh coffee. I'd love to have you stay for lunch." *Assuming there's something in the house to eat.*

"I picked up some lunch for us at Maria's Trattoria," Nancy said. "I figured it was the least I could do, since Charlie and I arrived unannounced." She beamed at Charlie. "You may not remember this from grammar school, but I was voted 'Most Domestic' in eighth grade."

Nancy's statement was so over-the-top ridiculous that I was surprised her nose didn't start to grow longer. (*Pinocchio* was one of our favorite fairy tales when we were kids.) I didn't call her out on it, though. If Nancy wanted to present herself as Harriet Nelson to my June Cleaver, I'd go right along with her. But I couldn't resist turning my face directly at her and rolling my eyes, which made Nancy blush. "I'll just buzz out to my car and bring in lunch," she said, recovering quickly. "I'll be right back." She shot me a dirty look on her way out, but I ignored it, good pal that I am.

"You have a beautiful home, Carol," Charlie said, pulling out a chair and making himself comfy at my kitchen table. "I remember delivering newspapers on this block when I was a kid. I always wondered what one of these antique houses looked like inside."

"Jim and I have lived here for over thirty years," I said. "He's not home at the moment, though. I know he'll be sorry to have missed you."

"I know," Charlie said. "He's at a marketing meeting with Mack about *The Second Honeymoon Game*. I arranged that. I wanted to talk to you privately, without your husband overhearing us. I have a proposition for you, and I hope you'll say yes. For old times' sake."

Chapter 20

Forget about the "new normal." My life's the "old abnormal."

Charlie followed his provocative remark with a wink and a big grin. I could tell that he was enjoying my reaction, which was a combination of shock and curiosity, mixed with a healthy dose of terror. I never was any good at hiding my feelings.

Maybe Charlie's been nursing an unrequited passion for you all these years, Carol. Naming his daughter after you was just the tip of the iceberg. Now he's going to declare his feelings, force you to leave Jim, and run away with him. It's a good thing Nancy's coming right back. He wouldn't dare sweep you away in front of a witness. Would he?

Oh for God's sake, get a grip, Carol.

Being fired from *The Second Honeymoon Game* had great appeal all of a sudden. I turned my back and busied myself making the coffee. Slowly. Very slowly, so I didn't have to respond to Charlie's admission that he had deliberately gotten Jim out of the house.

Hurry up, Nancy. Don't leave me alone with this guy.

"Here I am," my BFF said, breezing into the kitchen with a huge shopping bag. "Did I miss anything?"

You have no idea. I didn't really say that, of course.

"Nancy's been filling me in on what's going on with our classmates while we were waiting for you," Charlie said, taking the shopping bag from Nancy and helping to unload the food. "Whatever you brought smells delicious."

"Why don't we all sit down?" I suggested. "We can put the food out on the table and serve ourselves buffet-style."

I looked at Nancy and tilted my head in Charlie's direction, hoping she'd get the hint. *Take over, now. Say something.* Nancy shot me back a puzzled look, but fortunately, she's rarely at a loss for words for very long. Like, never.

"It's so wonderful to see you again, Chuckie. I mean, Charlie," she corrected. "I've seen several of your television shows over the years. But I never realized that you were the producer. I'm so excited to reconnect with you. And, despite what Carol may think, I have no intention of talking you into buying a house here in town. That is," she amended, "unless you want one, of course. I am one of the most successful real estate agents in Fairport, a town which is certainly a convenient commute to the city."

Charlie threw back his head and laughed. "I see you haven't changed a bit, Nancy. You always were a super salesperson. I remember you sold the most candy bars and wrapping paper during our class fundraiser. I think it was a school record."

Then, he turned to me. "And you haven't changed either, Carol. I told you that yesterday. That's why I came to see you today. As I said, I have a proposition for you."

I heard Nancy gasp. At least, I think it was Nancy. I was so nervous, it could have been me. *Oh lord, here it comes.* I licked my lips, which were suddenly very dry, and shifted in my chair.

"The suggestions you made in yesterday's meeting about the show's casting and direction were brilliant," Charlie continued, oblivious to my discomfort. "Right on. You always were creative. I want to hire you to be my right arm on *The Second Honeymoon Game.* Special Assistant to the Producer. What do you say? I hope it's yes."

I didn't know how to react. Probably jumping up and down and screaming, "Yes! Yes! Yes!" would be just a tad unprofessional.

"What about Carrie?" I asked. "Isn't that her job?"

"No, her duties are completely different. She's a technical wizard, and her job is to put the nuts and bolts of the show together under my direction. I want you to be part of my creative team."

"I don't know what to say," I responded.

I think I heard Nancy mutter, "That's a first." But I could have been mistaken.

"For heaven's sake, Carol. Why are you hesitating? You have to say yes. This is the chance of a lifetime," Nancy said. Then she batted her eyes at Charlie. "It's possible Carol may need an assistant of her own, Charlie. I'd be glad to offer my services. She and I work very well together."

I burst out laughing, and Nancy looked hurt. "It was just an idea," she huffed.

"Maybe this will help you make up your mind, Carol," Charlie said. He named a dollar figure for the position that would keep me, as well as Lucy and Ethel, in designer duds for the rest of our lives.

Nancy's eyes opened so wide I thought they'd pop right out of her head. And, true to form, before I could respond, she jumped right in with a suggestion of her own. "Carol would be great at that job," Nancy said. "She's super imaginative. And always so helpful. Of course, I'm very creative, too. You have to be if you want to be a top producer in today's cutthroat real estate market. It's all in knowing the proper way to put a spin on a property. That's the name of the game these days. Creativity and marketing. Perhaps there's a way I could be useful to you, too, Charlie. On the television show, I mean."

I had to hand it to Nancy. When she wants something, she doesn't give up until she gets it.

"I'm very flattered," I said to Charlie. "But don't you have people with professional experience already working on the project? I don't know anything about putting together a television show. I should have kept my big mouth shut and listened more at yesterday's meeting; I could have learned something. I'm too opinionated for my own good. It's one of my worst faults. At least, that's what Jim says."

Charlie waved away my objections. "As I said before, I don't need anyone else for the technical side of the show," he said, now turned in his chair to give me his full attention. "I want someone who understands the Boomer market, especially the females. That's who this show is aimed at. They're our target market for advertising revenue. You fit the bill perfectly. Your suggestions yesterday were spot on. I want to use your brain, Carol. Your creative energy. Your feminine intuition, if that doesn't sound too corny."

"I really have to talk to Jim before I give you my answer," I said. "Does he know anything about this?"

"I'm sure Mack is filling him in at the agency meeting. Do you think he'll have a problem with this? I hope you don't have one of those marriages where you have to check every little thing with your husband. You have a mind of your own, don't you?"

That frosted my cupcakes. I immediately felt defensive. Of myself. Of my husband. Of our marriage. I know what you're all thinking, and you're right. I was having another knee-jerk reaction without thinking first.

"I don't have to check every little thing with my husband, Chuckie," I said, deliberately choosing his grammar school nickname. "But a long-time, successful marriage like ours is a partnership, based on mutual respect for each other's opinions. I value Jim's. Plus, I'm sure he knows much more about television than I do."

I sat back, folded my arms, and fixed Charlie with an icy stare. "It's kind of ironic, isn't it?"

Charlie looked shocked at my over-the-top reaction.

"I mean, it's ironic that you're practically accusing me of being a doormat to my husband, yet at the same time, you want me to work on a television show called *The Second Honeymoon Game*. I would hope that only couples who have a solid marriage, like Jim's and mine, would be contestants on the show. And I have no intention of risking mine."

Silence. Even from Nancy.

Followed by tension. Lots and lots of that.

What are you trying to do, Carol? Sabotage the first real job offer you've gotten in more than twenty-five years? And isn't Jim always telling you to get a job? Boy, are you being stupid!

Lucy, who's always super sensitive to my mercurial moods, chose that moment to pad across the kitchen and lick my hand. Then, no kidding, she turned her attention to Charlie, and gave him a little doggie affection, too. *Play nice, kids. It's time to make up.*

Then she returned to my side and gave me a penetrating stare. *You know you want this job, so say yes. What are you waiting for?* Swear to God, that's what she was telling me.

I don't know if you've ever been in a staring contest with a canine, but believe me, they can hold eye contact forever! At least, it seems like that to me. Suffice to say, I got her message. Loud and clear.

"Okay, I'll do it," I said to Charlie.

"Yay!" said Nancy, jumping up and giving me a big smooch on the cheek. "I'm so excited! I can't wait. Bob will be thrilled."

"Whoa, Nancy," I said, at the same time that Charlie, now

looking very confused, asked, "Who's Bob?"

"Bob's my husband, sort of," Nancy explained. "We're separated, but dating. It's a great new way to be married, believe me. In fact," she wrinkled her brow in thought, carefully, so as not to cause any lasting damage, "that could be a whole new show for you, Charlie. *The Married but Dating Game.* I bet you'd get fabulous ratings."

Charlie's eyes glazed over and he shook his head a few times. Probably trying to clear it after being on the receiving end of yet another one of Nancy's enthusiastic outbursts. I knew exactly how he felt. I'd been in his position far too many times. So, I did what I usually do—took over the conversation.

"So, when do I start? Oh, and what exactly will I be doing?" I asked.

Charlie leaned back in his chair, clearly more comfortable. "I want to use you as a sounding board for any decisions involving the design of the show, starting with the pilot episode, especially the casting of the first contestants. There's no time to waste. Your opinion will be the most important one."

At last. Someone finally realized the value of my opinion. I was in my glory.

"Can you be ready to leave for Florida tomorrow morning?" Charlie asked me. "As you already know, we filming the pilot episode there. We've just picked up a major sponsor for the show, and he wants the first episode completed as soon as possible, so our whole timetable has been moved up. We'll also use snippets for a social media campaign when we get ready to launch the show. It's much more efficient to do it that way."

I blinked. Then blinked again.

"Florida? We're going to Florida?" I responded. "Tomorrow?" *I think I'm going to faint.*

I didn't really say the last part, of course.

Chapter 21

*When I was a little girl, I played monkey in
the middle. Now that I'm grown up, I play
muffin in my middle.*

My panic must have been reflected on my face. I totally zoned
out. Twenty-four hours wasn't nearly enough time for me to get
everything done before taking a trip like that. Plane reservations,
packing, losing twenty pounds to fit into last summer's bathing
suit—all these things demanded months of pre-planning. Plus,
Mark had been injured. How could I leave my daughter? She'd
need me to help nurse him back to health.

How long would I be away? And was Jim going with me, or would
I be on my own in a strange new land? With Charlie King, who'd
been harboring a yen for me since grade school.

Except, of course, my darling son Mike was already in Florida.
So I wouldn't be all alone. It was a great chance to have a special
mom/son bonding experience. I was sure he'd be thrilled. Once
I told him. At least, I hoped he would be.

I thought about the dogs—where could they go on such short
notice? I'd have to stop the mail and the newspapers. What if it
was too late to make those arrangements? Our front steps would
be littered with newspapers, and our mailbox would be bursting
at the seams. All dead giveaways that Carol and Jim Andrews were
away. An open invitation to any local burglar to stop by and steal
my Waterford and Wedgewood. How could I take that chance? I'd

have to ask the neighbors to help.

Hmmm. Wait a minute. Stop everything. I imagined the look on Phyllis Stevens's face when I told her Jim and I were flying to Florida tomorrow. And why. Maybe I could do this after all.

I came back from panic mode when I heard Nancy gush, "Oh, Charlie, you're the best. This is going to be such fun. And, you know, Claire and Larry McGee are in Florida for the winter. They'd be great contestants for the pilot of *The Second Honeymoon Game.* I'm sure you remember Claire from grammar school. Of course, she wasn't Claire McGee then. She was Claire Monahan. She transferred into our class in fourth grade."

Speak up, you doofus. Nancy's taking over everything.

I cleared my throat. Loudly. "Your suggestion certainly is interesting," I said. "But I'll have to think about using Claire and Larry for the show. There are so many factors to consider." I beamed the tiniest of fake smiles in her direction.

Nancy looked crestfallen that I had dismissed her ideas, and I immediately felt guilty. I got over it though. After all, I was the show's creative genius, not her. A muse, so to speak. Yes, I liked that image. I was Charlie King's muse. A muse who needed to get her act together ASAP.

"I don't know how Jim and I can possibly be ready to leave by tomorrow," I said, throwing in my husband's name so there would be no misunderstanding. This Florida trip would include both Jim and me, and not be a chance for Charlie to turn any imagined grammar school crush into a full-blown adult love affair.

"Men usually just throw a few things into a suitcase and they're ready to go," Charlie said. "That's what I do, and I'm sure Jim is the same way. Don't worry, Carol. He'll be packed in a jiffy. After all, the most important thing he's bringing is his laptop. Anything else he needs, he can buy in Florida."

Oh, yeah, right. I could just see my tightwad husband blowing big bucks on a completely new warm-weather wardrobe. Not going to happen.

"Do you think we can get last-minute plane reservations?" I asked, trying to get into the spirit of the thing. I had to admit, this was pretty exciting stuff for a late middle-aged housewife from the Connecticut sticks. I mean, suburbs.

"Don't worry about plane reservations for you and Jim," Charlie said with a mysterious smile. "That's all taken care of."

A vision of me flying first-class flashed in my mind. I was sipping a glass of imported champagne and helping myself to an hors d'oeuvre from a delicious assortment proffered by a handsome cabin attendant.

"You seem to have this all planned out, Charlie" Nancy said. "I guess I'll have to fly down separately. Assuming I'm included in this adventure, of course."

I tried to ignore Nancy's expression. She was pouting like a five-year-old child.

"We'll land at St. Pete-Clearwater Airport," Charlie continued. "My pilot has already made the arrangements."

"Your pilot?" I asked. "You know a pilot?"

"I guess you could put it that way," Charlie said. "He works for me. We're flying to Florida on my private jet." He looked down at Lucy and Ethel, now making themselves comfortable around his feet. "And we can't forget about these two beauties." He reached down and petted Lucy in her very favorite spot—the center of her head right behind her ears. If she'd been a cat, she would have been purring. "I insist that you bring the dogs with you. The hotel where you'll be staying is pet-friendly."

He waited just a beat. Or, maybe two beats.

"There's room on the plane for you, too, Nancy. That is, if you want to come along. The plane seats twenty comfortably, and it won't be full."

"OOOH," Nancy squealed. "That's fabulous. I'll have to clear my calendar, though. I have two house showings scheduled for tomorrow." She shrugged. "Oh, well. Somebody else in the office will have to handle them. I wouldn't miss this for the world."

"I just hope that, if either of the properties you have listed should sell while you're away, the agent who shows the house will share the commission with you," I said. All right, I was being petty. And slightly malicious.

Nancy's eyes narrowed. "You're always looking out for my best interests, Carol," she said, her voice tinged with a hint of sarcasm. "Thanks for the reminder. I'll be sure I make that perfectly clear."

Charlie turned to me. "Most of the people you and Jim met at yesterday's meeting are already in Florida," he said. "They flew down this morning. Including Carol Ann. She just couldn't get over meeting you. In fact, at dinner last night, she couldn't stop talking about you."

"Who's Carol Ann?" Nancy asked Charlie. "Your wife?" Then, she blushed. "I'm sorry. I'm being much too nosy." She looked at me. "Wait a second. Isn't Ann your middle name? Or am I remembering wrong? Oh, Charlie, don't tell me you married someone with the exact same name as Carol's. That would be too funny for words. One Carol Ann in the world is quite enough!"

King beamed. "Carol Ann's my daughter, the undisputed apple of my eye. My wife died when Carol Ann was just a baby. It's been just the two of us for a long time. She was named…"

Now it was my turn to look embarrassed. "I'm sure that's just a coincidence," I said quickly, before Charlie could spill his unrequited love for me all over my kitchen table. I don't know why I was so reluctant to tell Nancy that Charlie had named his daughter after me. After all, she'd been in grammar school with both of us and knew our history. Or, lack thereof. It just felt too intimate.

I know. I know. That really sounds weird. Especially since I've shared so many other intimate details of my life with my BFF for over fifty years.

I was saved from further comment by a text from Jim.

Him: *R u packed yet?*

Me: *Nope. Just found out about trip.*

Him: *Pack light. U always bring 2 much!*

My husband, the true romantic.

Chapter 22

The irony of life is that, by the time you're old enough to know your way around, you realize you're not going anywhere.

"This is the life," I said, leaning back in my seat and luxuriating in my surroundings. "I don't think I could ever fly commercial again after this experience."

Jim chuckled. "I never thought I'd hear you say that, Carol. Not with your fear of tight places."

I gave Jim a suspicious look. "I assume your reference to tight places isn't a comment about my gaining a few pounds over the winter." Hey, with guys, you never know. Best to get that out in the open right now.

"Because if you are," I continued, "I want you to know that most people pack on a few extra pounds during the holidays. And now that we'll be in a warmer climate, I plan to walk a few miles every day. That'll take the pounds off in a jiffy." Assuming I don't overindulge in some of the Sunshine State's well-known goodies, like key lime pie.

Jim's response was to throw back his head and laugh at me.

"Honestly, Carol, you really are the limit. I wasn't criticizing you. I was merely mentioning that you have a fear of being enclosed in a small space. Like elevators, for instance. You're much too sensitive."

"I just felt I should clarify what you were talking about," I said in my own defense. "Besides, this is no tight place. We could fit the entire neighborhood in this cabin." A brief picture of Phyllis and Bill Stevens flashed into my mind. "Not that I'd want to really bring the neighbors. I love Fairport, but it's nice to get away for a change. I'm glad we're having a new adventure together."

My husband leaned over, squeezed my knee and said, with a leer, "I'm looking forward to having some tried-and-true adventures while we're in Florida."

I swatted his hand away. "Jim, stop that. Someone will see us."

"Don't be silly, Carol. Lucy and Ethel don't care. Neither do Nancy and Charlie. They're too busy talking."

I leaned down and gave the snoozing canines a scratch on their heads, then turned in my seat and checked out my BFF. True to form, she was jabbering away with our host, whose eyes had once again taken on that glazed look. I figured it had been a long time since he'd heard so many words coming out of a single mouth in such rapid fire delivery. He started to get up, but Nancy laid a hand on his arm. "And do you remember…?"

Charlie laughed and sat down again. Well, that explained what they were talking about—our old grammar school class, not the casting of *The Second Honeymoon Game*. I needed to remind Nancy at the first opportunity that she was only along on this trip as a guest, not as an official member of the television show production team. That was my role. Oh, and Jim's. Of course.

"Did you let Mike know about our trip" I asked. "What did he say? Will he be able to sneak in a trip from Miami to the Gulf Coast to see us? He always seems so busy."

In fact, Mike had yet to respond to my own late-night text about our Florida trip. I didn't tell Jim that, though. In fact, lately it seemed that Mike was even less forthcoming about his life than usual. I was hoping he was more upfront with his father. Male bonding and all that stuff.

I frowned. *Perhaps you lean on Mike too much, Carol. He's not a kid anymore. He doesn't have to report to you on his every move. He's a successful business owner. An adult. Try treating him like one for a change.*

"I didn't get much of a response," Jim admitted. "He said, 'Cool.' That was it."

"Did you suggest our getting together?" I persisted. Honestly, sometimes men have to be spoon-fed like children even if, chronologically, they're supposed to be adults.

Jim shook his head. "No. I figured I couldn't until we had more of an idea what our schedule will be. And how long we'll be staying."

"As excited as I am to be getting away for a while," I said, "I felt really guilty leaving Jenny and Mark. It's much too soon to see how long Mark will be home convalescing after his accident. I'm worried that Jenny will need my help, and I won't be there for her. She depends on me."

"I'm sure Jenny and Mark will be fine without your assistance, Carol," Jim countered. "In fact, it's good for them to be totally on their own. They're a young married couple, and I've often thought that we see too much of them on a regular basis. Like having dinner together every Sunday night. We need to loosen the apron strings."

Jim's comments stung. "You mean, *I* need to loosen the apron strings, since I've never seen you put on an apron. For your information, Mr. Smarty Pants, Jenny and I are very close and we enjoy each other's company. That hasn't changed, even though she's now a grown-up married woman. And Mark has no close family anymore, in case you've forgotten. They want to spend time with us." Me.

Jim raised his eyebrows. "Okay, Carol. Maybe you're right. But I was just thinking back to the early days of our marriage. You resented it when my mother insisted that we spend every single holiday with her, no matter how inconvenient it was for us."

"That's not the same thing, at all," I shot back. At least, I hoped it wasn't.

"Look at it this way," my husband suggested gently. "Maybe without us old fogies around for a while, Jenny and Mark will have more of an opportunity to work on that special project you've been dreaming about."

"What project?"

"The one that you pray for every night. Grandchildren." He settled back in his seat with a satisfied smile and changed the subject.

"Who would have thought a week ago that we'd be on a private jet heading to Honeymoon Island in Florida?" he asked. "Certainly, not me."

"Honeymoon Island?" I squeaked. "You're kidding. Is that where we're going? I had no idea. All Charlie said yesterday was that we'd be landing at the St. Pete-Clearwater Airport. Where the heck is Honeymoon Island? What is it? Some sort of destination wedding place? We've already done that one, remember? On Nantucket, last

December for Jenny and Mark's wedding."

I have to confess that I have mixed feelings about that wedding. Don't get me wrong—I was thrilled that Jenny and Mark finally realized that they were meant for each other. Something I had known since the long-ago days when they were in the same grammar school class. But the wedding had its shares of ups and downs, to put it mildly. Especially for the poor wedding planner that Jenny had insisted on hiring. Perhaps some of you remember that. If not, I'll fill you in another time.

Jim, wise man that he was after so many years of marriage, allowed me the opportunity to wind down and take a breath without interrupting me.

Note to self: This might be a good practice for me to emulate. Sometime…in the far distant future.

"I'm surprised Charlie didn't tell you more about our Florida destination," Jim said. "Mack gave me all the details at yesterday's meeting." He rummaged in his ever-present briefcase and came up with a computer printout. "Here's some information about Honeymoon Island. You might want to read up on it before we land."

I whipped out my no-line bifocals so I could read without squinting. I never was good at retaining information the first time around. When I was cramming for exams back in school, it always took me hours and hours to make anything stick in my memory.

I have trouble reversing directions when I'm driving, too. Which is one reason why I let Jim do most of the driving on long trips. I know I should learn how to program a GPS, but I'm completely non-mechanical, and even if we had one in the car, Jim would constantly disagree with it and we'd probably end up getting lost anyway.

Now, where was I? Oh, yes. Honeymoon Island. Here's what Jim printed off the website. You may as well read it, too.

Florida's Honeymoon Island State Park
Honeymoon Island State Park is a destination for sun-sand-and-surf lovers along the Gulf of Mexico. Located on southwest Florida's barrier island chain and an easy drive from Dunedin, Clearwater, Tampa, and St. Petersburg, the island is reachable by following state road 586 over Causeway Boulevard.
History of Honeymoon Island

First mapped none-too-imaginatively as Sand Island and later given the less-elegant moniker, Hog Island (for a farm that came and went), Honeymoon Island got its current name in 1939.

To raise awareness of the area, New York developer Clinton Washburn purchased the island in 1939 for $30,000, and to attract newlyweds to the 50 thatched-roof villas he erected, he convinced Life *magazine and other media to publicize a contest, with the winners overnighting there— thus, the sandy stretch picked up its new name.*

Fascinating stuff. When I read a little further, I found out that many couples choose to marry and have their wedding receptions on Honeymoon Island. The park even offered a wedding planning service. That certainly explained why we were going to shoot the pilot of the television show there.

I had a brief moment when I thought I should share this information with Nancy. But when I turned around to see if she was still in her seat, I saw she was now cuddled against Charlie's shoulder, sound asleep. I squelched a brief pang of jealousy. After all, Charlie was *my* old sort-of boyfriend and *my* new boss, and here Nancy was, intruding on *my* trip and cozying up to him. Some nerve.

I was about to walk toward them and start a conversation with Charlie when Jim pulled me back. "Look, Carol," he said, gesturing out the plane window, "I think those are palm trees down there. We must be in Florida." Sure enough, I could see the palm trees, myself, and I forgot all about my petty jealousy. Yes, sometimes I can behave like an adult.

I grabbed the dogs' leashes for safety, then clung to Jim's arm. "I feel like we're getting lower. I hope that means we're near the airport and not that the plane has developed a problem." Departures and landings always freak me out, too. A therapist could have a field day with me and all my fears, real and imaginary. If I ever let the therapist get a word in edgewise, which I probably wouldn't.

I was in the middle of fervent prayers to whichever saint was in charge of airplanes when someone touched my shoulder, startling me. Yikes! It was our host. And boss.

"Time to put on seat belts," Charlie said. "And Lucy and Ethel have to go back in their safety harnesses. FAA regulations. We'll be landing in about five minutes."

Lucy growled a bit when I disturbed her. "Sorry, Luce, but this is for your own protection." Ethel, of course, submitted without an argument. Although I did catch her giving me a dirty look.

I settled back, my seat in an upright position and my seat belt securely fastened around my middle. I shut my eyes and began praying again. I hoped my personal protector didn't think I was being selfish by coming back with the same petition again and again.

Jim squeezed my hand. "Don't worry, Carol. We'll soon be on the ground and you can relax. Just take deep breaths. It'll all be worth it. I promise."

The next thing I knew, the plane had landed safely (I was certain it was through the intervention of my personal saint) and taxied to a stop. Eureka! We were in Florida and about to embark on a great adventure.

"Lead on, Jim," I said, releasing the dogs from their harnesses and clipping on their matching Lilly Pulitzer pink and green leashes. "We're right behind you. Let the fun and surprises begin! I can hardly wait."

Well, I didn't have to wait long. Walking out into the brilliant Florida sunshine hurt my eyes so much that I was squinting. But not so much that I couldn't make out a man and woman across the tarmac, holding up signs that read, "Welcome to Florida, Jim and Carol!" At first glance, I thought it was someone from *The Second Honeymoon Game* team. Then I blinked and realized it was Claire and Larry McGee.

And, standing right next to them, waving a sign which read, "Welcome to Florida, Mom and Dad," was our darling son, Mike.

Chapter 23

The only normal people in the world are the ones you haven't met yet or don't know very well.

I screamed. Well, wouldn't you have done the same thing? It had been over a year since I'd seen my only son. Letting go of the dogs' leashes in my excitement, I raced to my son and held him tight, tears streaming down my face. I didn't want to let go. Ever.

"Hey, Mom, take it easy," Mike said, hugging me back. "You may break something I'll need someday."

I felt a tap on my shoulder, and turned to see an airport attendant holding onto Lucy and Ethel's leashes. "I believe you dropped these, ma'am," he said. "You certainly don't want to lose these two."

"Thank you so much," I said, grabbing the leashes and wrapping them around my wrist for extra security. "I was just so excited to see my son again. It's been a long time."

"Hey, son, good to see you," Jim said, clapping Mike on the back in lieu of giving him a hug. The macho code of acceptable behavior between fathers and sons frowns on mushy gestures of affection, like hugging. Thank goodness it doesn't apply to mothers!

Lucy and Ethel could hardly contain their excitement at seeing Mike. They jumped up and down, begging for his attention until he sat down on the tarmac and gathered them both up in his arms. The dogs covered his face with sloppy kisses, practically knocking him flat. I didn't blame them. I wanted to do the same thing. The kissing part. Not the knocking flat part.

"Hey, girls, how are you? I missed seeing you last year."

I stepped back and surveyed my handsome son as he rose effortlessly to his feet. "You look like you've lost some weight," I said. "Are you eating enough? I hope we'll be staying at a place with a real kitchen, so I can whip you up some of your old favorite meals and put some pounds back on you. You're too thin. What do you want for supper tonight?" I frowned. "There better be a grocery store near where we're staying. I have food shopping to do."

Jim snorted. "Relax, Carol," he said. "We're supposed to be here on a working vacation. Let Mike have some space."

Never! At least, not right away.

I reached up and touched my son's face. "What's up with the stubbly look?" I asked, ignoring my husband. "The stubble hides your handsome face. I like the clean-shaven look much more."

Mike moved back from me. It was just a few inches, but for a mother like me it might as well have been a mile.

Oops. You're doing it again, Carol. Smothering your son, who is now a full-grown man, just in case you hadn't noticed. It's high time you started to treat him like one.

The old me, feeling rejected by my son, would have immediately burst into tears. The new me—less emotional, more rational (yeah, right!)—took a different, more adult tact. At least, I tried to. I hope I get points for effort.

"Sorry, sweetie," I said. "My maternal gene kicked in and I couldn't control it. Your new look just...surprised me, that's all. But I like it. I really do."

Mike laughed. "I know you're trying to convince yourself, Mom. You'll get used to it. Besides, the chicks love it."

"I just hope your father doesn't try to imitate you," I said. "He tried growing a beard on vacation years ago and it looked awful." I wrinkled my nose at the memory. "Don't give him any ideas."

"Don't worry about that," Jim chimed in. "I promise to shave every morning while we're in Florida. After all, we're here on our second honeymoon. Sort of. I want to keep you happy."

"Yeah, what exactly is going on? Your text didn't make much sense," Mike said. "And how'd you manage to arrive in such style?" He waved his hand in the direction of the private jet. "That's some fancy ride you hitched."

"We're here to produce the first episode of a television game show," I explained.

Jim, of course, immediately corrected me. "We're not here to *produce* the show," he said. "My old boss, Mack Whitman, recruited me to do the marketing for a television show aimed at Baby Boomers. The pilot episode is being shot here in Florida, and I was able to convince him to hire your mom to be my assistant on the project."

"But it didn't exactly work out that way," I interrupted. "I'm now the special assistant to the show's executive producer, Charlie King. We arrived in his private plane. Pretty cool, right?" I tried not to look smug. I failed.

"I want you to meet him," I said, grabbing Mike by the arm. "It turns out that he and I went to grammar school together. Can you believe it? And we've reconnected after all these years. Now, where did he go?" I scanned the tarmac and saw Charlie laughing and joking with Nancy, Claire and Larry. (Well, not Larry. Being a lawyer, he rarely laughs, much less shares jokes.) Nancy was hanging onto Charlie's arm like she was glued to him.

"That's Charlie King over there," I said. "Come on, I'll introduce you. I also need to say hello to Claire and Larry."

Jim excused himself, citing doggie responsibilities. "Lucy and Ethel have been cooped up for several hours. They need a good walk. You two go ahead. We'll catch up with you in a little while."

"Who's the hottie standing next to Mr. King?" Mike asked as we made our way across the tarmac.

"What? You mean you don't recognize Claire and Nancy?" I laughed. "It hasn't been that long since you've seen them."

"No, Mom," Mike said. "Be serious. I'm talking about the brunette on King's other side. The one in the white shorts with the great legs."

"Oh, you mean Carrie. That's Charlie's daughter. She works with her father on his television projects. I just met her the other day."

Although she's heard about me ever since she was born. I didn't really add that part, of course.

Claire threw her arms around me like she hadn't seen me in years. "Are you surprised to see us? I couldn't believe it when Nancy texted me yesterday about being on this television show. I'm so excited! Larry is, too. Aren't you, honey?"

The lawyer in question managed a small smile and nod of the

head. I had never seen him so demonstrative before. "It's nice to see you, Carol," he said. "Where's Jim?"

I returned Claire's hug, and shot Nancy a glare. If she thought she'd suddenly become *The Second Honeymoon Game* casting director, she had another thing coming. Claire and Larry would only make their television game show debut on *my* recommendation, not Nancy's.

"Jim's walking Lucy and Ethel," I said to Larry. "They needed their exercise after the plane ride. Charlie was kind enough to allow us to bring the dogs along on this *business* trip."

Charlie beamed. "They're very special canines, for sure. Maybe we can figure out a way to get them on the television show, too. Carrie, what do you think about that?"

I suddenly received a poke in my ribs from my darling son and realized I had committed a social gaffe. "My goodness, where are my manners?" I exclaimed. "Charlie, this is our son, Mike. He owns the most successful and 'in' restaurant in Miami, Cosmo's. You've probably heard of it. It's in South Beach."

Okay, I was laying that on a little thick. But hey, I'm his mother. Gushing is my right, right?

"Mike, I'd like you to meet my old grammar school chum, Charlie King."

"This is a real pleasure, Mike," Charlie said. "I'd like to say I've heard a lot about you from your parents, but since your mother and I just reconnected a few days ago, that's not exactly true. But I'm looking forward to getting to know you better while we're all in Florida. I hope you're planning on staying here on the Gulf Coast while we're filming the show." He turned to his right. "And this lovely young lady is my daughter, my only child, Carol Ann."

"It's Carrie now, remember, Dad?" Carrie said with a smile to show that she wasn't really angry.

Mike took Carrie's hand. "I had planned on heading back to Miami tonight. But I may change my mind." He had a goofy look on his face. You know the kind I mean, right? That "I've never seen anyone so gorgeous before and I think I'm in love" look.

"I'm looking forward to learning all about what happens behind the scenes on a television show from you, Carrie," Mike said. "And anything else you care to share with me."

Carrie dimpled, and I looked at the girl more closely. Mike was right. When she wasn't carrying a huge chip on her shoulder, and arguing with her father, Carrie was a real beauty. Mike was clearly attracted to her, and the feeling seemed to be mutual. Sizzle City, to coin a phrase.

I wondered if our family had room for another Carol Ann.

Chapter 24

Inside every old person is a young person
wondering what the heck happened.

"I've never seen anything more beautiful in my whole life," I said to Jim. "Just look at all these flowers. And in the middle of the winter! Up north, you'd be outside right now trying to get the snow blower going. Are we lucky or what?"

"I assume that was a rhetorical question," Jim replied with a smile. "But, you're right. We're pretty lucky."

"And look at all the palm trees everywhere," I said. "I wonder what Lucy and Ethel will make of all this new vegetation to explore."

"I'm sure they'll adjust just fine," Jim said. "Don't worry about everything so much."

Trust Jim to make me feel defensive about what really was an innocent remark. But, taking a page from the Jim Andrews School of Selective Hearing, I pretended I hadn't heard a word he said.

"I hope you'll give me a chance to drive this car," I said. "I've never been in a Mercedes before, and I've always dreamed about one."

"Then sit back and enjoy the ride," Jim said, hinting that perhaps my turn at the wheel would be a long time coming.

"If you plan on doing all the driving while we're here," I said with just a touch of annoyance, "be sure you don't lose the car keys. You know how you're always misplacing them at home."

"You don't have to worry about that, Carol," Jim said. "Charlie has the same problem with keys as I do, so Carrie figured out a way so that all the Mercedes can use the same key. She also had extra ones made, as a precaution. If one is lost, there'll always be a spare. Charlie told me she's a wiz at electronics."

"What a great idea. I bet she could make a fortune marketing her idea to all the wives in America." I laughed, to show my husband that I was only kidding.

"Charlie sure knows how to travel first-class," I continued. "First a private jet, then our own Mercedes. This is living. I never thought when we were in grammar school together that he'd be such a success. Just imagine. He has a fleet of four white Mercedes at his disposal, and we get to use one of them." I sighed in contentment.

"I bet they're all leased," Jim said, pouring a little cold water on me, figuratively speaking. "He probably charges them off as a business expense." Hmm. It sounded like my husband was just a teensy bit jealous.

"I don't care about that," I said. "A Mercedes by any means—leased or owned—is still a Mercedes. But I wish that Mike had come in our car. I wanted a chance to talk to him in private."

"You mean, grill him, don't you? Interrogate him about his life, especially, his love life?" When I didn't respond, especially since Jim was absolutely right, darn him, he added, "Mike seemed to be pretty taken with Carrie King. No wonder he jumped at the chance to ride with her instead of with his old fogey parents."

Cue selective hearing, Carol. Enjoy the beautiful scenery. And change the subject.

"Are you sure you know where we're going?" I asked my too-often directionally challenged husband. You know the story about men and asking for directions, so I don't need to remind you. Maybe you live with one of those, too.

"The directions were already programmed into the car's GPS," Jim replied. "I double checked before we left the airport. Charlie told me he had Carrie do that for all the cars, so nobody would get lost."

Jim gave me a sideways glance, which was safe since we were stopped at a traffic light. "Promise me you'll go easy on Mike, Carol. Don't fuss over him like he's still a child."

"All right, already. I promise," I said. "Ease up on me, okay? Mothers have the right to fuss over and worry about their children, no matter how old the children are. It's our reward for the hours of excruciating labor we go through to bring them into the world. Not that you'd know anything about that. You guys have it so easy."

I whipped out my phone. "Speaking of our children, I should text Jenny and tell her that we've gotten here safely. And find out how Mark is doing."

"I already did that," Jim said. "All is well."

Now I was really fuming. Still another example of Jim's usurping what should have been *my* job. *I* should have been the one to text Jenny first. I know. I know. Once again, I was being childish. But instead of snapping back at my husband, the way I wanted to, I put my head back and closed my eyes. I must have nodded off, because the next thing I remember, Jim was shaking me awake.

"Carol, wake up. We're here."

"I wasn't asleep, Jim," I lied. "I was closing my eyes because the sun is so bright."

A tasteful sign surrounded by palm trees and beautiful hibiscus welcomed us to the Honeymoon Island Resort. "I still can't believe it," I said to Jim, admiring the majestic pink stucco structure that would be our home base for our entire Florida stay. "We're here during one of the worst winters New England has seen in years. Pinch me to be sure I'm not dreaming."

Jim rolled to a stop in front of the main entrance to the hotel. In a flash, a staff member appeared to greet us, wearing a navy polo shirt emblazoned with the Honeymoon Island Resort logo, and khaki shorts that showed off tanned, muscular legs. Not that I paid much attention. Nor did I concentrate on his handsome face and eyes the color of melted chocolate. Not me.

Flashing a brilliant smile, he opened my door with a flourish and offered me his arm to help me out of the Mercedes. "Welcome, Mr. and Mrs. Andrews," he said. "Allow me to introduce myself. I am Bernardo, and I'll be your personal concierge during your stay with us. Anything you want, just ask." He gave me a wink, which I ignored. Honestly, I was old enough to be this man's…aunt.

"Although I appreciate the welcome," Jim said, "we won't need the services of a concierge. My wife and I are here on business. We're part of the team for a television show."

"I know," said Bernardo. "*The Second Honeymoon Game,* correct? You are with Charles King. He has reserved one of our best villas for your stay. If you remain here for just a moment, I'll return with a golf cart to drive you there. It's walking distance from the main building, but with the luggage, riding would be much simpler. In the meantime, please enjoy the scenery." He pointed in the direction of a magnificent beach with the whitest sand and the bluest water I'd ever seen.

I remember thinking at that moment that Jim and I were the closest to paradise we'd ever be while we were still on this earth, and felt pure joy and peace, looking out at that magnificent view.

Too bad I forgot about what happened to the first couple who visited paradise, Adam and Eve.

Chapter 25

My wife and I had words last night. Unfortunately, I didn't get to use any of mine.

"Whatever you're doing, it sure feels wonderful," I said to Jim. "And just look at that gorgeous sunset." I sighed in contentment and snuggled closer to my husband. "Here we are on a beach in Florida, it's after six o'clock at night, and the sun is just going down. In Connecticut, it would be dark already. And freezing cold."

It was our first night in Florida, and after settling into our luxurious villa, and a quick check with Charlie King to be sure there was no television show meeting until the following morning, Jim and I had decided to take a bottle of wine and two glasses to the beach.

OMG. The ramifications of what I'd just said rolled over me like a wave from the Gulf of Mexico. If the sun hadn't set, that meant we were visible to anyone strolling along the beach. I pulled myself away from my husband's amorous embrace and swatted him. "Stop that. Somebody might see us."

Jim rolled over on his side and gave me a "Look." "Carol, for heaven's sake. Even though we're down here for the television show, we're also on our own second honeymoon. And I hope you remember what we did on our first honeymoon. It was a lot more than what we're doing now."

I sat up and brushed the sand off my bathing suit. Truth to

tell, it fit a little tighter than it did when I tried it on at Suits R Us in Fairport, Connecticut, a few months ago. But I hope you won't tell anyone I admitted that.

Fortunately, from the way he was acting, Jim hadn't. And I intended to keep it that way. "I remember," I said with a smile to my husband of thirty-plus years. "But that was in the privacy of our hotel room, not in a public place."

I frowned. "I don't feel right about leaving Lucy and Ethel alone in the villa on our first night here. I hope they don't bark and disturb the neighbors. And we really should check on Mike. I wonder if he's planning on going back to Miami tonight."

"For heaven's sake, stop worrying about every little thing," Jim said with more than a trace of impatience. "I'm sure the dogs are fine. I asked Bernardo to check on them while we were out. And you promised to stay out of Mike's private life, remember?"

I nodded. Without enthusiasm. But I did make the effort.

"Why don't we go for a short walk?" I suggested, trying to get myself more into the vacation spirit. "I don't know about you, but I could use some exercise after that plane ride. And if we walk, we won't feel guilty about ordering dessert tonight."

Jim rolled over and got to his feet. With some difficulty, which I pretended not to notice.

"Why don't we walk that way?" I said, indicating a route that was in the direction of Honeymoon Island's rear parking lot. "It looks pretty level, and if one of us gets tired, we're close to the car."

I squinted, then said, "Wait a minute, Jim. Do you see something bright? And what's that smell? Is something burning?"

The next thing I heard was a loud *whoosh*. I'd never heard anything like it before.

Jim grabbed me. "Get down, Carol," he said, pushing me into the sand. "Our car's on fire. If the flames hit the gas tank, it'll explode."

There was a loud noise, then silence. I was lying face down in the sand, Jim on top of me. I opened my mouth to scream, but all that did was fill my mouth with sand. Ugh.

I could feel Jim shaking. He was just as frightened as I was, although, being a guy, he'd never admit it. "Are you okay, honey?" he asked. "I hope I didn't hurt you when I tackled you. I just wanted to protect you." Jim rolled over and got to his feet, offering me his hand to help me up.

I was trembling so hard that I probably lost five pounds from the exertion. I never thought of mindless terror as a weight-loss method before.

"What if we'd been in the car, Jim?" I said, sobbing. "We'd be dead by now. How could something like that happen?"

"It must have been a fluke," Jim said. "Some terrible mechanical failure. We need to contact the authorities right away, and Charlie, of course. He needs to know about this, so all the other cars in the fleet can be checked immediately. Oh, damn."

"What?"

"I left my phone in our room. There aren't any pockets in my bathing suit."

For some reason, that struck me as extremely funny. I guess I was bordering on hysteria by then. I couldn't stop laughing. A close encounter with death can do that to a person. You'll just have to take my word for that. I don't recommend you try it for yourself.

I cocked an ear and heard sirens in the distance. Help was on the way, thank God.

Two official-looking cars careened into the parking lot, almost hitting each other in their rush to get to the scene of the burning Mercedes. One was a ranger from the park's environmental police force; the other was from the county sheriff's department.

Jim and I hung back and let the officers do their job. Truth to tell, they hadn't even noticed us. I couldn't help but overhear that there seemed to be some difference of opinion as to which authority had jurisdiction in this situation.

"There's someone trapped inside the car!" I heard a deputy scream into his phone. "Get an emergency vehicle here right away!"

Chapter 26

I am the soul of discretion. Unfortunately, my mouth never follows suit.

I clung to my husband, and whispered, "Jim, did you hear that? There's someone trapped in the car. Oh, my God. It must be someone from the television show."

Jim disagreed, of course. "I'm sure it's nobody we know," he said. "I'm betting somebody saw the Mercedes in the parking lot and tried to steal it. These things happen all the time. And then, well...boom."

I swayed in the general direction of the ground, and moaned, "I think I'm going to be sick to my stomach." I promptly fainted. Right there in the parking lot. At least, that's what Jim told me later.

The next thing I remember was a light shining in my eyes, and a disembodied voice saying, "Ma'am, are you all right? Can you sit up?"

Man, how embarrassing. I now had the full attention of the park ranger who, having been summarily dismissed by the county sheriff personnel, had discovered me sprawled near the edge of the parking lot, my husband hovering above me.

"I'm all right," I said, pulling myself to a sitting position with some effort. "But this has been such a terrible shock. I've never seen anything like this before," I said, waving in the general direction of the burning car. "It's horrible."

"Can you tell me what you're still doing here?" the ranger asked.

"The park closes at dusk."

Jim took over the conversation, as he inevitably does. "We're staying at the Honeymoon Island Resort," he said. "It's our first night in Florida, and we decided to check out the beach. We didn't notice the sign that listed the park hours. The gate was open when we arrived, and nobody stopped us."

The ranger scribbled in his notebook, then asked for identification. Well, of course, both Jim and I were in our swim togs and weren't able to produce any.

More embarrassment.

Our interrogation was interrupted by the arrival of a fire truck and several more vehicles bearing the logo of the county sheriff's department, followed by an ambulance.

I burrowed my head in Jim's shoulder. "I don't think I can stand to watch this," I said, as several more deputies raced toward the burning vehicle. "Is it true that someone is in the car? Are they going to try and save him?"

The ranger immediately pounced on my choice of pronouns. "How do you know it's a man in there?"

"I don't know," I said, bristling at his accusatory tone. "Should I have said, 'Are they going to try to save him or her?' That sounds ridiculous under the circumstances."

My attention was drawn to another sheriff's deputy who was barking orders at all the other personnel on the scene. "Our first priority is to put out the fire, and then extricate the victim. Get to it. Immediately. We don't have all night to do this." Then the deputy caught sight of Jim, the park ranger, and me, and headed straight to us.

"Armstrong, Investigative Operations Bureau, County Sheriff's Office," the deputy said, flipping a badge so fast that I couldn't read it. "Who are you and what are you doing here? The park closes at sunset. You're trespassing. Show me some identification. Right now."

His high-and-mighty attitude really ticked me off. I've had lots of practice with law enforcement officials since Jim's retirement, and realized immediately that this pipsqueak was trying to intimidate us. Well, he wasn't going to get away with it.

Before I could respond, Jim did. "I'm Jim Andrews. My wife, Carol, and I are visiting here from Connecticut. We're staying at the Honeymoon Island Resort. We never thought to bring identification with us when we came to the beach. It's in our villa back at the Honeymoon Island Resort."

The deputy frowned and looked hard at Jim and me. "Where in Connecticut?"

"Fairport," I said. "It's just outside of New York City."

"I know exactly where it is," the deputy said. "I have a cousin who lives there. He's a detective on the local police force."

"What a coincidence," Jim said, smiling nervously. "Our son-in-law is a detective on the police force, too. His name's Mark Anderson."

I dug my fingers into Jim's arm to shut him up. But, of course, he didn't take the hint. In fact, he didn't have a clue where this conversation could end up. But I did. Now I knew why this twerp had ticked me off so quickly. I was pretty sure I was speaking to the cousin of Paul Wheeler.

Fortunately, Mark's name meant nothing to the officer. He didn't react at all. But I knew that he'd do a background check on us with the Fairport Police, and then he'd find out all about how I had "helped" them in some recent cases. And, unfortunately, the rocky relationship between Cousin Paul and me. Which was certainly putting it mildly. But maybe, since I had become Paul's confidante a few days ago because of his guilt over Mark's accident, he might not be so harsh in his comments about me.

Or, maybe, Paul would be even harsher, because he was embarrassed about what he'd told me. Oh, well. I couldn't control what Paul said. Unfortunately.

I always believe that, if you find yourself in a sticky situation—like, for example, if Jim finds out that I've maxed out my credit card due to circumstances (a.k.a. impulse purchases) beyond my control—the best defense is either a strong diversion or a strong offensive stance. I decided to go with Plan B.

"When you check us out with the Fairport Police," I said, looking the officer directly in the eye, which was easy to do since we were both about the same height, "you'll find that I was recently awarded a special citation from the department for my assistance in solving several cases. The chief is a very good friend of mine." Jim gave my hand a warning squeeze, but I ignored him and soldiered on.

"My husband and I are in Florida on business," I continued. "We're part of the marketing and production team for a new television show, *The Second Honeymoon Game*. The pilot episode is being filmed here. But, if you like, I'm sure I can carve out some time to be of assistance to you in this case."

"Lady, you must be delusional," the deputy said. "I don't give a hoot about your so-called relationship with the Fairport Police. You're in Florida now. And we don't take kindly to amateurs meddling in our official police business. Stay out of my way."

Before the deputy could continue to berate me, there was a shout from the direction of the ruined car. "Ma'am, we have successfully extricated the victim, and the photographers are through here. We're ready to take him away."

Ma'am? This deputy sheriff was a female? No way.

"Don't call me ma'am," the deputy ordered her subordinate. "I'll be right there. As for you two," addressing us, "I'm not through with you yet."

I started to sway again as the reality of the situation hit me. Jim grabbed onto me to stop me from falling. "Officer," he said, "is it possible for us to go back to our hotel now? I understand we have to make statements, but my wife really needs to lie down."

Deputy Armstrong's face softened, just for a minute. Then, she nodded. "Smith," she yelled to another deputy, "take these people's information. Then they're free to leave. For now. I'll see you both tomorrow. After I have the chance to check you out with the Fairport Police. And my Cousin Paul."

I'm sure it'll come as no surprise to you that I had a lot of trouble falling asleep that night. Even cuddling up to Jim, with Lucy and Ethel curled up between us, sleep refused to come. Every time I closed my eyes, I saw the burning car. And I said prayers of thanksgiving that Jim and I were safe.

I wasn't looking forward to being grilled by the local constabulary again. I even wondered if Charlie King would hold Jim and me responsible for the ruined Mercedes and make us pay to replace it.

Don't be stupid, Carol. Jim's right. Someone saw a Mercedes in the parking lot and tried to steal it. There was a weird mechanical glitch and the car ignited. What happened isn't your fault.

I rolled over on my other side, trying to make myself comfortable in a strange bed. This second honeymoon was turning out to be the trip from hell. And we hadn't even been in Florida for twenty-four hours.

I cheered myself up a little when I remembered how wonderful it was to see Mike again. I wondered if he was still here, or if he'd flown back to Miami without saying goodbye to his parents. Or did he decide to stay and get better acquainted with the lovely Carrie King?

Then, I mentally slapped myself. Jim was right again, darn it. Mike was a grown man and what he chose to do in his free time, and with whom he chose to do it, was none of my business. I was also sure that, if I reminded myself of this fact approximately a million times a day, I'd start to believe it.

I realized it was a blessing to have some of our close friends here. Especially Nancy. Wait until she found out what happened to us tonight. Heck, she'd probably be angry that she'd missed all the excitement.

I smiled at that. Knowing Nancy, she could be cheering herself up a little with Charlie. They certainly seemed to be cozy on the plane ride down here.

I was even glad that Claire and Larry were here. After what happened tonight, Jim and I might need a very good lawyer.

Chapter 27

Sometimes I pretend to be normal, but it gets boring, so I go back to being me.

"I'm not hungry," I said to Jim. "After what happened last night, I may never eat again." I pushed my breakfast toward him. "Here. You have my permission to eat all the food on my plate. You don't have to wait for my leftovers."

Jim gave me a skeptical look. "This is a first, Carol. Are you sure about this? Here. Drink some coffee. It'll perk you right up."

I took a small sip and grimaced, either from the coffee—which was definitely not as good as the coffee we had at home—or from my husband's atrocious pun.

Home. That's where I wanted to be this morning. Sitting in my own kitchen in my own beautiful house in Fairport, Connecticut, instead of the dining room of the Honeymoon Island Resort, sipping coffee made by my personal barista. That would be Jim, in case you don't get the reference. I pushed away the thought that the temperature was probably ten degrees with blizzard conditions in Fairport this morning, while here in Florida, the sun was shining brilliantly outside and the weather forecasters had promised temperatures in the mid-80s.

I put the cup down, and announced, "I want to go home. Today. Right now." Cue automatic tears. "I wish we'd never come here. I wish we'd never gotten involved with this stupid television show. I wish…"

Jim reached over and grabbed my hand. "Honey, I know how upset you are. What happened last night was terrible. But we're here and, you know the old saying, 'The show must go on.' I got a text that there's a production meeting scheduled at nine. We don't want to be late. I see Mack in the doorway, waving at us right now. We have to go."

I sighed. Jim was right.

"I didn't know Mack was already here," I said, grabbing a piece of fruit to take with me to the meeting so I wouldn't starve to death. "In fact, except for Charlie and Carrie, I haven't seen anyone from the production team so far."

"I'm sure they'll all be at the meeting," Jim said, as we followed Mack's disappearing back down the hotel hallway leading to The Flamingo Room.

For once, my chubby legs beat Jim's long-legged stride, and I got to the meeting room first, immediately wishing I hadn't. All thoughts of planning the television pilot vanished when I saw who was sitting at the head of the table—two representatives from the County Sheriff's Department. And, of course, one of them, looking as intimidating as possible, was Deputy Armstrong.

I nodded nervously at the rest of the staff, some of whom I didn't remember meeting in New York, then pulled out a chair at the opposite end of the table from the deputy. Jim took a seat next to me, and Kurt Armitage sat on my other side. For once, the genial Gene Richmond, television host extraordinaire with a quip for every occasion, had nothing to say. Even Mack was subdued; he didn't make eye contact with Jim and me. Definitely not a good sign.

I could hear the clock on the wall ticking. Or, maybe that sound was my knees knocking together. Were we going to be fired? Or, even worse, arrested?

The meeting room door opened again, and Carrie King walked in, supported by—of all people—our son. The little devil. So that's why he'd become the Invisible Man last night.

Carrie and Mike took seats next to Deputy Sheriff Armstrong. I realized that Carrie looked terrible. Her eyes were red-rimmed (from lack of sleep?) and she was not wearing any makeup. Trust me. When a woman doesn't bother to put on makeup, especially if she's in a public situation with a potential new boyfriend, she's got a lot on her mind.

The deputy sheriff cleared her throat and began to speak.

"Good morning, everyone. I'm Deputy Sheriff Armstrong from the County Sheriff's office. I'm here to get more information from you about what happened to one of your company cars last night at the beach. Perhaps you've already heard about the incident?"

Cue staff shifting in their chairs.

I looked around and suddenly realized someone was missing. So, of course, I raised my hand, requesting permission to speak—as any other good little Catholic girl who'd been trained by the nuns would do.

Detective Armstrong sighed. Deeply and loudly. "Yes, Mrs. Andrews," she said. "Do you have something to say?"

"It's more of a question," I said. "I'm sorry to interrupt, but how can we start this meeting without Charlie King here? He's the executive producer of *The Second Honeymoon Game*," I clarified for the deputy, "and his company, Charles King Productions, owns the Mercedes that was destroyed last night."

Which was not our fault, so don't try to pin the blame on Jim and me. I didn't really say that last part, of course.

"I'm sure he can answer many of your questions. I think we should wait for him."

My innocent suggestion produced uncontrolled sobbing from Carrie. Mike put his arm around her protectively and whispered something in her ear.

"What?" I asked. "What did I say?"

Detective Armstrong cleared her throat again. "Mr. King will be unable to join us," she said. "He died in last night's explosion."

My eyes welled up and spilled over. I was so shocked, I couldn't speak.

"Charlie's dead?" Kurt repeated. "Are you sure?"

Deputy Armstrong directed her laser stare at him. "Of course I'm sure," she snapped back. "And who are you?"

Kurt sat up straight in his chair and tried not to show how uncomfortable he was at being singled out by the deputy. I sympathized with him. I'd been in that particular hot seat far too many times. "My name is Kurt Armitage. I coordinate the talent for *The Second Honeymoon Game*. I've worked with Charlie for years. I just can't believe...I can't believe any of this."

I couldn't believe it, either. I buried my head in the comfort of Jim's familiar shoulder, not caring if I got his brand new golf shirt soaked with my tears.

"But what about the show?" asked Gene Richmond. "How can we continue without Charlie? He was the visionary, the guiding light, the..." He struggled to control his emotions, then added, "But we must go on. As a tribute to Charlie and his genius."

"Oh, shut up, Gene," said Kurt. "You're just worried that your little television comeback won't happen after all. That's certainly no loss to America's viewing audience. Just think of all the publicity Mack would have to do to remind everybody who you are. Or maybe, I should say, who you *were*."

Gene sprang out of his chair, his face purple with rage. "You little twit. How dare you speak to me like that?" I shrank back against Jim. I was sure the two men were going to end up in a fistfight.

"Enough!" said Deputy Armstrong. "Both of you sit down and get hold of yourselves. I've got an investigation to conduct, and neither of you are helping." She nodded at the other deputy. "But I hope you've made a note of this behavior."

"I'll need to interview each of you separately," she continued. "And until I'm finished with all of you, no one is allowed to leave this room. For any reason. Got that?"

Satisfied that she had made her point crystal clear, Deputy Armstrong turned her attention to me. Unfortunately. "You're first up, Mrs. Andrews. Follow me."

Rats. But there was no way, short of faking a complete collapse on The Flamingo Room floor, that I could avoid this interview. Of course, even if I did collapse, and an ambulance was called to take me to a local hospital, with my luck Deputy Armstrong would go with me, interrogating me all the way to the emergency room.

All through the shocking announcement of Charlie's death, and Kurt and Gene's angry exchange, Carrie had remained quiet. No doubt due to the comforting presence of Mike, who continued to have his arm around her shoulder. As I rose to follow Deputy Armstrong, I felt I had to express my condolences to her. Even if Armstrong yelled at me to "hurry up."

"Carrie," I said, "you and I may not know each other very well, but I feel we're connected because of your dad. I know how much he loved you. If there's anything, anything at all, I can do to make this terrible ordeal easier for you, well...I'm here for you. Jim is, too."

Carrie dissolved into tears. Then she grabbed my hand, pulled me down so we were eyeball to eyeball, and whispered in my ear,

"Please, help me. How could this happen? Why did my father die?"

Chapter 28

I don't let anything or anybody get me down.
At my age, it's too hard to get back up again.

I stared at her, unsure about what she was asking. I glanced at my son, who said in a low voice, "I told Carrie about your new career. And how good you are at it." He raised his eyebrows and, for a split second, looked so much like his father that I couldn't believe it. Except, of course, that Mike was encouraging me to pursue my so-called detective vocation, while Jim would have an absolute fit if he knew I was involved in another police investigation.

I had to give this some serious thought before I committed to helping Carrie. I didn't want to risk Jim's ire, and Deputy Armstrong had made it pretty clear last night that my offer of unofficial assistance wouldn't be tolerated here in Florida. Under any circumstances.

Come on, Carol. You're not going to let a little obstacle like that get in your way, are you? Jim always comes around in the end. He's even proud of your snooping when you solve the case. And if you're really clever, Deputy Armstrong won't ever catch on to what you're up to.

All this musing flashed across my brain in a millisecond, believe it or not.

"Mrs. Andrews, we're waiting for you!"

I snapped to attention and turned around to see Deputy Armstrong standing at the doorway, tapping her foot in impatience. *Uh oh. Better not aggravate her any more than you already have.*

"Sorry for the delay," I said, following her down the hallway to a smaller conference room. "I stopped to give my condolences to Carrie King, since she's just lost her dad in a very shocking manner." *Take that, Deputy Bossy Pants.*

I noted that this time, we were in The Pelican Room. My goodness. Was every meeting room in this hotel named after a bird?

"Sit," Armstrong said, pointing to a chair. "Now."

Well! I didn't take kindly to being ordered about so cavalierly. This "interrogation" was going downhill fast. But, I sat. I am an obedient, cooperative person. Especially when facing a person who could change my Florida accommodations from a five-star resort to a jail cell.

"Deputy Lewis will take notes during this interview," Armstrong said, nodding at the other law enforcement officer. "But before we begin the questioning, Lewis, I could use some coffee, and I'm sure Mrs. Andrews could, too. I believe I saw some at the refreshment stand near the pool area. Get some for yourself, as well. Here." She pressed a ten-dollar-bill into his hand, then added, "Be sure you get a receipt."

Deputy Lewis was clearly unhappy at this unusual request. But rather than argue, he nodded and skedaddled out of the room in search of some fresh caffeine.

As soon as the door to The Pelican Room closed, Deputy Armstrong said, "I just love sending a man out to get coffee, don't you? It's sort of a small payback for all the years that the secretaries of the world were required to do it as part of their job descriptions."

She gave me a big grin. "We don't have much time before Lewis gets back. Even though I sent him as far away from here as I could."

"Time?" I asked. I was totally confused. "Time for what?"

Armstrong grinned again. "I talked to my cousin Paul about you last night."

Oh, boy. Here it comes. Slap on the handcuffs and get the jail cell ready.

"He doesn't think too kindly of you."

"The feeling's mutual," I said. "He's a real twit." Then I clapped my hands over my mouth. "Oops. Sorry. I shouldn't have said that."

"On the contrary, Mrs. Andrews," Armstrong said, "I completely agree with you. Strictly between us, of course." She cleared her throat, then continued, "He called you an old, interfering busybody with nothing better to do with your time than interfere in the official work of the Fairport Police Department."

"I'm not old," I snapped back. "I'm mature. In age, anyway." I could feel a flush of embarrassment spread across my face. "But I can't deny that I'm, well...curious. And what I told you last night is the absolute truth. I have helped the Fairport police solve some cases. People talk to me. I'm non-threatening. I've been able to find out things that the police never would have."

Armstrong smiled and leaned back in her chair. "I believe you. Especially if Paul was the detective in charge of any cases you were involved in. I'm sure he's not the brightest member of the force. I probably shouldn't be telling you this, but Paul's always been a pain in my posterior. He and I have been in competition since our nursery school days. In fact, that's why he went into law enforcement. Because I did it first."

She leaned closer. "He had this terrible rhyme he used to torment me with when we were growing up. 'Terri, Terri, quite contrary, how does your waistline grow?' Etc. etc. I was heavy as a child, and he never let me forget it. In fact, the only way I could get him to stop was to pop him one." Her face darkened at the memory. "He'd always cry and tell our mothers that I was beating him up for no reason. They usually took his side."

She stopped herself. "But you don't need to hear about my family history. I just wanted to explain to you that if Paul tells me something is black, then I immediately know it's white. So if he tells me that you're an old, interfering busybody, then I know that you're a good judge of people, someone who has a sharp mind and isn't afraid to use it."

While part of me appreciated the compliment, another part of me was suspicious. Why was Deputy Armstrong buttering me up, as my late mother would have so quaintly put it?

"I can see that you're wondering why I'm talking to you this way," Armstrong said, correctly reading my mind. "So I'll get right to the point before Lewis gets back with the coffee. I want you to be my unofficial eyes and ears in this investigation. You know these television people. I don't. I need somebody connected with the show to feed me information. But this is strictly between us. I'd lose my job if this got out. So, are you game?"

"Whoa," I said. "Stop a minute. I have no idea what you're talking about. You're not suggesting that somebody deliberately rigged the car to explode, are you? Jim drove the same car to the beach an hour before, and nothing happened to us." Oops. I didn't mean to let that slip. Oh, well.

"It's still early in the investigation, Mrs. Andrews," Armstrong replied. "The lab has to examine what's left of the car to see if the source of the explosion can be identified. The explosion could have been caused by a mechanical malfunction. But we're not ruling anything out. And I can tell already from preliminary conversations with the television show staff that they're not going to be as forthright with me as they could be. That's where you come in. I just want you to keep your ears open, and if you hear anything that you think I should know about, contact me immediately."

Armstrong fixed me with a hard stare. "Let me be perfectly clear. Under *no* circumstances are you to start asking questions on your own. Just listen, and share anything you think could be relevant with me right away. Wrapping up such a high profile case quickly would go a long way toward improving my image in the Sheriff's Office."

"Your image? What do you mean?"

"You must be one of the few people who didn't hear about The Big Rug Fiasco. Our headquarters went through a major renovation last year, and part of the job included purchasing two new area rugs for the lobby. The rugs were supposed to have been printed with the seal of the department and the words 'In God We Trust.' Unfortunately, one of the rugs said, 'In Dog We Trust' instead. I had signed off on the rug purchase, and never noticed the typo. Unfortunately, a reporter from one of the local papers came in to do an interview several months later and saw the typo. He wrote a story about it, including a picture of the rug and of me; the story went viral, and I'm now the laughing stock of the office. I want to solve this case ASAP to get back my cred. I'm tired of people snickering behind my back."

That made sense to me. I figured that being a female in what's traditionally a male-dominated profession would be hard enough. To be ridiculed by her male colleagues for what was an honest mistake must be super embarrassing.

I thought about Armstrong's request for about half a second. I bet you're surprised it took me that long, but that little annoying voice that pops up now and then (it sounds a lot like Jim's) yelled, "No, Carol! Don't do this."

Of course, I ignored that voice as I have for years, and said, "I'm in. And I already have some information for you."

"I knew this was a good idea," Armstrong said. "Go on. What do you know?"

"When I was on my way out of The Flamingo Room, and stopped to talk to Carrie King, she asked me to do pretty much the same thing you are."

Armstrong raised her eyebrows so high that they practically disappeared into her hairline. "She asked you to snoop on other members of the television show production team?"

"Well," I said, "not exactly. She asked me to find out who was responsible for her father's death. I think her exact words were, 'Why did my father die?' "

"Interesting," Armstrong said. "But why would she ask you that? I didn't realize your reputation was so well-known."

"My son, Mike, suggested it," I said. "He's the good-looking young guy who was sitting right next to Carrie," I added with a touch of maternal pride. "They just met yesterday, but apparently have really hit it off, if you get my meaning."

"Even more interesting," Armstrong said. "Maybe he can be of some help in this investigation, too."

"Oh, no," I said in alarm. "Please don't get him involved. Jim will have a fit if he finds out what I'm doing, but he'd be apoplectic if he thought Mike was involved, too."

"But he is involved, Mrs. Andrews. From what you've told me, your son is Carrie King's alibi."

"Alibi? What do you mean? Surely you don't think that Carrie would want to harm her own father? That's just crazy."

"As I said before, this is very early in the investigation," Armstrong replied. "For all we know, she had a huge fight with her father. Maybe he told her she was off the show. Who knows? Anything is possible."

I shook my head. No way.

"It's important that we get a timetable of King's movements last night," Armstrong said. "And why he went to the beach."

"I may be able to help you with that," I said. Nancy was going to kill me, but I heard myself saying, "I think he spent some quality time with my best friend, Nancy Green. In case you didn't know, Nancy, Charlie and I all went to grammar school together, and we reconnected after all these years because of *The Second Honeymoon Game.*"

And I bet that Nancy and Charlie really reconnected. But I didn't say that out loud. Of course.

Our conversation was interrupted by a tap on the door, followed by the reappearance of Deputy Lewis bearing three cups of coffee in a carryout box. "Sorry I took so long," he said, looking embarrassed. "I took a wrong turn and got lost finding my way back here from the pool." For a split second, Armstrong and I shared a knowing look.

Men never ask for directions.

Chapter 29

My husband and I have an unspoken pact.
He pretends not to notice my thickening
waistline, and I pretend not to notice his
thinning hair.

Instead of going back to The Flamingo Room to rejoin the rest of *The Second Honeymoon Game* production staff, I took a detour and headed straight toward our villa, snagging a sweet roll and fresh coffee on my way. I had some serious thinking to do before I faced anyone else. Especially my husband, who could read my face like the proverbial book when I didn't want him to.

This was a lot more serious than my usual list of sins, which included snapping up a bargain or two (or five) on things I never realized I needed but now that I'd seen them, I absolutely had to have. Maybe a few of you can identify with that situation. Hey, if any of you have tips on how you deal with your husbands, email me privately, okay?

Jim was probably next on Deputy Armstrong's interview list. I was betting his questioning wouldn't take nearly as long as mine did, so I figured I had half an hour tops to get my act together. Despite what you may think about me, I do not like to lie to my husband. (Especially when there's more than a fifty percent chance that I'm going to get caught.)

Lucy and Ethel, clearly in vacation mode, barely acknowledged my presence. I envied them. Maybe in my next life I'd come back as an English cocker spaniel.

I was just settling myself at the desk in the living room when there was a loud banging at the door, accompanied by a familiar voice that was verging on hysteria. "Carol, are you there? Let me in! I have terrible news!"

It was Nancy. Rats. From the way she was carrying on, she'd just found out about Charlie's unfortunate demise. "Calm down, Nancy," I hissed, grabbing her arm and pulling her into the villa before anyone else heard her.

"Calm down?" she said, her voice shaking. "How can I calm down? The man of my dreams is dead. Oh my God. What am I going to do?"

Good heavens. This was too much, even for Nancy.

"The man of your dreams?" I asked. "Has something terrible happened to Bob? Your husband," I added, just for the sake of clarification.

I know, I know. I shouldn't have said that, because, of course I knew who Nancy was crying about. But when Nancy slips into her drama queen persona she risks bringing out my evil twin, who sometimes takes over my usually sweet and caring BFF persona.

"No, not Bob," Nancy said, scowling at the mention of her occasionally two-timing husband. "Since when is Bob the man of my dreams? I'm talking about Charlie King, for heaven's sake. He died last night. I just found out about it. There's nothing wrong with Bob."

"Well, you and Bob are still legally married, in case you've forgotten," I said. "I believe you called it, 'married but dating.' And you said the arrangement was working out great. You can't blame me for being confused."

"Oh, pish," Nancy said. "Leave it to you to pour cold water on my fantasy life." Then, she burst into tears. "But Charlie and I were just starting to get reacquainted after all these years. I felt such a cosmic connection with him, and I could just tell that he felt the same way. And now, he's gone. Poof! Just like that." Nancy snapped her fingers for emphasis. "I had to come and tell you right away."

I handed Nancy a paper napkin to dry her eyes—leave it to her to have the foresight to wear waterproof mascara so her makeup still looked perfect—and made a quick decision to keep my big mouth shut for once and let Nancy talk. Big surprise, right? I am nothing if not spontaneous.

"We had such a lovely time last night," Nancy said. "I never suspected it would be Charlie's last meal."

"I'm sure he didn't suspect that, either," I said. "I hope he had dessert."

"You are just awful," Nancy said, swatting me with the now-soggy napkin. "For your information, Charlie did have dessert. Key lime pie, which he shared with me. Claire and Larry had their own."

"Claire and Larry? They were with you?"

"Of course they were," Nancy said. "Charlie was thrilled to see Claire again, and he insisted that the four of us have an early dinner together and talk about old times." Nancy frowned a little. "I'm afraid Larry was a little bored by all our reminiscing, but he was a good sport about it."

Nice change for Larry. Usually he was the boring one. Maybe now he knew how the rest of us felt when he went into one of his dry as dust legal monologues.

"We were all having such a good time," Nancy continued, smiling at the memory. "Charlie was, well, charming. A perfect host. But then, he got this text, which seemed to really upset him. He excused himself, jumped up, and raced out of the restaurant. That was the last I saw of him." She dissolved into tears again.

My brain ramped up to warp speed. This was important information. Now, if I could figure out who'd sent Charlie that text, I could solve the riddle of Charlie's untimely death. (I'm never comfortable with using the word "murder.") Piece of cake. Because there had to be a connection. Somebody sent Charlie a text, lured him to the beach on some pretext, and then, bam! Bye, bye, Charlie.

"And before you ask me, Carol, the answer is no. I have no idea who sent Charlie that text." Nancy's eyes filled with tears again and threatened to spill over.

I poured a little of my now lukewarm coffee into another cup and handed it to Nancy. "Here. Drink this. Maybe it'll help."

Nancy grabbed the cup like it was a lifeline—she's a caffeine junky, too—and downed it in one quick gulp. "Are you going to eat that sweet roll?" she asked. Wordlessly, I passed it to her. The mark of true friendship, right?

Nancy broke off a tiny piece of the roll and popped it into her mouth. "You're right, I do feel a little better now," she said. "Thanks." And then, instead of polishing off the rest of the roll, she began shredding it into a million pieces. My sweet roll! Which I hadn't even tasted yet!

"Nancy," I said, "that's my breakfast you're demolishing."

"Huh?" she asked, then looked down at the mess on the desk. "Oh, sorry. Here." She pushed the crumbs toward me. "You know I always play with my food when I'm nervous." She looked at me with the laser vision that only one BFF can have for the other, and said, "You've got a funny look on your face all of a sudden, which means something's up. What is it?"

To tell, or not to tell. That was the question. On the one hand, Nancy's always been a key member of my sleuthing team, and I can never keep a secret from her. (Unlike Jim. I've been keeping secrets from him for years.)

On the other hand, I was pretty sure Deputy Armstrong told me not to advertise my collaboration with the sheriff's office. Didn't she? Or, did she just tell me not to ask any questions? Maybe if I told Nancy what I knew, I could get her to ask some questions for me, so I couldn't get into trouble. That's the kind of thinking that would even impress St. Thomas Aquinas. I knew that course in logic I took back in college would one day come in handy.

On the other hand, well...I only have two hands. So, thanks to St. Thomas Aquinas, I made my decision.

I took a deep breath, then said, "Jim and I were at the beach last night when the car exploded. But I didn't find out about Charlie's death until this morning at the program meeting. Deputy Armstrong from the county sheriff's office made the announcement. We were all in shock."

Now, it was my turn to turn on the waterworks. "It was horrible last night, Nancy. Seeing the car explode and burn, and now finding out that Charlie was in it. I'll have nightmares about it for a long time."

Nancy passed me back the soggy napkin. "You need this more than I do now."

"There's more," I said. "Mike spent the night with Carrie King."

Nancy raised her perfectly sculpted eyebrows at this bit of news. "So what? He's over twenty-one. They both are. Don't tell me you have a problem with that, Carol. You've just got to get over this hang-up you have about..."

"Oh, for Pete's sake, Nancy," I said in exasperation. "I don't care about the overnight part. As everyone I know keeps pointing out to me, my two kids are adults now and what they do with their lives is none of my business. Mostly. But when Carrie found out that her father was dead, Mike told her about my amateur sleuthing career. She wants me to find out what happened."

Nancy's eyes, so recently filled with tears, now sparkled with interest. "Of course, you said, yes, right? And I'll help you. Like I always do. So will Claire."

I held up my hand. "I'm not finished telling you what happened, yet. There's more." I told her about Deputy Armstrong, her relationship to Paul Wheeler, and the request she'd made of me.

"This is exciting," Nancy said. "It's the first time anyone actually on a police force has asked us to get involved. So, how do we start the investigation, chief? Tell me what you want me to do."

Oops. I had to be very careful with what I said next. If you think I'm the queen of jumping to conclusions, wait'll you see how Nancy operates.

"Tell me everything you can remember about the text Charlie got last night," I said. "It might be a clue."

"Wow, I had a clue and didn't even know it," Nancy said. Was that a trace of sarcasm I detected in her voice?

"Are you making fun of me?"

"Of course I'm not," Nancy said, wrinkling her brow in concentration. "I don't know much. Charlie got a text, read it, then jumped up and ran out of the restaurant like his pants were on fire." She clapped her hands over her mouth when she realized what she'd said. "Ooooh, I'm sorry. I didn't mean to put it that way. But you get the picture, right? He was in a big hurry."

"Did he mention a name?" I asked. "Was there anything that might tell us whether the text was from a man or a woman?"

"Nope," Nancy said, shaking her head. "I don't think so. Maybe Claire or Larry would remember something. Claire was sitting the closest to Charlie."

Aha. Now we were getting somewhere.

"Have you seen them this morning?" I asked. "Maybe we should track them down. They may not even know about Charlie yet."

"Good idea," Nancy said. "Just give me a sec to fix my makeup. I like to look my best all the time. You ought to know that. I never know who I might meet." With that, my recently distraught BFF gave me a wink and disappeared into the bathroom.

Honestly, that Nancy.

Chapter 30

At my age, "getting lucky" means walking into a room and remembering why I went in there.

You've heard the old saying about the best-laid plans, right? That they always go astray. Or life is what happens when you're making other plans. Etc. etc. Nancy and I had just started toward Claire and Larry's villa when an excited Jim came barreling our way and headed us off.

"Whoa, Carol, where are you and Nancy going? I need to talk to you. Right away." He shot Nancy a look that translated to, "Alone, please."

Now, Nancy is almost as adept at reading Jim as I am. And since we had already made a plan (sort of), she gave us a wave, and said, "I'm off to see if Claire and Larry want to have some breakfast. See you later."

Darn it. Nancy was going to have all the fun. I just hoped that, if she found out anything important, she remembered it. Like me, her short-term memory sometimes fails her.

Jim grabbed my hand and propelled me back to our own villa. I swear, the guy was so excited I thought he might explode himself. (I know. Slap me for that one.)

"I just came from talking with Deputy Armstrong," Jim said, once we were safely inside and away from prying ears. Lucy and Ethel don't count—they never reveal any of our secrets. At least, I

143

hope they don't. "And you'll never guess what! Go ahead, guess."

I surveyed my husband of thirty-plus years. I hadn't seen him this energized since he found out there was a BOGO sale at our local supermarket. Except for...never mind. That's none of your business.

"I have no idea, Jim," I said. "And I'm not in the mood to play Twenty Questions. It's been a very upsetting twelve hours. Not exactly the second honeymoon I was expecting. Poor Charlie."

Jim's face clouded over. "You're right, Carol. I wasn't thinking about how this mess has affected you. After all, you knew Charlie far longer than I did. But..."

"Yes, Jim? But, what?"

"I just came from an interesting meeting with that female deputy sheriff. She's pretty sharp. She checked with the Fairport Police, and was very impressed with what she found out. She's asked us to let her know immediately if we hear anything that could be helpful to her investigation. Isn't that something?"

Without giving me a second to absorb this information and come up with one of my usual zippy comebacks (such as, "She meant *me*, not *us*,"), he went on, "So, here's where we'll start. I want you to..."

I stiffened. No way was my dear husband going to be the captain of this sleuthing team, no matter what he thought. *I* was still in charge.

"You know, Carol," Jim went on, oblivious to my reaction, "I never understood before how exhilarating going undercover could be. I'm sorry for all the times I criticized you for getting involved in police investigations. I was wrong."

I was wrong. Three little words that I'd never heard Jim say before. This was a golden moment for me. I wanted to savor it as long as possible.

But just to be sure I understood Jim correctly, I asked, "Are you admitting that I'm right and you're wrong? That my so-called female intuition usually leads to a solution to a mystery that's stumped the police? Is that what you're saying?"

"I don't know anything about feminine intuition," Jim said.

You got that right, buster.

"But I do know that it's our civic duty to assist the authorities when we're asked to," Jim continued. "I'm not giving you a free ticket to poke your nose in where it's not wanted, so don't get any ideas."

"Understood, Jim," I said. Of course, I didn't agree with him. I'm sure that comes as no surprise to any of you.

"I'm glad we had this conversation so we could clear the air," Jim said, giving me a kiss on the cheek. He checked his watch. "Larry and Mack will be here any minute. We're going to have a brainstorming session about this case. The television show pilot is on hold until further notice, in case you hadn't heard. So you have the day all to yourself to sit by the pool and work on your tan. Have fun." On that note, my husband, the Great Wannabe Detective, practically pushed me out the door.

Now, if you've known me for a while, you know how I usually deal with situations like this. I either burst into tears, carry a grudge until it hurts, or come up with a devious plan to do what I want without Jim being the wiser. And if you know me REALLY well, you'll have no trouble at all figuring out which method I chose.

But, first things first. I was still hungry. Starving, actually, and I think much better on a full stomach. In fact, I'm known to be positively brilliant if my tummy is happy. So off I went to the hotel dining room, hoping against hope that I had timed it correctly and lunch service was about to start. The place was empty, except for a few servers clearing off the remains of breakfast from tables and re-setting them for noontime.

Onward to the pool area, even though I was sure my chino slacks and pullover cotton sweater were bound to get some curious looks. Dressed for Florida sunbathing, I was not. I comforted myself with the knowledge that what I was wearing covered mostly everything up, unlike several other sunbathers, both male and female, who obviously hadn't checked themselves in a full-length mirror before heading out into the bright sunshine.

I squinted against the sudden glare, hoping to find a food service cart. No luck. Maybe this forced dieting would result in an immediate weight loss.

I heard someone call my name, and I shrank back in the shadow of the doorway. No way did I want to talk to anyone now, especially someone from *The Second Honeymoon Game.* I needed a quiet corner, caffeine, and something to write on so I could jot down everything that I had seen last night before I forgot it completely.

"Carol! Over here!" the person said, holding up a carafe. "Want coffee? I scored a fresh pot. You look like you could use some."

"Claire!" I said, scurrying to the shady side of the pool deck. "You're a lifesaver. But where's Nancy? The last time I saw her, she was on her way to your villa."

"Nancy's dealing with some real estate emergency back home," Claire said with a disapproving sniff. "As if we don't have a real emergency to deal with right here. I assume you heard what happened to poor Charlie."

"I not only heard about it, I was there," I replied, taking a welcome sip of piping hot coffee. "Man, does this taste great."

"What do you mean, you were there?" Claire demanded, taking away my cup and setting it back on the saucer. "Not another sip until you tell me everything."

So...I went through last night all over again. But this time, because Claire has become super anal in her advancing years and doesn't travel anywhere without a notebook and pen, my whole nightmare was consigned to paper. Claire, of course, was the scribe. All my friends know that my penmanship is atrocious.

When I had finished talking, I grabbed my cup of now tepid coffee and took a welcome swallow. Then another. I waited for Claire's reaction.

"I don't know how you do it, Carol," Claire finally said. "You always seem to be involved with something tragic these days." She shuddered. "I suppose you're used to discovering dead bodies by now. You're probably immune. Better you than me."

"I didn't actually discover a dead body this time, Claire," I said frostily. Trust Claire to make me feel defensive. "When Jim and I went to the beach last night, witnessing a car explosion was not exactly what we had in mind. And remember, it was our car. We could have been killed, instead of poor Charlie. I could use a little sympathy and support from you for a change, instead of criticism."

"You didn't say it was the Mercedes you and Jim drove to the beach that exploded," Claire said, looking chagrined. "I'm sorry. That must have been very scary." She scribbled something additional in her notebook, then circled it.

"It was," I said, mollified by the apology that I felt I had coming to me.

"Of course, one white Mercedes looks just like all the others," Claire continued. "How was I to know it was yours unless you told me? There could have been more than one in the parking lot at the time." Claire hates to be wrong; she only admits it if she absolutely has to.

Hey, wait a minute. That sounds too familiar for comfort. But I'd never tell anybody else that, so mum's the word, okay?

"Let's not argue," I said. "The question is, where do we go from here? The television show pilot is on indefinite hold, and both Charlie's daughter and the deputy sheriff assigned to the case have asked for my help in figuring out what happened last night." I sat back and tried not to look smug. But I hoped Claire got the point that I was now "officially" on the case. To my complete annoyance, Claire didn't even react, except to make another note.

"Deputy Armstrong is the chief investigating officer on the case," I clarified, "and just happens to be Detective Paul Wheeler's cousin."

Claire raised her eyebrows at that one. "Paul Wheeler from Fairport? His cousin asked for your help? Are you sure? Paul Wheeler thinks you're an interfering busybody, if I remember correctly."

"Thank you for reminding me," I said sweetly. "But as it happens, the two cousins can't stand each other. And Deputy Armstrong is a 'she.' "

"Now, that's interesting," Claire said.

"I'm so glad you think so," I said with just a touch of sarcasm. "Hey, wait a minute. What are you doing?"

Claire was squeezing my right arm so hard that it hurt. She leaned over and hissed in my ear, "Do you see who just came out to the pool? It's Gene Richmond. I just love him. I never missed him on *Funtastic Trivia*. I'm his biggest fan. OMG, this is so thrilling." My normally unflappable friend was trembling with excitement. She reminded me of Lucy and Ethel when they see me go for the box of Milk Bones.

"If you let go of my arm, I'd be glad to introduce you," I said. "He's the host of *The Second Honeymoon Game*. I know him well."

Just a tiny exaggeration. But forgivable, right?

Thank goodness Gene remembered to wear his hairpiece this morning. I figured he was afraid of getting his head sunburned.

I waved and, to my embarrassment, Gene ignored me. Instead

of heading in our direction, he settled himself on a chaise at the opposite side of the pool and opened a book.

"I can tell you know him very well," Claire snorted. "That's why he came right over to say hello."

Well! I wasn't going to take any more nonsense from Claire. Why was everybody on my case today, anyway? First Jim, and now Claire. So I marched over to Gene's chaise and smiled as sincerely as I could. "Good morning, Gene," I said. "Although it's not a good morning for any of us on *The Second Honeymoon Game,* right? With dear Charlie's tragic death?"

Gene looked up from his book and acknowledged me. Finally.

"Hello, Carol. Please forgive me for being so rude. It's just that Charlie's unfortunate demise has been such a shock, I thought I'd come out here by myself and try to make some sense of it. Then I saw you, and I wasn't up to talking. I'm so upset."

Truthfully, Gene didn't seem upset at all. Instead of looking at me while we were talking, his eyes kept darting around the area, checking out everyone else who was there. I hate people who do that. How rude! It's like I'm not important enough to focus on when someone more interesting might be available.

And, by the way, if Gene was so upset about Charlie's death, why didn't he just stay in his own villa and hang a "Do Not Disturb" sign on the door so he could mourn in private? Unless he wanted to mourn in a public place, in front of an audience. I wondered if he'd been questioned by Deputy Armstrong, and what he'd told her.

I snuck a quick peek and saw that Claire was now standing, her eyes fixated on Gene and me. I knew she was dying to meet her idol, and I couldn't bear it if Gene was rude to her. So I played the flattery card.

"Your biggest fan is coming this way," I said, beckoning Claire to join us. "Her name is Claire McGee. I just know that meeting you in person will be the highlight of her trip to Florida. Maybe, even the highlight of her life!"

Okay, I was laying it on a little thick. But Gene immediately responded, just as I thought he would. He plastered a huge smile on his face and smoothed his hair. I mean, hairpiece. "Any friend of yours is a friend of mine, Carol. I'm always delighted to meet a fan."

I just bet you are, and I'm sure it doesn't happen to you very often these days, you old has-been. I didn't really say that out loud, of course.

"Claire was also one of Charlie's grammar school classmates,"

I said as Claire approached. "His death has been a huge shock to her, too. She and her husband Larry were going to be contestants on the pilot. I don't know what's going to happen with that now."

"Oh, the show will definitely go on," Gene assured me. "It always does. That's an old show business tradition, you know."

"I'm not so sure about that," I countered. "At least, I bet it won't go on until the authorities are convinced that Charlie's death was an accident. What do you think about the explosion, Gene?"

I know. I know. Subtlety is not my strong suit.

I could swear that Gene had that "deer trapped in the headlights of an oncoming car" look, just for a millisecond. But it was gone so quickly that I could have imagined it. I do that a lot. Imagine things, I mean.

Claire came up behind me and hissed in my ear. "Introduce me."

"You must be Claire McGee," Gene said, taking Claire's hand and making my usually composed friend blush. "Carol has told me all about you. The pleasure is all mine, lovely lady. In fact...." He broke off mid-sentence and dropped Claire's hand like the proverbial hot potato.

"Something has come up. I have to leave." Gene immediately vanished in the direction of the dining room, abandoning Claire and me without a second glance. Or an apology. What a jerk.

Chapter 31

If God wanted me to touch my toes, He would have put them on my knees.

"I'm beginning to get a complex," Claire said. "First, Larry abandons me to meet Jim, then Gene Richmond runs away from me like I've got a communicable disease."

"I wouldn't take it personally, Claire. Something obviously came up that Gene had to deal with right away. Probably something to do with the television show." My voice trailed off. I wasn't very convincing, even to myself. I had also caught a quick glimpse of the person Gene went rushing off to meet. I just couldn't figure out why it would be so urgent for Gene to talk to Bernardo, the ever helpful concierge.

Unless there was an emergency at Gene's villa. Maybe the air conditioning wasn't working, and Bernardo had arranged for a repairman. That may be why Gene was doing his mourning for Charlie poolside, instead of in the privacy of his villa. Yes, that had to be it. I just love it when I can figure things out so quickly. Especially since it doesn't happen to me that often. Besides, I couldn't think of any other reason why Gene would abandon an adoring fan for a hotel concierge. I doubted that Bernardo was a longtime fan of Gene's, and he certainly had nothing to do with the television show.

Naturally, Claire blamed me for Gene's abrupt departure. "Honestly, Carol," she said, as we headed back to our shady table, "was it too much to ask for you to arrange a few minutes for me to talk with a man I've admired for so long? What did you say to him to make him leave so suddenly?"

Oh, for Pete's sake.

"I asked him to meet one of my dearest friends, who'd been a fan of his for years," I said. "You came over, said hello, and then he left."

"Well, now I understand," Claire said. "When you said I'd been a fan of his for years, you insulted him. You all but called him an old man. How could you do that? I barely got to shake his hand."

"You are completely ridiculous," I said. "Gene Richmond's been a fixture on television for decades. That's not insulting. It's a fact. You should be thanking me for introducing you instead of blaming me. Gene was rude."

I paused to digest Claire's accusation and realized there might be a grain of truth in it. Darn it.

"You know, you may be right," I said. "I've learned that these show business types are very sensitive, and they have huge egos. Maybe I did insult him. But I certainly didn't mean to."

I gave Claire a few seconds for what I hoped she'd interpret as my apology to sink in. I was much more interested in Claire's take on Charlie King's sudden departure last night from dinner than Gene's vanishing act today. Despite her tart tongue (aimed at me far too often), her powers of observation are excellent. Which is why she's always been such an important part of my sleuthing team.

I needed to get her back on track, so I sighed. Deeply and loudly.

"I feel so terrible about Charlie," I said. "What a horrible way to die."

To my surprise, Claire's eyes filled with tears, which rarely happens. Like, never. "Larry and I were just getting to know him last night," she said. "We were having such a nice time." She paused, then added, "You know that Larry isn't much for small talk."

A minor understatement. Larry's idea of making social chit-chat bores most people to tears. I didn't really say that, of course.

"I love my husband," Claire went on, "but I know he's not that good at making friends. All the friends we socialize with are my friends, like you and Jim. Maybe that's because Larry always sounds like he's giving a lecture or a presentation to a jury. I've reminded him that he really doesn't know everything about everything. I've even suggested that people get turned off by his know-it-all attitude, and a lot of what he talks about is really boring, even to me. I try to take an interest but…"

"But it's hard sometimes," I finished. "I understand exactly what you mean. It happens in my house, too. It really galls me when Jim takes over some of the household tasks I've been doing for years. He thinks he knows everything and I know nothing. As a matter of fact," I stopped, remembering Jim's usurping of my Great Detective mantle, "Jim now fancies himself the next Sherlock Holmes. Deputy Armstrong asked him to keep an eye out for any information that could help in the investigation about Charlie's death, and to pass it along to her. When I pointed out that the deputy had asked me to do the same thing, Jim just brushed me off, and said he doubted we women would have much to contribute to the investigation. Can you imagine? He called a meeting of his so-called detective brain trust—Larry and Mack Whitman. That's why Larry and Jim got together today."

I could feel my blood pressure shoot up. The longer I thought about Jim's attitude, the madder I got.

"That's downright insulting," Claire said. "What do they want us to do? Go to the hotel kitchen and bake an apple pie?"

"I figured you'd agree with me, Claire," I said. "If you, Nancy and I put our heads together, we can probably figure out this whole thing before the guys get fitted for trench coats and fedoras."

Claire looked at me, puzzled. "You lost me."

"Humphrey Bogart as Sam Spade in *The Maltese Falcon*," I clarified. "Now, tell me everything you can think of about your dinner with Charlie last night. Especially, about the text he got. Nancy said he read the text and then bolted out of the restaurant. Do you have any idea who sent it? Did Charlie say anything? Could you see a name or a number on his phone's screen?"

Claire shut her eyes tight and seemed lost in concentration. Finally, she said, "When Charlie read the text, he muttered something that sounded like, 'No way.' " She shook her head in frustration. "I'm sorry, Carol, I know that's not much, but it's the best I can do. I never realized it would be so important. Too bad I didn't pay more attention."

"You're doing fine," I said. "Better than Nancy. Did you get a look at the actual text? Did it list the sender's phone number?"

Claire looked at me like I was daft. "There isn't always a number for a text, Carol. Unless the text is from someone you don't know.

There's usually a name." She shut her eyes again, then opened them wide. "This time, the sender had initials, not an actual name. I think it was MPR. But I have no idea what that means."

"MPR?" I repeated. "Are you sure it wasn't NPR? Could Charlie have gotten a text from National Public Radio?"

"Beats me," Claire said. "And why would that get Charlie so riled up?"

"His pledge bounced?" I suggested.

"Now you're really being ridiculous!" Claire said. "Oh, there's one thing more. I just remembered that when Charlie was rushing out of the restaurant, someone stopped him, but Charlie just shrugged him off and kept on walking. It probably means nothing."

"This could be important, Claire," I said. "Who was it? Anyone you recognized?"

Claire didn't respond, so I asked again. "Come on, Claire. Who was it? This could be a clue. Who stopped Charlie on the way out of the restaurant?"

Claire looked miserable. Then she said, "It was Mike." At my blank look, she clarified. "Your son."

Chapter 32

Lord, give me patience... and give it to me NOW!

"I'm sure that means nothing, Claire," I said with a confidence I didn't feel. "Mike was quite taken with Charlie's daughter, Carrie, at the airport yesterday, in case you didn't notice. In fact, Mike didn't go back to Miami last night like he'd originally planned. I'm sure he stayed with Carrie. Not that I quizzed him about where he spent the night, of course. You know that I would never do that."

That was an outrageous lie, and Claire knew it, but she didn't bother with one of her famous comebacks.

"Mike probably wanted to tell Charlie what a wonderful daughter he had," I continued. "I'm sure it was perfectly innocent. But since Charlie was in a big hurry, he couldn't stop to chat."

"As I remember it, Mike grabbed Charlie's arm and tried to stop him from leaving," Claire continued. "I guess it could have been innocent. But I thought you should know about it. Especially because of the timing."

"Timing?" I repeated. "What do you mean?"

"Well, Mike must have been one of the last people to talk to Charlie before he died. Maybe that's significant."

Now, I was getting angry. "What exactly are you implying, Claire?" I demanded. "Are you suggesting that my son had something to do with Charlie's death? Because if you are, you're way out of line. He even encouraged Carrie King to ask me to investigate how her father died. Mike has absolutely nothing to do with this whole mess, and absolutely nothing to hide. I'm getting a headache. I need some aspirin." I stomped away before Claire could answer me, or apologize.

I started in the direction of our villa, then thought better of it. With my luck, Jim and his crime-solving henchmen would still be hashing out plans to solve the riddle of Charlie King's sudden death. Heaven forbid I should interrupt them. I reversed direction and headed to the calm oasis of the hotel lobby, where I could snag a comfortable chair and process what I'd just been told.

As I know I've told you countless times before, I *never* interfere in the private lives of my two adult children. (Please forgive me if I'm repeating myself.) Particularly my son's. After all, he lived more than a thousand miles away, so it wasn't like I could peer over his shoulder all the time and know what he was up to. But this was an emergency situation. And if I—his own mother—had questions about Mike's encounter with the late Charlie King last night, it was my right to ask them.

No, it was more than a right. It was my maternal duty. Especially if Deputy Armstrong planned to cross-examine Mike herself. Which I was sure she would, especially if my former friend Claire blabbed about what she'd observed last night.

The plush overstuffed chair that I chose was in the darkest reaches of the lobby. It was so comfortable that I couldn't help but close my eyes, just for a second, to rest them. Oh, heck. Who was I kidding? I hadn't slept well the night before, and a brief snooze might be just what I needed to refresh and jump start my addled brain.

I confess I did nod off (I hope I didn't snore!) and I had the most wonderful dream. Jenny and Mark arrived at our house with the momentous news that they were expecting my first grandchild. I was beyond overjoyed! As my dream continued, I was figuring out which room I'd have Jim repaint to use as a nursery for the baby. I knew I'd be called on for lots of childcare because of Jenny's demanding college teaching schedule, and I do like to be prepared. It was such a happy dream. But it didn't last as long as I wanted it to. Like, forever.

I was in my happy dream place when I became aware of whispered voices. A man and woman were having a disagreement. In my fuzzy state, I thought that it was part of my dream, and that Jenny and Mark were arguing, since I recognized one of the voices. This was no time for them to have a disagreement of any kind. We had a baby on the way.

I heard the woman (Jenny?) speak to the man (Mark?). "All I'm saying is that you don't have to tell Deputy Armstrong you talked to Dad last night. But the longer you wait, something that was totally innocent could end up looking like you have something to hide. She's talking to everyone who's part of the television show. There's no reason why you should freak out."

"I'm not freaking out," the man said. "But I'm not part of the television show. My parents are. I just came to Honeymoon Island to see them. Your father and I barely spoke last night. He was in a hurry. He did jerk his arm and push me away, though. Under the circumstances, that could be misunderstood by anyone who saw us. What a mess. I don't know what to do."

"I'm sure Deputy Armstrong will understand if you decide to tell her," the woman said. "And I'll be with you, Mike. After all, you only saw my dad to help me. I'll back you up, no matter what you say."

"I'm pretty nervous," the man said. "I'm glad you're going with me."

My eyes snapped open as the couple disappeared from my line of vision. But not so quickly that I couldn't identify them as Carrie King and Mike.

So, Claire was right. Mike had seen Charlie last night, and was now on his way to see Deputy Armstrong, What the heck had he gotten himself into?

I'm not proud of what I did next. But I'm not ashamed, either. If any of you are mothers of so-called adult children, I hope you won't criticize me. In fact, you'd probably do the exact same thing if you were in the exact same set of circumstances.

I know. I'm stalling. Deep breath.

I followed them. Carrie and Mike, I mean. At a discreet distance, so they wouldn't see me. Hey, I don't read all those mystery stories for nothing. I have picked up some handy tips, on the art of surveillance, for instance.

Fortunately, the hotel hallway was thickly carpeted so I was saved from having to flatten myself against a wall and hide in case they noticed me. Which was a good thing, because flattening my pudgy body against a wall would require an act of God.

I heard Mike say, "Okay, I'm ready." He knocked on the door of The Pelican Room where Deputy Armstrong and I had our cozy chat just a short while ago. After he and Carrie went inside, I knelt down in front of the door and pressed my ear against the wood, straining to hear what was going on inside. I figured that, if anybody saw me, I could say I'd lost an earring and was looking for it. Lame, I know. But it was the best I could come up with.

The voices were muffled at first. Or maybe my hearing was going, too, along with other aging body parts. Then, I heard Deputy Armstrong say, "Nobody's accusing you of anything, Mr. Andrews. We're interviewing anyone who might have had any interaction with Mr. King before he died last night."

"I barely knew the man," Mike said. "I only saw him once, at the airport, when I came to meet my parents."

"Mr. Andrews," Deputy Armstrong replied, "I got a phone call from a server in the hotel dining room. She told me that you had a brief altercation with Mr. King last night as he was leaving the restaurant. She described you quite clearly."

"That wasn't me," Mike protested. "It must have been someone who looked like me. I was with Carrie King. Alone. Right, Carrie?"

"That's right, Deputy Armstrong," Carrie said. "We were together from when we met at the airport yesterday. All day. And, all night. Mike never saw my father after we got to the hotel."

I almost lost my cool right there in the hall. I wanted to run into The Pelican Room and shake Mike until his teeth rattled. Carrie, too. Fortunately, good sense prevailed. For once.

Deputy Armstrong responded in a quieter voice, so I didn't quite catch all she said. But she ended the interview with a warning that scared me down to my toes: "I hope you plan on staying around, Mr. Andrews. I'll be talking to you again. Very soon." Then, I heard the sound of chairs moving in The Pelican Room, and realized the interview was over. Man, that was quick. I had to get out of there pronto, before I got named Eavesdropper-in-Chief. I had some serious thinking to do.

Chapter 33

The only exercise I get these days is jumping to conclusions.

"Take deep breaths," I ordered myself. "Maybe you misheard. Or misunderstood."

Nah. Who was I kidding? Not even myself. Mike had lied, and as a consequence, had probably shot to the top of Deputy Armstrong's suspect list. Assuming she figured it out, of course. And I couldn't count on her being as clueless as her Fairport cousin.

I wanted to find Claire and demand an explanation from her. I was sure she had ratted out Mike. That was the end of our lifelong friendship, without question. How could she do that? She'd known Mike since he was in utero. She was practically another mother to him. What a traitor. I guess I was muttering all the way across the lobby, because I suddenly realized that several strangers were giving me curious looks. I just glared at them and refused to be embarrassed. Let them think what they wanted. I bet most of them talked to themselves, too.

I really missed Jenny. Mark, too, of course. But talking to my daughter always cleared my head and helped me focus. I wondered if she and Mike had been in touch since he'd surprised us at the airport yesterday.

Was it only yesterday? It seemed like a whole year had passed since then.

Then I made a decision that I'm sure will surprise you. I wanted to talk to Jim. Right now. After all, he was Mike's father, and Mike was in deep trouble, whether he realized it or not. I hoped Jim's so-called brain trust meeting was over. I needed my husband and the father of my children right now, not an imitation Hercule Poirot. We had to work together. For once. And if I couldn't find Jim, I had another option. My two favorite canine co-conspirators, Lucy and Ethel. They were always available for a heart-to-heart chat; they never blabbed about any secrets I spilled, and were never judgmental. No matter what.

Of course, the dogs couldn't always be counted on to come up with surefire solutions to my problems. But at least they were willing to listen. Assuming they weren't hungry, of course. If they were, all bets were off.

"Be calm," I told myself. "You have to present the facts to Jim in a rational manner. Don't get emotional and start blubbering the way you usually do. That kind of behavior makes him nuts. Start with what Claire told you about what she saw last night, and go from there. Jim will know what to do next. Maybe he'll even talk to Mike himself." I nodded in satisfaction. Yes, that was a great idea. This situation definitely called for a man-to-man talk.

Which got me off the hook.

Imagine my frustration when I reached our villa and found a folded note with my name on it taped to the door. *Off for a quick lunch meeting about the show. We need to put out some sort of press release about Charlie's death. The media is all over this and Mack is worried about damage control. Be back as soon as I can. Detecting is on hold for now. Don't do anything until we talk. Oh, Lucy and Ethel need a walk. I didn't have time to take them out. See you later.*

Well, there was nothing I could do about my missing husband. Maybe this was even a blessing in disguise. I could use the time to organize the facts in an orderly manner, like the agenda system I've used under similar circumstances.

"Lucy, Ethel, time to go out," I said, opening the door and closing it quickly so the canines couldn't pull one of their frequent escapes. But there was none of the usual scurrying to greet me. In fact, there was nothing at all. Only silence. Lucy and Ethel were gone. OMG. They'd been dognapped!

I let out a scream that was loud enough to be heard from Honeymoon Island clear to Tallahassee. (That would be the state capital of Florida, and several hundred miles north of here, in case you're geographically challenged.)

Be rational, Carol. Maybe Jim changed his mind and decided to take the dogs with him to the meeting.

No way, I argued back. *Dogs aren't allowed in the dining room. Or around the pool area. In fact, dogs are only supposed to be walked in a few clearly designated areas.*

I checked around the villa. No leashes, anywhere. Then, I started to cry. Deep, gulping sobs. There wasn't a doubt in my mind that something terrible had happened to my dogs, and it was all Jim's fault. Don't ask me why. It just was.

Okay, I wasn't being rational.

I thought of calling Nancy and Claire to help me search for Lucy and Ethel. They loved the dogs almost as much as Jim and I did. But Nancy has a tendency to get even more hysterical than I do, believe it or not. Her presence would only add to my panic. As for Claire, well…I wasn't sure I was even speaking to her right now.

Mike! I could call him. He'd be here in a heartbeat.

And then what, Carol? First, you're going to ask him to help find the dogs, and then you'll browbeat him into explaining why he lied to Deputy Armstrong? Tell him what a jerk he is?

Even in my panicky state, I knew that was a very bad plan.

Call your new best friend Deputy Armstrong, Carol. She's right here, and she's a trained professional.

Oh, yeah? And say what? Would you mind terribly dropping your investigation into a possible murder to help me find my two dogs? She'd really think you were a loony tune then.

All these thoughts raced through my brain at warp speed, and I still didn't know what had happened to my dogs, and how to get them back.

Then, I had a brilliant idea. Lucy and Ethel were motivated by food more than anything else. I rummaged in the refrigerator and found some extra sharp cheddar cheese that must have been left by a previous guest. Bonanza! I was sure the smell would attract them.

Unless they'd been taken away in a car, or worse.

Stop it, Carol. Get outside and find your dogs.

I stuffed my pocket with the package of cheese and raced for the door, running smack into our concierge, Bernardo, with Lucy and Ethel in tow.

I was so shocked, thrilled, angry, relieved—you name an emotion and I felt it at that moment—that I didn't know what to say. The dogs, however, danced around my legs and telegraphed, loud and clear, what a great time they'd had on their walk with a new friend. I grabbed their leashes and said to Bernardo, "Wait here. I'll be right back."

Bernardo grinned. I was sure he was expecting a tip. Well, he was going to get one. But not the kind he usually got from hotel guests.

The two dogs trotted into the villa and flopped down on the cool tile floor, exhausted from the exercise. "I'll deal with you two later," I said. "I may have to get you both cell phones so you can keep in constant touch and not scare me to death the way you just did. Stay here."

It was clear that neither Lucy nor Ethel were planning to go anywhere at the moment. They were so pooped they didn't even beg for biscuits, the way they always did.

I gave the dogs a big bowl of cool water and two Milk Bones apiece (I would have given them the whole box of dog biscuits— that's how relieved I was that they were safe), then confronted Bernardo and let him have it, right between his big brown eyes.

"Just what the heck did you think you were doing?" I demanded, stepping outside and slamming the villa's door behind me. Usually, I shrink from confrontation of any kind. But this situation was different. My family's safety, and our private space, had been violated.

"What's wrong?" Bernardo asked, clearly perplexed at both my question and my incredibly angry tone of voice. "I was making my usual rounds to check on the villa guests," he continued, "and see if anyone needed anything. I saw the note on your door, so I took your two dogs for a little walk. That's all."

I narrowed my eyes and took a deep breath. "First of all, Bernardo, you read a private note from my husband that was clearly addressed to me. You had no right to do that."

"But...."

"That's just the beginning," I said. "Next, you took it upon yourself to enter our villa, when neither of us were there, and without our permission, take our two dogs out of the villa without leaving any information about what you were doing. Do you have any idea how upset I was when I got back and couldn't find them? Do you?" By this time I was so angry that I was ready to throttle the obviously clueless concierge. Because, from his expression, he had absolutely no idea what I was talking about. Or why I was so upset.

"But, Mrs. Andrews, I was only doing my job," he protested. "Helping the guests. Making their time here as pleasant as possible. I don't think I did anything wrong."

"Well, I do," I screamed. "You scared me to death. You took my dogs without permission, and you better not do it again or I'll report you to the manager. The next time you want to 'help' one of the guests, you'd better check with them first and see if they want your help. Understood?" I vamoosed into the villa and slammed the door, leaving Bernardo standing on the front step, his mouth wide open.

It was a few minutes later that it dawned on me. If Bernardo had come into our villa without permission and taken our dogs out, how many other times had he secretly been inside other guests' villas? What else had the over-helpful concierge been up to?

Chapter 34

Old age is coming at a really bad time.

"You know you're not supposed to talk to strangers," I said to Lucy and Ethel. "Much less go for a walk with anyone we don't know. What in the heck were you thinking?"

I know. Some of you, who might not know me very well, probably think I'm crazy, talking to my dogs that way, expecting they'd understand what I was saying and actually answer me back. But years of living with canines have convinced me that dogs are very effective communicators if we humans know how to read their signs. Especially Lucy, who never lets me get away with anything without a comment. And if you've never seen a dog do an eye roll, you're definitely not paying attention. Or you've never met Lucy.

So, naturally, Ethel immediately jumped up on the sofa beside me, nestled into the curve of my shoulder, and covered my face with sloppy doggy kisses. She knew she was in big trouble, and was telling me she was sorry in the only way she could. By showing me unconditional love.

Not Lucy, though. Lucy never apologizes. Instead, she yawned, turned around in a circle three times, and settled down for a snooze.

"Now that you're back safe and sound," I continued, "I want you to promise that you'll never go anywhere with anyone without my permission. Or Jim's," I added. Sometimes I forget that he's part of the pack, too.

"I forgive you," I said. "I guess I overreacted. But I'm just so worried about Mike. You won't believe what he did this morning."

Lucy cocked her head. Mike is one of her very favorite humans, and she doesn't get to see him as much as she'd like. She joined Ethel and me on the sofa and gave me her non-blinking doggy stare, inviting me to continue.

So I did. I talked about Mike's burgeoning romance with Carrie, his supposed encounter with Charlie King right before he died, Claire's possible betrayal (Lucy bared her teeth at that part and growled), and, finally, Mike's outright lie to Deputy Armstrong. By the time I'd finished, I was crying. No big surprise there, right?

"I don't know what to do," I said to the dogs. "I don't know whether to talk to Claire, confront Mike, tell Jim what's going on, or get on the next plane back to Connecticut. I wish we'd never come to Florida! This trip is a nightmare. I miss my house. I miss Jenny and Mark. I even think I miss Paul Wheeler. That's how upset I am."

The dogs let me continue my tirade. They knew I'd eventually calm down and come up with a plan, just like I always did. And this time, I had the personal permission of the deputy sheriff assigned to the case to nose around and see what information I could come up with. That was a first for me. It didn't matter that Jim had been asked to do the exact same thing, because the dead man's daughter had also begged me to figure out what had happened to her dad. Not Jim. Not that I was keeping score, understand. But just saying.

Above all, I knew my son was innocent. Stupid, yes. But innocent of any wrongdoing.

Lucy must have sensed that my brain was starting to percolate, but I needed a shove in the right direction. So she hopped off the coach and made a beeline for the leashes. Then, she turned around and stared at me.

"What?" I asked. "You must be kidding. Aren't you exhausted? You and Ethel were just out. Besides, there isn't one person out there I want to talk to right now. I'm too upset. I am not taking you out again."

Lucy dragged the leashes over to the sofa and dropped them on my feet. Then, she raced toward the door, sat and stared at me.

Oh, wow. I finally got the message. "You're right, Lucy. As always. There's one person here I can count on to jump in and help, no matter what. Assuming she's finished with her real estate emergencies by now. Let's go find Nancy."

My BFF greeted me at the door of her villa, cell phone plastered to her ear. "Yes, that's exactly what I think," she said into the phone, giving the dogs an absent-minded pat and waving me into a nearby wicker chair that looked extremely uncomfortable. I settled myself as best I could, the dogs curled at my feet, and prepared to wait until Nancy was finished talking. Correction: until Nancy was finished with her phone conversation. Like me, Nancy is NEVER finished talking. Which is probably why we're BFFs.

Anyway, I know the real estate business is very demanding (at least, that's what Nancy always tells me), and since I figured she was still dealing with a long-distance crisis, I ordered myself to be patient.

"You've got that right," she continued, the phone bobbing up and down for emphasis. "Both of them are as stubborn as mules. And neither one of them ever wants to admit that they're in the wrong."

Boy, this must be some crisis. Probably some seller who refused to drop the price on a listing, plus a potential buyer who'd made an offer and wouldn't go a penny more. Good luck with that one.

Nancy eyed me, then said, "Things were bad enough when Charlie died so suddenly last night. But now, they're even worse. Boy, do I ever wish you were here with us, Mary Alice. Maybe you could calm Carol and Claire down and get them talking to each other again."

"Mary Alice!" I shrieked. "Give me that phone." I yanked it out of Nancy's hand. "Hello, sweetie. We miss you so much. And don't believe a word of what Nancy's been telling you. Claire and I just had a minor disagreement. We'll work it out. We always do. Of course, it was all her fault."

I put my hand over the phone and said to Nancy, "How did you hear about this, anyway? It just happened a little while ago."

"How do you think I heard?" Nancy said. "Claire came here right after your argument. She was very upset."

"Humph," I said. "I'll bet she was."

"Hello? Hello? Are you still there, Carol?" Mary Alice said. "I can't hear you."

"Sorry. Nancy asked me a question and I got distracted," I said.

"But I'm back now."

"Tell me what you know about poor Charlie," Mary Alice said. "What a terrible way to die."

"I'm sure Nancy has already given you the details," I said, "but she may not have told you that Jim and I were actually there when the car exploded. It was horrible. And the local authorities, as well as Charlie's daughter, have asked for my help in the investigation. It's possible someone tampered with the car. His poor daughter is distraught." I didn't add anything about Mike's possible involvement. That would only upset Mary Alice even more.

"I wish so much that I was there to help you," Mary Alice said. "Even just for moral support. And that poor daughter. Now she's lost both her parents tragically."

"What do you mean, Mary Alice?" I asked, waving Nancy away as she attempted to grab her phone back. "What do you know? This could be very important."

"If you give me my phone," Nancy said, clearly losing patience, "I'll put Mary Alice on speaker. That way, we can both hear her at the same time."

I hate it when someone else makes sense.

"Hang on a sec," I said to Mary Alice. "We both want to hear what you've got to tell us."

"Charlie married a local girl named Hope Maxwell," Mary Alice said, her voice now booming thanks to modern technology.

"Who's Hope Maxwell?" Nancy asked. "Are we supposed to know? I never heard of her."

"Don't tell me she went to grammar school with us, too," I said. "I thought I knew the names of everyone in our class."

"No, silly," Mary Alice said. "But she was from Fairport. Her father owned the drug store in town. Don't you remember Maxwell Drugs? We all used to go to there after school for ice cream floats."

"I remember that place," Nancy exclaimed. "It's where I bought my first tube of lipstick. I think it was called Fire Engine Red."

"Trust you to remember that piece of trivia, and not Hope Maxwell," I said. Nancy retaliated by sticking her tongue out at me. I know what you're thinking, and you're right. Sometimes we're not very mature.

"Can we get back on track here?" Mary Alice asked. "I have to get to the hospital in fifteen minutes. Private duty today."

"I remember that Maxwell Drugs closed in the late nineties,"

Nancy said. "I think there's a bank there now."

"I remember something else about that place," I said, searching my memory bank. "Wasn't there a poster of a girl on an easel right at the entrance of the store?"

"You're right," Nancy said. "It was sort of a shrine to someone who'd died. I stopped shopping there when the owner put it up. I thought it was too creepy for words."

"That's Hope Maxwell," Mary Alice said. "She was married only a few years before she died. Her father put the poster in the store to honor her memory."

"How come you remember this so well and I don't?" I asked. "I didn't realize you read the obituaries so carefully. I thought only old people did that, to be sure their name wasn't there."

The next thing we heard was a sound I couldn't identify. Unless....

"Mary Alice? Are you crying? What did I say to upset you? I certainly didn't mean to."

I looked at Nancy, who was as mystified as I was at Mary Alice's reaction.

"I don't read the obituary page every day," Mary Alice said, her voice quivering as she fought for control. "But I'll never forget this one. The notice about Hope's death was in the paper the same day as Brian's. And I remember thinking how doubly tragic it was that two young families had been torn apart by a sudden death at the exact same time."

Jim and I had been away on a trip when Mary Alice's husband, Brian, had died suddenly in a car crash. I'd felt guilty about not being there for my friend for years. And now I'd quintupled my guilt by throwing out careless remark that had upset one of the dearest people in my life.

"Oh, Mary Alice, I'm so sorry," I said. "Open mouth, insert flip flop. Please forgive me."

"You couldn't know, Carol. Of course, I forgive you. But there's one thing you can do for me, to make things right."

"Anything," I said fervently. "Anything at all. Just ask me."

"Make up with Claire," Mary Alice said. "Right now. It doesn't matter who was right and who was wrong. Just make up with her, right now. I mean it."

The next thing we heard was the dial tone.

Chapter 35

I don't have gray hair. I have "wisdom highlights."

"Mary Alice is right, you know," Nancy said. "You and Claire have to make up, and the sooner the better. What the heck are you so mad at her for, anyway?"

"Claire had the nerve to imply that Mike could be involved in Charlie's death. She saw the two of them together for a split second when Charlie was leaving the restaurant in such a hurry last night," I said, my face flushing. Saying it out loud to Nancy made me even madder. "And to make matters worse, someone tipped Deputy Armstrong off about a supposed confrontation between Mike and Charlie."

"Carol, be reasonable," Nancy said. "I'm sure Claire didn't mean to suggest Mike was involved in Charlie's death. And you know there's no way Claire would tell Deputy whatserhername anything that could get Mike in trouble. She'd never do that."

"Armstrong," I said. "Deputy Sheriff Armstrong." I ran my fingers through my hair in a gesture of complete frustration. Nancy grabbed my hand and commanded, "Stop that. Right now. You're not in Fairport now, and Deanna's not here to perform miracles with your hair, the way she always does. Even though she's a hair styling wizard, she doesn't have the magical power to teleport herself to Florida."

"I guess I do owe Claire an apology," I said with some reluctance.

"I shouldn't have yelled at her like that."

"I forgive you, Carol," said a familiar voice. "I've been eavesdropping for the last ten minutes."

"You really are the limit," Nancy said, as Claire joined us inside the villa. I took a close look at her. She sure didn't look upset to me. But then, she's a lot better at hiding her feelings than I am.

"I figured you'd head over here eventually, Carol," Claire said, obviously pleased with herself for figuring out my whereabouts. "And you know that we can never stay mad at each other for long." She gave me a hug. "I'm sorry I didn't get the chance to say hello to Mary Alice."

"Me, too," Nancy said. "I think we're always better behaved when she's around."

I laughed. I couldn't help it. Because it was true. There was something about Mary Alice that always brought out the best parts of our personalities. "She's always calm in a crisis, that's for sure," I said. "I think that's why she's such a good nurse."

"I wish she was here with us," Nancy said. "But she had some interesting information about Charlie's late wife." She brought Claire up to speed about Hope Maxwell, and what I had said that upset Mary Alice so much.

"I didn't realize that Charlie married a local girl," Claire said.

"Why would you?" Nancy asked. "We'd been out of touch with him for years."

"All right, enough of this memory lane stuff," I said before Nancy began to wax poetic again about Maxwell Drugs and lipstick. "Mike's in big trouble. I need your help to get him out of it. The big jerk."

"I don't know how you could think I'd go to the authorities with incriminating information about Mike," Claire said, not letting me off the hook completely. "How the heck did you jump to such a ridiculous conclusion?"

"*Someone* told Deputy Armstrong about seeing Mike with Charlie at the restaurant last night," I said. "She claimed that Mike and Charlie had an argument. Deputy Armstrong questioned Mike about it, and Mike lied. He said that he hadn't seen Charlie since we all met at the airport earlier in the day." I turned my baby blues on Claire. "I figured you were the person who snitched on Mike." I conveniently ignored the fact that the information purportedly came from a server in the restaurant. Right now, I was a lioness protecting her cub, and was entitled to use any weapon I could think of to get at the truth. Including ignoring the truth, if necessary.

"Me? No way," Claire protested, echoing Nancy word for word. "I haven't even met this Deputy Armstrong. I didn't see Charlie and Mike arguing, either. They were together for about a millisecond, and then Charlie left. He was in a big hurry, remember?"

"That's the best piece of news I've heard all day, Claire," I said. "You have to talk to Deputy Armstrong right away. Let's go."

I raced toward the door, the dogs at my heels. When I turned around, Claire hadn't moved. Neither had Nancy.

"Come on, Claire. Let's go. What are you waiting for? You have information that will clear Mike."

"You are such a doofus," Nancy said. "You don't get it, do you Carol?"

"What? What don't I get?"

"What Nancy means by her indelicate remark, Carol, is that my going to the authorities won't help Mike at all," Claire said. "In fact, it'll probably make things worse for him."

"That's not true, Claire. How could it?" I asked.

"Because, if I say that I saw Mike and Charlie together, but *not* having an argument last night, that means I saw Mike and Charlie together last night. Period. And that also means that Mike lied about it when he was questioned by Deputy Armstrong. Now do you get it?"

"Oh." I sat down, deflated. "You're right. I didn't think of it that way. So, what do we do now?"

"I suggest you go talk to your son," Claire said. "As soon as possible to find out what the heck is going on."

"And I suggest that you find Jim, clue him in about Mike, and involve him in that conversation, too," Nancy said.

"I agree," said Claire. "After all, he is Mike's father. He has a right to know."

"I already decided to tell Jim what was going on," I said, "and to talk to Mike as soon as possible. I'm not looking forward to any of this." I grabbed the dogs' leashes. "We're leaving. Come on, girls." As we were headed out the door, I turned back. "Just out of curiosity, what will you two be doing while I'm having the most difficult conversation of my life with the two guys I love most in the world? Swimming laps in the hotel pool?"

I know. I shouldn't have said that. Nancy and Claire were only trying to help.

"Very funny, Carol," Nancy said. "I can't speak for Claire, but I'm going to check out the late Charlie King on the Internet using my special contact group."

Claire raised her eyebrows. "And what would that be, pray tell?"

"The Realtors Network, of course."

Of course.

Chapter 36

I joined a support group for procrastinators.
We haven't met yet.

"Feel free to take your time on our walk," I said to Lucy and Ethel. "As a matter of fact, you have my permission to sniff every single blade of grass and check out every bush and palm tree on the hotel property. Heaven knows, I'm not in any hurry to find Mike. And Jim is probably still hammering out a press release about Charlie King's death. You know how he hates to be interrupted while he's writing."

I glanced down and realized Lucy was panting from all this unexpected exercise. It was hot outside, and she and Ethel needed water right away. I did, too. And this was a perfect excuse to waste more time while I figured out how to have The Conversation. I have a black belt in Procrastination 101.

I reversed course and started in the direction of the hotel restaurant, then stopped. I realized I couldn't bring the dogs in there. "Come on, girls," I said, heading toward the swimming pool, "we have to stay outside. I hope there's an empty table in the shade."

Otherwise, I'd have no choice but to head back to our villa and risk running into Jim. I still had no idea how I was going to tell him about Mike's stupidity.

"Bummer," I muttered. All the shady tables were already occupied. I scanned the area, and saw a table for two that had a single vacant seat. The lone occupant was slouched in his chair, baseball cap tipped over his eyes to block out any spare sunlight. He appeared to be napping.

Well, there was no choice. I'd have to see if this total stranger was a dog lover who'd be willing to share his table with me. Correction: with us.

"Behave yourselves," I warned the girls. "If we're lucky, we're going to make a new friend, and I'm going to get your water."

My stomach grumbled. Most unattractive, I know. But I suddenly realized I hadn't had lunch. In fact, I hadn't had much to eat for breakfast, either. Which proves how upset I was. I rarely miss a meal, especially one I don't have to cook.

The closer we got to the table, the less sure I was that this was a good idea. There was something odd about the way the man was seated in the chair. I realized he hadn't moved since I'd first spotted him a few minutes before. In a flash of complete panic, I realized that he could be dead. OMG. I'd had my fill of discovering dead bodies, thank you very much. I was taking no chances. I had to get out of there, pronto.

I slowed my steps, not wanting to call attention to myself. Or the possibly deceased man in the chair. And then, I saw his hand snake out toward a glass filled with amber liquid. He lifted the glass to his lips, took a large swig of whatever was in it, and placed it unsteadily back on the table. Then, he pulled out the vacant chair and gestured toward me.

"I see you standing there staring at me, Carol Andrews. Come on over and let's have a little chat."

The man took off his cap. "It's your pal Kurt Armitage. From *The Second Honeymoon Game*. Sit down and keep me company for a little while."

Well, why not? I had lots of questions, and my pal, Kurt, could be just the one to answer some of them.

I held up the two dog leashes. "I'm not alone. Do you like dogs?"

Kurt sat up straight in his chair. "They don't bite, do they? I was bitten by a cocker spaniel when I was a kid."

"These are *English* cocker spaniels," I said, parking myself in the other chair before Kurt could take back his invitation. "They're very gentle. Not at all snappish, like some of the American cockers can be. Their names are Lucy and Ethel. Put out your hand and let them say hello. I promise it will be okay."

Lucy and Ethel gave Kurt's hand a cursory sniff, deemed it

acceptable, and plopped down at my feet, exhausted. I tried not to notice how quickly Kurt snatched his hand away from the dogs. Normally, I have nothing to do with anyone who didn't immediately love Lucy and Ethel. But not this time. I was on a mission.

"They really need water," I said. "And I wouldn't mind something cold to drink, myself. Can you flag down a server?"

"Sure thing," Kurt said. "I know 'em all. I've been here for a while." He held up his glass. "This is iced tea, in case you were wondering."

I'll bet.

Kurt waved his hand and in a flash a server appeared. From his eagerness to please, I figured Kurt was a pretty good tipper.

Then, the server spotted Lucy and Ethel. "No dogs are allowed here at the pool. It's a hotel rule." He looked at me and flushed with embarrassment. "I'm really sorry. I love dogs, myself."

Bummer. There went my big chance to pump good old Kurt for some juicy background information. I started to get up, but Kurt stopped me. He peeled a twenty-dollar bill off a money clip and handed it to the server. "There aren't any dogs here. Your eyes are playing tricks on you. It must be the heat. My friend Carol would like something cold to drink. Perhaps a large glass of water. Or two. And a large bowl of ice. And I'll have another iced tea. All right?"

"Yes, sir," the server said, pocketing the money. With a glance at the dogs resting beneath my feet, he added, "I guess I was mistaken. I hope no one else makes the same mistake I did."

Kurt peeled off two more twenties. "Share these with your friends. Just to be sure their eyes don't play tricks on them, too."

Wow. Kurt must be loaded, possibly in more ways than one. But I knew I had no time to waste on a friendly little chat. I had to get right down to business. I squeezed my baby blues tight, willing some tears to come, for effect. Then I said, "I feel so terrible about Charlie's death."

Kurt snorted. "Yeah, good old Charlie. He sure went out with a bang."

I was incensed. "What a horrible thing to say, Kurt! And truly tasteless." I stood up. "I think we should go back to our villa. I can give the dogs their water there."

"I'm sorry, Carol," Kurt said, suddenly appearing more with-it. "You're right. I shouldn't have said that. I'm going to miss Charlie, too."

"How long did you and he work together?" I asked, sitting back down and seizing the opportunity to probe some more.

"Too long," Kurt snapped. "I'm sorry. I shouldn't have said that, either. Charlie and I worked together for eight years. But he just didn't keep up with the times."

"He had some great shows," I protested. "Like...." I cast around in my brain and couldn't come up with a single one.

"The most important word in that sentence is 'had,'" Kurt said. "People don't want game shows anymore. They may watch *Wheel of Fortune* and *Jeopardy!*, but those are classics. People are hooked on reality shows now. That's what drives up the ratings and gets the big bucks sponsors. Do you know what I mean?"

I knew all too well. But I wasn't going to share my taste with Kurt, so I just nodded.

"Charlie was a genius at concept back when we first started working together," Kurt continued, "and he did produce a few reality shows. *Gold Coast Confidential was his most recent one.* None of them lasted too long. He just didn't understand the current trends. Or, maybe he understood them, but didn't want to accept them."

"What about *The Second Honeymoon Game?*" I asked, trying to steer the conversation back to why we were all here in Florida. "I think that's a great idea for a television show."

"Yeah, *The Second Honeymoon Game*," Kurt said. "A great idea with real potential to become a mega hit." He fixed me with a level gaze. "Do you know anything about history?"

"Well," I said, not quite sure why the conversation had taken a sudden veer off the track, "I took a few courses in college. Why?"

"Do you remember Custer's Last Stand? Well, *The Second Honeymoon Game* was Charlie King's Last Stand. And Charlie ended up the exact same way Custer did. Poor guy."

Kurt fiddled with his glass, which was now empty. I prayed he was drinking traditional iced tea, because this talk was proving to be very informative and I didn't want him to lose his focus. I've heard that certain kinds of iced tea can do that to a person. Like Long Island, for example.

"I figured you'd know all about the show," he finally said. "You and Charlie being such old friends."

"I hadn't seen Charlie since we graduated from grammar school, which was a long time ago," I said. There was no sense in telling Kurt exactly how long. He was in no shape to figure out any math problems. "What do you mean about this television show being Charlie's Last Stand?"

"Nobody in the business would talk to him," Kurt said. "They thought he was all washed-up. He pitched *The Second Honeymoon Game* to the networks, and they laughed at him. Even FOX." Kurt shook his head. "And heaven knows, they'll put *anything* on the air these days. Of course, their focus is on younger viewers. Like everyone else."

"But we're here to film the pilot episode," I said. "Someone must have thought Charlie's idea was a good one."

"Yeah, you're right," Kurt said. "Someone did. But I have no idea who it was. All of a sudden, Charlie came up with a mysterious backer who agreed to bankroll the pilot." He fixed me with a stare. "In case you don't know, television is a very expensive medium. Some of the budgets, even for the reality shows, are through the roof. Of course, Charlie had cut some corners by hiring a few people who worked cheap and jumped at the chance to be involved. Like Gene Richmond, for instance. He hasn't been on television for years. And, of course, Carrie. Because she's Charlie's daughter, he didn't have to pay her a huge salary. Too bad she doesn't have a clue about what a television show is all about."

"Now, wait a minute," I said. "I understand that Gene Richmond hasn't been on television for a long time, but Carrie made a very good presentation at the meeting we all had in New York. She really impressed me with her knowledge of log lines and all that other jargon."

Kurt laughed. "Lady, Carrie's 'presentation' was a rehash of what she found on Google. She didn't know what she was talking about. Didn't you notice a few folks rolling their eyes during it?" He held up his hand. "Wait a minute. How could you? You were too busy interrupting her with ideas of your own."

I was saved from saying something I'd probably regret later by the arrival of our helpful server with a large plastic bowl filed with chipped ice and four bottles of water bearing the hotel logo. "Never mind the iced tea," Kurt said as the server turned to make his escape. "I want a large pot of extra strong coffee. I need caffeine so I can write a tribute to Charlie for tomorrow morning's event."

"Tomorrow morning?" I repeated. "What's happening then?"

"There's going to be a memorial service on the beach in honor of Charlie. We all have to be there. Mack Whitman's called local media contacts, and some of them have promised to provide coverage. What ghouls. But, I guess there's no such thing as bad publicity, right? And the show must go on. Welcome to the wonderful world of television."

Kurt paused and gave me a quizzical look. "I'm surprised you don't know about this already. Don't you and your husband talk to each other? He's up to his eyeballs planning this thing."

Jim and I may talk to each other, but we don't usually listen to each other. I didn't really say that, of course.

"I didn't know the time was definitely set," I said. "There was some discussion about a memorial tribute, but Deputy Armstrong had suggested it be delayed until she had more information about how Charlie died."

I always say, if you're going to tell a lie, make it a whopper. And this one would rival anything Burger King has on its menu, for sure.

"Oh, that's not going to be a problem," Kurt assured me. "I've heard that Deputy Armstrong got a tip about a young guy who got in a big fight with Charlie last night in the hotel restaurant. Wouldn't it be cool if Armstrong arrested him on-camera during the memorial service? Wow, the show would be a hit before we even did the pilot. We'd have even more big bucks sponsors begging to get on board."

OMG.

Chapter 37

I'm not a snob. I'm just really good at figuring out who's worth talking to and who isn't.

I knew I had to find Jim and Mike. No more procrastinating. Jim needed to know that our son was at the top of Deputy Armstrong's suspect list, and Mike needed to explain why he lied. Or else both the men in my life would find themselves starring in a very unpleasant reality television show of their own tomorrow morning.

I found a stone bench shaded by a friendly palm tree and plunked my derriere down, wrapping the dog leashes around my wrist to be sure they didn't get any funny ideas about exploring the area. First, I fired off a text to Jim. After all, I'd been married to him longer than I'd been a mother to Mike. Just in case you're keeping score.

Me: *Need to talk to u asap. Where r u?*

Jim: *With Mack. No time now. Can you wait an hour?*

Me: *No way.*

Jim: *Why?*

Me: *Emergency.*

Jim: *R u sick? Dogs?*

Me: *No. It's Mike.*

Jim: *Mike's sick?*

Me: *No. Not sick.*

Jim: *Up to my eyeballs planning press conference for tomorrow. Will meet u at villa in an hour. Okay?*

Me: *Sigh. Okay.*

I clicked off. "I guess one person's press conference is another person's memorial service," I said to the dogs. That sounded so ridiculous that even Ethel gave me a skeptical look.

"Maybe it's better if Jim and I don't catch up for another hour," I said, determined to put a positive spin on what was basically my husband brushing me off. "If I'm lucky, we'll find Mike and clear this whole mess up and Jim won't ever have to know."

And I can add this to the ever growing list of things I've never told Jim.

I wondered if sins of omission counted as much as sins of commission. If they did, I was in big trouble.

"I guess my text to Jim didn't sound urgent enough," I said to the dogs. "I'm not making the same mistake with Mike. I have to make it clear I'm not taking no for an answer. I have to see him right away."

Me: *I know what you did. Meet me at Villa C in ten minutes.*

I pressed Send.

I got an immediate *ping* back, indicating a response.

Mike: *What I did? What did I do?*

Me: *Nine minutes. No excuses. And you know what I'm talking about, buster.*

When I pressed Send this time, I felt a tiny prickle of guilt. But I got over it. Mothers usually know best. They just have to prove it to their offspring.

By the time we got to the villa, Mike was already there, sweaty and red-faced. My first inclination was to hand him something to wipe off his face—an automatic "mommie" response. But I stopped myself. This was an inquisition, not a mother-son bonding session.

Mike gave me a weak grin. "What's up, Cosmo Girl? Are you mad at me for something?" Under normal circumstances, Mike's use of my special nickname would make my heart melt. But not today.

"Come in," I said, opening the villa door and going into the blessed air-conditioning. Mike followed, more obediently than I would have expected. I guess he finally realized he was in big trouble.

I pulled out a chair at the dining room table. "Sit." Lucy and

Ethel immediately sat, which struck me funny. I turned my head away from Mike so he couldn't see me laughing. When I turned back to face him, I was all business.

"Let's cut out all the nonsense and get right to it," I said. "You lied to Deputy Armstrong about seeing Charlie King last night. I want to know why."

Mike's face flushed red. A sure sign that I had hit the mark.

"I don't know what you're talking about, Mom," Mike said. He shifted in his chair and refused to meet my gaze. Exactly the same body language he used when he was a little boy and I'd caught him in some minor transgression.

"I said, cut the nonsense," I repeated. "You lied, and I know you lied. I want to know why. Don't you realize how bad that makes you look to the authorities?"

In a true example of the apple (Mike) not falling far from the tree (me), my son immediately went on the offensive and began to question me.

"How do you know I lied?" he challenged. "How do you know I saw Charlie King again after we all met at the airport yesterday? If anyone says I did, they're a damn liar." Mike sat back in his chair, satisfied that he had successfully stonewalled my interrogation.

"Are you calling Claire McGee a liar?" I shot back. "One of the people who's known you since the day you were born?"

"She's wrong," Mike insisted. "It must have been someone who looked like me. And where does she claim she saw me?" He sat back in his chair and crossed his arms, daring me to answer.

"Claire *saw* you last night at the entrance to the hotel restaurant. And don't try to deny it. Nancy was there, too. Are you saying two of our closest friends in the whole world mistook you for a stranger? You've got to be kidding."

Notice I didn't say that Nancy also saw Mike. Because I wasn't sure that she had. And I didn't want Deputy Armstrong to think she had another potential witness against Mike and question her, too. I just threw Nancy's name into the mix to scare Mike.

"I don't know why everyone's making such a big deal out of this," Mike said.

Honest to goodness, it took all the self-control I had in my whole body to resist taking Mike by the shoulders and shaking him. How could he be so clueless?

"Are you out of your mind?" I said through clenched teeth.

"People saw you and Charlie King together right before he died. And I'm told that you and he had a shoving match. That can be interpreted as a fight. Within an hour, the man was dead. How can you say that's no big deal? And why did you lie about it when you were questioned by Deputy Armstrong?"

I hoped that Mike would infer that Deputy Armstrong was the source of my information. In a way, of course, she was. But I didn't want to admit that I eavesdropped on Mike's interrogation.

"I was with Carrie King ever since I met her at the airport yesterday," Mike said. "She can vouch for me." He gave me a defiant look, daring me to argue with him. I recognized that look. It was the same one he used when he got caught driving the family car without a license. Too bad Mike was too old now to be grounded or sent to his room as punishment.

"That look didn't work on me when you were thirteen and it's not going to work now," I said, with as much force as I could muster.

"Oh, yeah? Why don't you ask Carrie if you don't believe me?" Mike said. "Maybe you want details about what we were doing, too. Is that right, *Mother?*"

Mike has never called me Mother, no matter what. Now he'd really pushed all my buttons. I turned purple, not my best color. Obviously, it was time for me to change tactics, because this line of conversation wasn't getting me anywhere.

"Carrie seems like a lovely girl," I said, leaning down to pat the dogs and give my blood pressure a chance to come down a few points. "It's a good thing you were with her when she got the terrible news about her father's death. I'm sure you've been a big support to her."

"I hope I've helped her," Mike said. "I really like her a lot. Meeting her has been the only good thing that's happened since I got here yesterday. This isn't exactly what I bargained for when I decided to surprise you and Dad."

I decided to ignore the implication that Mike wasn't happy to have special time with Jim and me. A beautiful girl trumps elderly parents every time.

"None of us bargained for this tragedy," I said to my son. "Dad and I were there when the car exploded and killed Charlie, in case you didn't know that. It was horrible. I can't stop thinking about that poor man. I hope he didn't suffer." This time, the tears in my eyes were genuine.

"It's true that Deputy Armstrong asked me a few questions about last night," Mike admitted. "But when I told her I hadn't seen Mr. King since the airport, she seemed satisfied. And Carrie backed me up. So it's our word against whoever claims they saw me with him. And that person's wrong. How many times do I have to tell you that before you get off my case?"

I pounced. "That's the whole point, Mike. I don't want there to be a case against you. And you're not helping yourself. Please, tell me the truth. What really happened last night? I'm your mother. I love you unconditionally. No matter what you tell me, I'm on your side."

Those tears were threatening to spill down my cheeks. When I looked at my son, I saw tears in his eyes, too.

"Like I said, I don't know why everyone's making a big deal about this," he finally said. "I did see Mr. King very briefly as he was leaving the restaurant last night. I started to ask him something, but he was in a terrific hurry and pushed me aside." His face darkened. "There certainly was no fight."

Now, we were getting somewhere.

"Did you push him back?" I demanded.

"No, Mom, not really. But I was so startled I might have given him a tap on his arm. It was an automatic response."

"A tap?" I persisted. "How hard a tap?"

"Gosh, Mom, ease up. Not hard enough to make anyone think we were fighting."

"Well, someone said it was a fight," I said. "And I know for a fact it wasn't Claire or Nancy." Especially not Nancy.

"Ask Carrie what happened if you don't believe me," Mike shot back. "She was right there."

"That's great, Mike," I said. "So she can corroborate that nothing really happened between you and her father?"

Mike looked miserable. "Yeah, she could have. Except for one thing. She and I decided it was best to deny that I'd been there at all. Carrie was worried that I might get in trouble otherwise. And I agreed."

I held up my hand. "Wait just a minute, please, while I process this." I took a deep breath, then continued, "Are you telling me that someone you barely know has talked you into lying to the authorities?"

"Mom, after all, it was her father who died. She wants to find out how he died more than anyone else. That's why she asked you to help. And she was afraid that if the sheriff's office got sidetracked with me, the guilty person would get away. After all, from everything I've heard, the first twenty-four hours after a crime is committed is critical. Why confuse Deputy Armstrong? It makes perfect sense."

"On the contrary," I said, struggling to keep my voice level and not scream, "this makes you look guilty as hell. Do you know there's going to be a memorial service for Charlie tomorrow morning at the beach? And Deputy Armstrong may name a 'person of interest' in the case at that service? Maybe even announce an arrest? Any idea who that might be?"

Mike shook his head.

"It's you!" I exploded. "I hope I'm wrong, but I'm betting it's you! How could you let Carrie influence you into making such a bad decision? What is the matter with you? We raised you to make intelligent choices. Not stupid ones."

Mike glared at me. "That's exactly right, Mom. You and Dad raised me. But I'm grown up now, and capable of making my own decisions. Even if you think they're the wrong ones. If you want to tell Deputy Armstrong what I admitted to you, go ahead. I don't care. I'm outta here."

My only son stalked out of the villa, slamming the door behind him.

Chapter 38

My new computer said, "Press Any Key" to start. But I couldn't find the button that said, "Any Key."

"This has to be the longest twenty-four hours of my whole life," I said to Lucy and Ethel. "And the worst. You both know that I hate arguing with anybody. Even when I'm positive I'm right. And I was right this time. Wasn't I?"

Jeez, Carol. Get a grip. You're asking for reinforcement from the dogs again. That's a little over the top, even for you.

I was about a millisecond away from sobbing my eyes out. "I don't think either of the kids have ever been so angry at me. Even Jenny, the time I caught her sneaking out of the house when she was a freshman in high school to meet a guy who was ten years older than she was. Gosh, we sure had a huge fight. But it was nothing like this. Jenny knew she was wrong, and she admitted it. Not until both of us had shed lots of tears, though." I frowned as the memory of that incident flooded my brain. It was one of the many family crises that I'd had to handle all on my own, because Jim was out of town on business.

Ping. I squinted at my phone. Speak of the devil (metaphorically, of course), I had a text from my husband.

Jim: *All hell breaking here over Charlie's death. Will be working a while longer. Networks sending reporters to cover tomorrow's event. It's morphed into a huge story. I'm sure Mike's problem will straighten itself out. Don't interfere, and don't be mad at me.*

Me: *Mad? Why should I be mad? I need you and you're not here. It's the same old story. AND I NEVER INTERFERE!*

But something stopped me (possibly, a drop of common sense?), and instead of clicking the Send button, I clicked Cancel. I couldn't take the chance of having the two most important men in my life both mad at me at the same time.

But I knew I had to do something fast to help Mike, even if he didn't know how much he needed my help. And preventing an impending disaster isn't the same as interfering in someone's life, right? Of course, right.

I was so good at crisis management that I once considered offering my services to the federal government during the next budget crunch. But I didn't do it. I realized I had enough to worry about without adding the entire weight of the country to my already full plate. But should any of you decide to send an email to the White House on my behalf, well, I can't stop you.

I knew I would solve this with the help of the people I've always turned to when I'm in trouble, and who are always there for me, no matter what: Nancy, Claire, and Mary Alice.

I waved leashes and said the magic words, "Want to go for another walk?"

"You just missed Carrie King," Nancy said, welcoming us with a hug. Well, to clarify, she didn't hug Lucy and Ethel. But she did give them a few scratches behind their ears. That, a large bowl of spring water, and a comfortable place to snooze seemed to satisfy them just fine.

"Carrie King?" I said, settling myself on the sofa beside Claire and preparing to unburden myself. "What the heck was she doing here? I didn't realize she even knew who you were."

"Well, of course she knows me," Nancy huffed, taking offense at my remark. "You're not the only one who went to grammar school with her father, in case you've forgotten. She stopped by to be sure I was all right."

"Huh? You've lost me," I said. "Why was she so concerned about you?"

"Charlie told her that I'd become very special to him," Nancy said, dabbing at her eyes. "He said it would mean a lot to him if she and I became good friends. Who knows what would have happened between Charlie and me if he hadn't died so suddenly? We could have had a grand love affair."

I didn't dare look at Claire, but I was sure she was rolling her eyes at Nancy's outrageous version of her newfound relationship with our late classmate.

"Pardon my skepticism," I said, "but you'd only seen the man a few times since we graduated from eighth grade, more than forty-five years ago. Do the math. It's been a long, long time. You hardly knew each other. That doesn't sound like the beginning of a grand romance to me."

"Ha!" Nancy said, tossing her head in a gesture that always drives me nuts. "You're just jealous, because you thought Charlie had been carrying a torch for you all these years. But then he saw me and, bingo! It could have been love at first sight for him."

"That's doubtful," I said. "Second sight, maybe. And, anyway, we're arguing over a dead man, for heaven's sakes."

"Oh, puleez," Claire said. "Could we get back on track, please? Carol, did you catch up with Mike and Jim? What happened?"

"Well," I said slowly, "that's kind of a long story."

"Big surprise," said Claire. "All your stories are long."

I tried to look angry, but failed. Because Claire was right. I do take a long time to get to the point. Like now, for instance. I settled for sticking my tongue out at Claire, which made her laugh and broke any tension left between us.

"Before I tell you about Mike," I said, "I want to know more about Carrie's visit here. Was it only because she was worried about you, Nancy?"

Nancy started to answer, but Claire interrupted, "She was looking for you," Claire said. "She said she'd knocked on the door of your villa and you weren't there."

"Carrie's so upset about her father's death," Nancy said. "When she first got here, she couldn't stop crying. I'm sure Carrie was looking for emotional support. The unconditional kind that mothers always give to their kids, no matter how old they are, and she had nowhere else to turn."

Of course, that made me feel very guilty about the tongue lashing I'd recently given my only son.

Maybe you were wrong to interfere, Carol. What if you've damaged your relationship forever?

I added that worry to my fear about Mike being charged with a crime he didn't commit. What a mess.

I came back to earth when I heard Claire say, "And with her father gone, and her mother's death when she was so young, now Carrie has no family at all. It's very sad."

"She has no siblings?" I asked.

Nancy shook her head. "Nope. She was an only child. Just like you, Carol."

"She must have been very close to her father," I said. "Charlie had to be both mother and father to her. Did she talk about her relationship with her dad?"

"Not really," Claire said. "She was more interested in having us tell her stories about Charlie from our grammar school days. I think talking about her father with us cheered her up a little."

"Carrie couldn't believe that we've been best friends for so many years," Nancy said. "I guess she never developed any really close relationships with other girls her age."

"Carrie went to several different schools all over the country while she was growing up," Claire added. "Charlie traveled a lot for work, and he always took her with him. She even had private tutors for a while."

"It doesn't sound like the kind of childhood I'd want," I said.

"Me, either," Nancy agreed.

"Carrie wanted to know what it was like to have best girlfriends," Claire said. "We told her about some of our adventures."

"Like the time we were going to New York to see a play, and you got locked in the bathroom at the Fairport train station, Carol. You were screaming blue murder before somebody heard you and let you out. You almost missed the train."

"I don't think that was very funny," I said. "I had nightmares about it for a long time."

"Well, it made Carrie laugh," Nancy said. "I told her that you don't like self-service elevators, either. Especially in older buildings."

"And let's not forget about the swimming test at Mount Saint Francis Academy," Claire said. "Remember how freaked out you were when you thought we had to pass that test to graduate?"

"Yeah, we were lucky that requirement was discontinued," Nancy added. "Especially since you never did learn how to swim,

Carol."

"I'm glad I could be the subject of so much lively conversation," I said. "What an honor."

"Oh, sweetie, we didn't mean to make fun of you," Nancy said, realizing that my feelings were hurt. "We were just trying to cheer Carrie up, and one thing led to another."

"Enough of this," Claire said. "Back to you, Carol. What happened with Mike and Jim?"

"I never connected with Jim," I said slowly. "Except by text. And my talk with Mike was horrible." I started to cry. "I don't know if he'll ever speak to me again."

"Oh, honey," Nancy said, immediately wrapping me in a big hug. "That's not possible. He loves you. You're his 'Cosmo Girl.' "

"I think my subscription to *Cosmo* may have reached its expiration date," I said, grabbing a tissue from the box Claire was holding out to me.

"We ought to have stock in Kimberly Clark," she said, "with the way we're going through tissues on this trip."

"I'm sure you only use store brand at your house though, right, Carol?" Nancy said.

"Unless Jim has a coupon," Claire added, never missing a chance to have the last word.

Their wisecracks produced the desired effect. I stopped sniffling and made an effort to get myself under control.

"So, what happened with Mike?" Nancy asked.

"And please, try not to cry again when you tell us," Claire said. "But, just in case," she plopped the entire box of tissues on my lap, then said, "Talk."

So, I did. And I hope you were all paying attention the first time, because I have no intention of going through it all over again for you. Claire was taking notes throughout. Maybe, if you're really nice to her, she'll share them with you.

When I had finished what I hoped was a succinct version of my conversation with Mike, Claire summarized as only someone who's been married to a lawyer for more than three decades could. "Mike admitted to you that he did see Charlie last night. Charlie was in a big hurry, and brushed Mike away when he tried to talk to him." Claire looked up at me over her reading glasses. "Which is exactly what I told you in the first place, Carol. There was no fight."

"But someone told Deputy Armstrong there was a fight," I said.

"That's the part I don't understand."

"Someone's obviously lying," Claire said. "Because I know what I saw." She turned to Nancy. "What about you? Did you see anything?"

Nancy shook her head. "That was when I got a text from the office about one of my listings," she said. "I'm sorry that I can't help."

Claire returned to her scribbled notes. "Mike lied to Deputy Armstrong about seeing Charlie last night. And that was Carrie's idea? Are you sure that's what he said?"

"I'm sure. She was worried that if he admitted he'd seen her father, he'd get in trouble." I looked at my two friends. "For heaven's sake, how stupid can a guy be? Now Mike's in even more trouble. What the heck was he thinking? Where was his brain?"

"I suspect that Mike wasn't thinking with his brain, Carol," Claire said. "Especially if he spent the whole night with Carrie. If you get my drift."

"Claire's right," Nancy said. "The brain isn't the only body part that influences a guy's judgment."

I chose to ignore the implication. After all, this was my baby boy we were talking about. Don't misunderstand—I got what they were referring to. I just...chose to ignore it. Especially since I suspected they were right. I did what I always do when the subject gets too intimate; I changed it.

"I also had a talk with Kurt Armitage," I said. "This was before I saw Mike. Kurt's part of the television show staff," I clarified. "He told me some interesting things about Charlie's business history. Apparently, *The Second Honeymoon Game* was Charlie's desperate shot at making a comeback on television. Kurt called it Charlie's Last Stand. He said Charlie had been all washed up in television for years. Nobody would talk to him. But he found some mysterious guy with deep pockets to bankroll the pilot of the show. Kurt had no idea who it was."

Nancy thought for a minute, then said, "Actually, this information goes along with what I found out about Charlie through my real estate connections." She waited for just a beat, to be sure Claire and I were paying close attention. "Charlie's house was in foreclosure. It looks like he was broke."

"What do you mean, Charlie was broke?" Claire asked. "What about his private jet? And his fleet of Mercedes? That doesn't make any sense."

Nancy shook her head. "It gets even weirder. Except for the house that's currently in foreclosure, there's no record of Charlie owning any other property, including houses, even when he lived in California."

"I didn't know he ever lived in California," I said. "But I guess that makes sense. That's where most television shows are produced, right?"

"Most wealthy people set up a realty trust for their holdings," Nancy said, continuing with her Real Estate 101 for Dummies lecture. "Buying property is a good investment. At least, it was years ago. And I'm assuming that Charlie was making big bucks in the television business. But I couldn't find anything except the foreclosure. It's very odd."

"I'm not so sure Charlie was making big bucks, even back then," I said. "None of the shows he produced were real mega hits, and the entertainment business is pretty cutthroat. At least, that's what I've heard. One day, you're a big star; the next—you're a has-been. Like Gene Richmond."

"Humph," Claire said, remembering her embarrassing encounter earlier today. Which I'm sure she'd hold me, and only me, responsible for until my dying breath. "Some people are just plain rude. To walk away in the middle of a conversation with no explanation or apology."

"I saw that creepy Bernardo beckoning to him," I said. "You know who I mean, right? The so-called 'concierge,' who's always popping up all over the place, offering services that nobody wants. Or asks for. Like taking Lucy and Ethel for a walk without permission earlier today and scaring me to death. I thought they'd been dognapped."

Nancy patted my hand in sympathy. She knows how much I love the girls. Then, she said, "Maybe Bernardo had made an appointment for Gene to pick out a new hairpiece."

"Humph," Claire said again. But this time, she grinned when she said it. "Do either of you have anything else to report?"

"Kurt Armitage also told me there's a big deal memorial service scheduled for Charlie tomorrow morning at the beach," I said. "In fact, that's what Jim's working on right now. It's going to be a huge media event."

"Why do I get the feeling from the expression on your face that this is not good news?" Nancy asked. "There's more to this event than a memorial service, right?"

I nodded. "Unfortunately, you're right. According to Kurt, Deputy Sheriff Armstrong may make a big announcement at the service. She's honing in on a particular young man who was seen arguing with Charlie right before he died." I choked back a sob.

"By this time tomorrow, Mike could be in jail."

Chapter 39

Don't be so serious all the time. If you can't laugh at yourself, give me a call. I'll be glad to laugh at you.

"Well, we're not going to let that happen," Claire said firmly. "Mike needs legal representation, right away. I'll find Larry and he'll get to the bottom of this." She whipped out her phone and started typing a text.

"That's a brilliant idea," Nancy said.

"There are only two things wrong with your suggestion," I said, stopping Claire's busy fingers in mid-flight. "First of all, is Larry licensed to practice law in the state of Florida?"

"Well, no," Claire admitted. "I didn't think of that part."

"What's the second problem?" Nancy asked.

"I bet Mike won't even talk to Larry," I said. "He's refused to admit that he saw Charlie last night, remember? Except to me, and I had to practically force it out of him. He has no idea the trouble he could be in."

"Then it's up to us to clear Mike," Claire said. "And we can do it." She grabbed my hands and repeated, "We can do it. Believe that, Carol. But there's no time to waste. We're going to figure this whole mess out before tomorrow morning's memorial service."

"I wish I had your confidence, Claire," I said.

Nancy checked her phone. "Mary Alice just sent a text. She says she has something she wants to tell us. She wants to be sure we're all together, and then she'll FaceTime us."

Nancy tapped a quick reply into her phone. "I told her to call now."

"Since when does Mary Alice know how to text?" I asked, happy to focus on another topic besides my soon-to-be-wearing-an-orange-jumpsuit son. "And what the heck is FaceTime?"

"She took a computer course at the Fairport Senior Center this winter," Claire said. "FaceTime means you can make a call on your Smartphone and actually see the person you're talking to."

"FaceTime is a great idea, as long as my hair and makeup look good," Nancy added. "I just don't use it too early in the day." I shot her a quick look and realized she wasn't kidding.

Nancy's phone trilled, she pressed a few buttons, and through the wonders of technology, Mary Alice appeared on the screen, waving at us.

"We're putting you on the dining table so we can all see you," Nancy said. "You're our centerpiece."

"This is probably the closest I'll get to Florida for a long time," Mary Alice said. "And I guess I won't get a tan today, right?"

Claire and Nancy both laughed, but I didn't. I was too impatient for mindless chatter, so I grabbed the phone. "Mary Alice, Mike is in big trouble. I don't know what you've found out, but I sure hope it will help him."

"What?" Mary Alice asked. "What's going on?"

Nancy yanked the phone from my hand and put it back on the table. "Here's the short version. Some idiot claims that Mike and Charlie King had a fight last night. Mike lied to the deputy sheriff about seeing Charlie. Carol thinks Mike's going to be arrested and charged with Charlie's death." She looked at me. "Have I left out anything important?"

I shook my head.

"Now," Claire said, leaning forward toward the phone so Mary Alice could see her, "what have you found out?"

"Give me a second," Mary Alice said. "I'm trying to process what you've told me. Oh, Carol, I wish I was there to give you a hug."

"Hugs are great," Claire said, "but information is even better. What do you want to tell us?"

Mary Alice held up a yellowed newspaper clipping. "Remember I told you that the obituary for Charlie's wife was in the paper the same day as Brian's?"

"We're all nodding," Nancy said, speaking for everyone.

"I found the obituary and re-read it." Mary Alice's voice wobbled. "It was very hard for me to look at that paper again. But I forced myself. The obituary was very short. But there was something about the way it was written that made me suspicious. I know a few nurses who've been on staff here at the hospital for years. One of them, Rita Monroe, was a goldmine of information. She remembered that Charlie's wife was a very troubled person after she had her baby. Today she'd probably be diagnosed with postpartum depression, but back in those days, nobody knew what that was."

By this time, Claire, Nancy and I were jockeying to get as close to the phone as possible. Stupid, I know. Like that'd make any difference in Mary Alice's story.

"Rita told me that Charlie's wife committed suicide. And the family hushed it up. That's why her father had that memorial to her at his drug store. It was the only way he could think of to honor her life....And her memory."

"How tragic for Carrie," Nancy said, echoing all our thoughts.

"Postpartum depression can sometimes last for years," Mary Alice added. "Nobody understood it back then."

"I didn't know much about it until that actress, Brooke Shields, wrote a book about her own experience with it," Claire said. "Remember the furor that caused?"

"This is all very sad," I said, directing my comments toward the phone, "but I don't see how this relates to Mike. Helping him is my number one priority right now. I feel bad for Carrie, but.... I hope the rest of you understand."

"Of course we do," Nancy said. "Mary Alice, we wish you were here with us so much."

"Believe me, so do I," Mary Alice said with a laugh. "We had five more inches of snow last night."

"Thanks for the information about Carrie's mother," I said, not wanting to appear ungrateful. "We'll be home soon."

After a flurry of air kisses, Nancy clicked her phone off and looked at Claire and me. "So, where are we? Did that help at all?"

"I don't see how," I repeated, shaking my head in frustration. "I'm worried to death about Mike, and I don't think either of you are helping. You just don't understand." I could feel a major pity party starting.

"I'm going to ignore that remark," Claire said. "Because we

both know how upset you are. And maybe Mike isn't our birth son, but that doesn't mean we don't love him. So quit feeling sorry for yourself and let's get back to work."

She wrote NEXT STEPS in bold writing on the notepad, then looked at me. "So…what next? Or, should I say, who next? As in, who else do we talk to?"

"Whom," I said automatically. "Whom is the direct object of 'talk.' "

Nancy rolled her eyes.

"I'd sure like to find out who that dining room server was who started all this trouble," I said. "In fact, I'd like to wring her neck, the liar."

Claire wrote: FIND OUT WHO SERVER IS.

Nancy said, "That's a great idea. And I don't know about the rest of you, but I'm hungry. What do you say we make a quick trip to the dining room ourselves? We can grab a bite and ask a few questions. Multi-talking at its best."

"Great idea," Claire said. "Just give me a minute to freshen up, and text Larry, in case he's looking for me."

"What about the dogs?" I said, gesturing to Lucy and Ethel who were snoozing by the sliding glass door.

"I bet they won't even miss us," Nancy said. "Come on."

"I don't know," I said. "I hate to leave them. They may start to bark because they're in a strange place."

"Then we'll take them with us and eat outside by the pool," Nancy said in frustration. "Let's go."

Lucy gave me a doggy stare and a huge yawn. Then she rolled over and went back to sleep.

"She's telling us she's had enough exercise, and needs her rest, Carol," Nancy said. "I don't blame her. Bye, Lucy. We'll bring you and Ethel a treat from the dining room."

Honestly, that Nancy. Sometimes I think she knows my dogs better than I do.

Chapter 40

Chocolate comes from cocoa, which is a tree. That makes it a plant, which means that chocolate is a vegetable. Therefore, eating a whole bag of M&Ms is actually eating a salad.

"I'm sorry, hon, but we are closed," the self-important young man said, halting us at the entrance to the dining room. "We begin dinner service at five o'clock. I suggest you try the poolside bar."

Never mess with three post-menopausal women. Especially if they're hungry. And, above all, never call us "hon."

I peeked around the little twerp's shoulder. There were four men sitting at a table in the corner of the dining room, enjoying a late lunch.

"I'm certain I didn't hear you correctly," I said in my most lady-of-the-manor voice. "Or, perhaps you've been misinformed. Those four gentlemen are obviously eating. I assume that's food from your hotel kitchen. We would like to do the same. So please seat us. Now. Unless the dining room only serves men at this hour, which is a form of discrimination. In that case, we could sue. And my friend Claire just happens to be married to a prominent Florida attorney. I'm certain he'd be happy to take on the case. Am I right, Claire?"

Claire nodded her head in agreement. "Discrimination cases are his specialty, as you know, Carol. In fact, he's slated to argue a suit against the Happy Holidays Hotel chain at the U.S. Supreme Court in two weeks."

Nancy suppressed a giggle. With a great deal of effort.

Well, what else could the poor guy do, when faced with a possible lawsuit, but open the velvet rope he'd been hiding behind, reach for some menus, and say, "Sorry for the misunderstanding. Please, follow me. I'll alert the kitchen that you are here. Also, please enjoy an iced coffee or tea on the house."

"That's more like it," I said, settling into a seat and preparing to look at the menu. "What a jerk."

"I just hope somebody comes to take our order," Nancy said. "There don't seem to be any servers around."

"Those four men over in the corner have food," Claire said. "I doubt they went into the kitchen and made it themselves."

"Fat chance," Nancy said. "There aren't a lot of men who'd make their own lunch, even in their own house."

I laughed in spite of myself. "Trust you to make me feel better."

"You know the old saying, 'Marriage is for better and for worse, but not for lunch,' " Claire added. "Although retirement sure changes that in a hurry."

Our conversation was interrupted by a burst of laughter coming from the other table.

"You know," I said, turning around and craning my neck with some effort, "there's something about one of those men over there that looks familiar. I think I've seen him some place before." I whipped out my bifocals for a better look.

"Well, how about that," I said. "I not only know that guy, I've been married to him for more than thirty years."

"What? You're kidding," Nancy said.

"I think I know my own husband," I said, pushing back my chair and standing up. "Even from the back. I'm going over there to see what's going on. Are you two coming with me?"

"Why not?" said Nancy. "I just love drama. Come on, Claire."

I wasn't surprised to see that two of Jim's tablemates were Mack and Kurt Armitage. But his third companion was a shock. It was Bernardo, that shifty concierge, who'd recently kidnapped my dogs. What the heck was he doing there? Had he served lunch, then pulled up a chair and made himself comfy? That'd be just like him.

Their table was littered with empty glasses and plates, which didn't seem to bother the men at all. They were all having a jolly time, judging by the continuous laughter. This was a serious business meeting to plan a memorial service? I didn't think so.

I tapped Jim on the shoulder. "Working hard, dear?" I was pleased to see that I had successfully embarrassed my husband, which was evident from the red flush that crept up around his shirt collar.

Gotcha!

All four men immediately sprang to their feet. Just like four little boys whose mothers had caught them raiding the cookie jar just before supper.

"Carol," Mack said, recovering the quickest, "we were just talking about you. We need your input on tomorrow's memorial service. You know, the woman's touch. Especially since you and Charlie had such an intimate history."

"I'd hardy characterize my relationship with Charlie as intimate, Mack," I said. "Unless you want to include my friends, Nancy Green, Claire McGee, and the entire graduating class of Mount St. Francis Grammar School in…well, never mind what year.

"This is Nancy," I continued, pulling her forward, "and this is Claire. In case you haven't met them before. In fact, Claire and her husband Larry may be the first contestants on *The Second Honeymoon Game*." I looked at Kurt. "Assuming the show's pilot ever happens."

"The show always goes on," Kurt hastened to assure me. "It may be delayed a bit, but it will go on."

"We don't mean to interrupt your *business* meeting," I said, dripping with an excessive amount of sarcasm that I was sure even my clueless husband couldn't miss, "which is obviously important and very serious, judging by the amount of laughter we heard from the other side of the dining room. When you have a second to spare, Jim, I'd like to have a brief conversation about our son. I promise I won't take up too much of your valuable time. And, Bernardo, if you could find it in your heart to take our lunch orders—at your convenience, of course—I would really appreciate it. Oh, and Lucy and Ethel send their best."

Then I turned and made my way, head held high, in the direction of my own table. At least, I started to make my way. It would have been so much more dramatic if I hadn't held my head up quite so high, which caused to bang right into a pile of extra chairs and spill them all over the place.

My gallant husband immediately sprang to my rescue, even

though I'm sure what Jim really wanted to do was smack me upside the head, figuratively speaking. As he grabbed me to save me from falling, he hissed in my ear, "This better be good." Then he gave me a quick peck on the cheek, and said to his tablemates, "Carol and I need some time to catch up. We haven't seen each other for most of the day."

And whose fault is that, dear?

I didn't really say that, of course. No sense adding more logs to the fire. So to speak. But boy, I wanted to. I glared at Jim, which I hoped telegraphed how angry I was.

Bernardo rose from his chair. "While you and your wife talk, I'll tell the kitchen to prepare a special meal for all you lovely ladies."

I gaped at him, and repeated, "You'll tell the kitchen? I don't understand."

Bernardo looked apologetic. And embarrassed.

"I didn't mean to mislead you, Carol. Or your friends. But sometimes I like to go incognito to see how well one of my properties is running. I actually own this hotel."

Kurt spoke up. "It turns out that Bernardo owns this one, and several others. He also happens to be the mysterious backer of *The Second Honeymoon Game* that Charlie talked about but wouldn't identify. I guess you could say that Bernardo's our boss."

"And a fine one he is, too," Mack said. "We've just been kicking around some new ideas for the show. Bernardo has some terrific ones."

I'll just bet he does. And even if he didn't, you'd say so anyway.

Nancy immediately pulled up a chair beside Bernardo. "I'd love to hear some of them," she said. "I find television so fascinating. I know Claire does, too. Right, Claire?" She gave me a wink, and I realized that Nancy was creating a diversion so Jim and I could slip away and have a private conversation. If there's one thing that men like to talk about, it's how brilliant they are.

"Well, I don't pretend to be an expert," I heard Bernardo say as I dragged Jim to a deserted corner of the restaurant.

"Do you have any idea how much you humiliated me in front of everybody just now?" Jim asked angrily. "Mack and Kurt and I were trying hard to make a good impression on Bernardo, and you had to come along and ruin it."

"I refuse to let you intimidate me into apologizing for my behavior," I said, looking my husband squarely in the face. "I was totally justified, in my opinion. And I'm sure every other wife in the world would agree with me if she knew the circumstances. Now, be quiet and let me talk. It's about Mike. He's in real trouble, and he doesn't even realize it."

I filled Jim in as best I could about Deputy Armstrong's suspicions, that Mike had lied to her, and her possible announcement of Mike's arrest at tomorrow's memorial service. Of course, Jim interrupted me every other minute with questions, accusations, and more questions, so my sad tale took even longer than usual.

But I didn't cry. Not once. Points for me, right?

When I had finally finished, Jim sighed. "Carol you're doing it again. When are you going to stop jumping to these ridiculous conclusions? There is absolutely no truth to this, whatsoever. And I should know. After all, I've been working on the logistics of tomorrow's event, not you."

"That's another thing," I said. "Why wasn't I involved in planning this event? Have I been fired from *The Second Honeymoon Game* team and nobody bothered to tell me?"

Isn't it impressive, the way I can switch gears in mid-argument? It's taken years of practice.

"Carrie asked Mack to handle the memorial service details," Jim said. "And, naturally, Mack involved me. We've been working on it most of the day."

"Yeah, I can see how hard you've been working," I said. "Well, what about Mike? Will you talk to him? You're his father. Maybe he'll listen to you."

"Let it go, Carol. I'm sure you misunderstood. Who told you about this so-called announcement from Deputy Armstrong?"

I had to think for a minute, then said, "It was Kurt. Yes, I'm sure it was him."

Jim relaxed. "Well, that explains it."

Huh?

"We were kicking around some ideas to ensure coverage for tomorrow, and Mack came up with the outrageous idea of leaking to the press that an arrest would be made during the service. It was a publicity stunt, pure and simple. But we finally decided it was a ridiculous idea, and decided not to go through with it. Kurt must have misunderstood."

I gasped. "Do you mean to tell me that I've been on the edge of a nervous breakdown for most of the afternoon and this whole thing was a stupid publicity stunt? How was I supposed to know that, when I wasn't included in the planning meeting in the first place?" I glared at my husband.

Jim had the grace to look embarrassed. I decided it was a good look for him, and pressed on with my questions.

"What about the phone tip Deputy Armstrong got from one of the servers? Is that made up, too?"

Jim shook his head. "You've lost me, Carol. I don't know anything about any phone tip. Are you sure? How did you hear about this?"

Well, I certainly wasn't going to admit to my husband that I had been kneeling down with my ear pressed to the door during Deputy Armstrong's conversation with Mike. So I played the "I can't remember" card which, as I get older, is popping up with increasing regularity in my personal deck of cards.

I frowned, feigning concentration, then said, "Sorry, Jim. I don't remember who said it. Maybe Kurt?" I shook my head. "Nope, it wasn't him. But wherever I heard it, I remember very clearly that there was a phone call to Deputy Armstrong from one of the servers who was working in the dining room last night. She said she witnessed a fight between a young man and Charlie as Charlie was leaving the dining room. Don't you get it? The young man was Mike. And when he was questioned by Deputy Armstrong, he lied about it."

Jim looked exasperated. "Even for you, that's a huge jump to an illogical conclusion. Why do you assume the young man is Mike?"

"Because Claire saw Mike and Charlie together, too. Although she says that there was no fight. Charlie was in a hurry, Mike stopped him to talk, and Charlie brushed him off and raced out of the restaurant."

"So nothing really happened," Jim said. "I'm sure Mike meant that there was no fight, not that he didn't see Charlie at all last night. You misunderstood. Again. And Claire can tell Deputy Armstrong that there was no fight, and the whole matter will be dropped before it even starts. You were worried for nothing." He gave me a smooch on the cheek.

"Nothing? How can you say I was worried for nothing?" I was so mad that I wanted to stamp my foot in frustration. But I didn't. The way my day was going, I'd probably break a toe.

"Because there's also a hole in what you told me that's big

enough to drive a tractor trailer through. Trust me, there was definitely no phone call from a female server who was working here last night, because the dining room only has male servers at the moment. Again, you must have misunderstood."

Jim patted my cheek. "But if it'll make you feel any better, by all means, nose around and see what else you can find out."

"What about your detective career, Jim?" I asked. "Aren't you Deputy Armstrong's number one honcho on this case?"

"I guess I deserved that shot, Carol. I was wrong to take over the way I did. So let's call a truce. How about I do what I do best, and you do what you do best? Just be sure you get the facts straight this time. Now, I have to get back to work."

Chapter 41

I'm going to retire to Florida and live off my savings. I'm not sure what I'm going to do the second week, though.

"I know what I heard," I insisted to Nancy and Claire. Having been summarily dismissed by my husband, the three of us (well, the five of us—Lucy and Ethel were present, too) were having yet another council of war back in Nancy's villa.

Correction: We'd have a council of war once my two friends quit complaining and I got them to focus.

"It's too bad we had to leave so fast," Nancy said, ignoring me as she frequently does. "We were just getting our food. I barely had time to eat a single bite."

"That's all you ever eat," I said.

"I'm careful about what I eat," Nancy admitted, "but I do eat. Just in small portions. I intend to live to a ripe old age, and Mary Alice is always warning us about the dangers of too much red meat and fatty foods."

"Hey, look what I found," Claire said. "It's a room service menu. Let's order something." She waved it in my direction. "You too, Carol. You need to celebrate. It looks like Mike's off the hook."

"But he's not," I insisted, grabbing the menu from Claire and venturing a peek. Hey, I'm only human.

"Then you really need to order something," Nancy said. "You always think better when you're not hungry." Her look turned thoughtful. "I wonder if there's a way to have Bernardo pay for this. After all, we now know he's the big cheese around here."

"But maybe nobody else does," Claire said. "Or, at least, only a few other people do. Remember, Bernardo said he was here on the q.t. to check out his property investment and see how well the hotel was run."

"Well, he must have told the kitchen staff," Nancy said.

"Not necessarily," Claire said. "Bernardo was wearing his concierge uniform when we saw him in the dining room, remember?"

"I still can't get over the fact that he really owns this place. And that he was Charlie's secret backer," I said. "I know this must mean something important, if I could just figure out what."

"Key lime pie and a big pot of coffee," Nancy announced, picking up the house phone to call room service. "That'll get our little grey cells percolating, for sure." She paused, then said, "I wonder if there's such a thing as a low-fat version of key lime pie."

"You're no fun at all," I said. "If there's one time we need extra calories, this is it."

"Carol's right," Claire said. "Key lime pie is the Florida version of our northern cure-all, a big bowl of ice cream. I've always wanted to eat dessert first. And while we're waiting," she took out her notebook again, "let's go through this one more time."

I groaned. "I'm not sure I can right now. My head is all fuzzy."

"I'll resist pointing out that your head is frequently fuzzy," Claire said with a smile that I hoped was sincere. With Claire, you never know.

"Did you add what Mary Alice told us about Carrie's mother to your notes?" Nancy asked.

Claire nodded. "Of course I did."

"I felt so sorry for Carrie when she came to see us a while ago," Nancy said. "I just wanted to hug her." She looked at me. "Carol, you really need to reach out to her. She needs a lot of emotional support right now. And remember, you were the person she really wanted to see, not Claire and me. We were just poor substitutes."

Of course, that made me feel guilty. I just can't help myself—it's an uncontrollable, automatic response. And Carrie had been named after me, which meant we were practically related.

But then, my rational side (which I do listen to on very rare occasions) kicked in, and I remembered that Carrie had also been the one behind Mike's decision to lie to Deputy Armstrong. What kind of a game was Carrie playing, anyway? Was she really the distraught daughter, or was there something more going on that I hadn't figured out yet?

I decided to raise the question with Nancy and Claire. After all, they'd just seen Carrie, and my only recent interaction with her (eavesdropping at keyholes doesn't really count, even in my world) had been at the early morning meeting with the television show staff and Deputy Armstrong, when Carrie had begged me to help. I tried to remember the way she'd asked me, but her exact words eluded me. I shook my head. It probably didn't matter, anyway.

My phone bleated, startling me out of my musings. I was thrilled to see that it was my darling daughter, calling from the frozen north. At least one of my two children was still speaking to me. Unless she was calling to bawl me out for overstepping my maternal bounds once too often.

"Hello, sweetie," I said, mouthing, "It's Jenny," to Claire and Nancy before heading into the bedroom for privacy. I closed the door and sat down on the bed, trying not to wrinkle (or allow myself to be distracted by) the gorgeous pink and green patterned Lilly Pulitzer quilt that covered it.

"Hi, Mom," Jenny said. "I'm calling to check up on you. How's the second honeymoon going? Or can't you share those intimate details?"

I was glad Jenny didn't see me blush. "It's a lot different from our first honeymoon," I said, not quite sure where this conversation was headed.

"Well, I should hope so, Mom," Jenny said, laughing. "You and Daddy aren't newlyweds anymore. And I don't think there was a television show involved in the first one. Or, was there?"

I laughed back. "Not that I know of. In fact, I'm not sure television was even invented all those years ago. And if it was, I bet all the broadcasts were still in black and white. So, how are you doing? How's Mark? Is he back to work yet, or still recovering from his accident? I worry so because I'm not there to help you."

"No worries, Mom," Jenny said. "Mark's doing very well. He expects to get back to his regular police schedule next Monday. He's also helping me with a little home improvement project while he's convalescing. Nothing too strenuous, so don't worry."

There was a brief pause, and then Jenny said, "I hear that you've been up to your old tricks down there in Florida. My sources tell me you're involved in another suspicious death."

"It's not like I go looking for these situations," I said, trying not to sound overly defensive.

"I know that, Mom. But you have to admit, you have a knack for being in the wrong place at the wrong time."

"Even though Charlie King and I hadn't seen each other since our grade school days," I said, "he was a good man, and witnessing the car exploding, then finding out that Charlie was inside, is something I'll never forget. It was terrible. I didn't sleep at all last night." I choked back a sob.

"I'm sorry, Mom," Jenny said. "I didn't realize you'd actually witnessed the explosion. Mike didn't tell me that."

"Mike?" I said. "You've talked to him? When? What did he say? How did he sound?"

"Easy, Mom," Jenny said. "That's really why I'm calling you. Not that I didn't want to talk to you, of course, but Mike texted me a little while ago and told me about the mess he's gotten himself into down there. How you found out about it and yelled at him, and you had a terrible fight. He's very upset."

"Well, he should be," I snapped back. "Mike's never talked to me like that before."

"What did Dad say?" Jenny asked.

Hmm. How could I explain Jim's total lack of involvement in Mike's crisis without making him look bad in his daughter's eyes? That was the question. Especially since I didn't understand it, myself.

"Your dad's back in full public relations mode," I said. "It's like watching a retired race horse suddenly being tapped to run in the Kentucky Derby. He's spending a lot of time with his boss, organizing tomorrow's memorial service for Charlie King, doing some damage control about how Charlie's death will affect the television show, and handling loads of media. He's left the family business up to me, because he knows I have more experience with this kind of thing."

I paused for a minute and hoped Jenny would accept this load of outdoor fertilizer that I was spreading as the truth.

"It's nice that Dad has such faith in you," Jenny said. "Especially since he usually spends most of his time forbidding you to get involved in any kind of investigations."

"We respect what each of us is good at," I said, shoveling another load of fertilizer in the direction of Fairport, Connecticut.

"I don't know exactly what you're doing, Mom," Jenny said. "But please, please make up with Mike. I know you just want to help him. Deep down, I'm sure he knows that, too."

"Don't worry about my relationship with your brother," I said with more confidence than I felt. "We both needed to blow off a little steam. I'll text him and see when we can get together tonight. I guess it's up to me to make the first move."

"That makes me feel better, Mom," Jenny said. "Keep me posted. I'm sure that things aren't as bad for Mike as he said. He always did have a flair for the dramatic, even when we were kids."

"So, tell me about this home improvement project you and Mark are working on," I said, switching the conversation to a much safer topic. "Can you send me any pictures? I'm not sure how long we'll be in Florida, and I hate to be out of the loop. I wish Dad and I were there to help you."

Jenny laughed. "Actually, Mom, you and Dad have helped. In fact, it's safe to say that you inspired this project. I think you'll love it, and be very surprised. But you have to be a little patient. We've just started it."

It was nice to get positive feedback from at least one of my children. Although patience isn't one of my well-known virtues.

"I'll contact Mike right away," I said. "Don't worry. And I'll do my best to be patient about your project."

"Love you, Mom. Give Dad a kiss from me." She clicked off. Leaving me with plenty of food for thought. So to speak.

Chapter 42

When I was a child, nap time was a punishment. Now, at my age, it's a mini vacation.

A loud knock on the bedroom door interrupted my musings. Nancy stuck her head inside and announced, "Food's here! And you'll never guess who delivered it. You better hurry up before Claire and I eat it all." You can bet that Nancy's threat got me moving pretty quickly. If I have a choice between thinking and eating, I'm sure you can figure out what I always choose.

"Well, if it isn't our very own version of *Undercover Boss*," I said, settling myself in the chair closest to the food cart. "How nice of you to take such a personal interest in our cuisine." Just in case my sarcasm was lost on Bernardo, I couldn't resist adding, "Oh, now I understand. You're still playing your concierge role, right? Delivering food to guests is all part of the job, I assume."

I took a closer look at the room service cart, overflowing with delicacies of all kinds. "I don't remember any of this food being on the menu, and we certainly didn't ask for this flower arrangement. Or the box of Milk Bone dog biscuits. Don't expect us to pay for any of this, because we didn't order it."

I sat back, folded my arms, and glared at Bernardo. Unfortunately, Lucy, who had been snoozing nearby, heard the words "Milk Bone," perked right up, and make a beeline for the cart. Like me, she rarely resists the siren call of food. I grabbed her collar before she did any damage, and said, "No. Sit." Surprisingly, she did. But not before she gave me a very dirty look.

Bernardo didn't miss a beat. "I've made sure none of this will be added to your bill," he said. "And you're right to be angry, Carol. I deceived you and I owe you all an explanation. Most of the staff here don't know who I really am, and I prefer to keep it that way for another few days. I hope I can count on your discretion. Going 'undercover,' as you call it, is one foolproof way I can check on how my properties are being run. And the fact that Charlie was shooting the pilot of the television show here was an added incentive for me to come. I like to protect my investments."

"Do tell," I said, helping myself to a chocolate-covered strawberry.

"Yes," Claire said, speaking up at last and—surprise of surprises!—for once, agreeing with me. "Do tell. We're all dying to know about your business relationship with Charlie. Pun definitely intended. Especially since Carol's son, Mike, seems to be at the top of Deputy Armstrong's suspect list for Charlie's untimely death. There's a whole lot going on here that none of us understand, and you seem to be right in the middle of the action."

I flashed Claire a look of gratitude.

"How rich are you, really?" Nancy asked.

I choked on the remains of a strawberry. Yes, I'd had another one. All right, two.

"Did that private jet that flew us to Florida yesterday really belong to you?" Nancy continued, oblivious to my coughing fit. "And the fleet of white Mercedes, too?"

Trust Nancy to get to the crux of the matter. But I had to stop her before she offered to help him buy some expensive beachfront property in Florida. She is, after all, a Realtor.

"Well, I'm not in the same class as Bill Gates or Warren Buffett," Bernardo said. "But, I guess by most people's standards, I'm considered well-off."

"So, you're rich," Nancy pressed, not willing to let the subject go until she had a real answer.

"Yes, I'm rich now," Bernardo said. "But I wasn't always so wealthy. It's only in the past five years or so that my company, Mature Property Resorts, became successful. My hotels cater to the over-fifty crowd, and I prefer to hire them as my employees, too, whenever I can. In fact, Carol, I'm very impressed with your husband. Once this terrible situation about Charlie's death is cleared up, I plan to offer Jim a full-time job. I need a good public relations person, and he's just the man I've been looking for."

My heart dropped to my shoes. This would mean that Jim would be working full-time, non-stop, just like he used to do when he worked at Gibson Gillespie. We'd have no family life at all. I could drop dead on the kitchen floor when he was off on a business trip, and he wouldn't find my body for days. I choked back a sob, just thinking about it.

I pushed those ghoulish thoughts out of my mind, saving them for another time. For now, I needed to get back on the conversation track Claire had started.

"What about you and Charlie King?" I asked. "You were his secret money man. Why secret? What did you have to hide?"

"You don't understand how the entertainment business works," Bernardo said. "It's not who you are. It's who the people in the industry think you are. It was Charlie's idea to keep my investment private, not mine. He wanted to make a big comeback. Even more, he wanted to make it appear that he was doing it on his own."

"Why you? How did you two get together?" I asked, trying not to talk with my mouth full, as my late mother taught me.

"As I said, my properties are targeted at Boomers. We offer wellness opportunities and amenities that most other hotels don't. Like classes in water aerobics to help with arthritis, for example. Charlie found me online, contacted me, we met, he talked, I listened, and I was in. He was quite persuasive."

"And charming," Nancy added.

"I guess I always wanted to be in show business," Bernardo admitted. "Investing money in *The Second Honeymoon Game* was as close as I could get."

"This is all very interesting," I said, trying to tamp down my annoyance at Lucy, now snuggled at Bernardo's side and gazing up at him adoringly, "but what do you know about Charlie's death?"

Now it was Bernardo's turn to look uncomfortable. I realized that I had scored a direct hit.

"Were you working in the dining room last night?" Claire asked. "Did you see us there?" She gestured at Nancy. "We were having an early dinner with my husband and Charlie. Then, Charlie got a text and dashed out. That was the last we saw of him."

I picked up the line of questioning. "My son is being accused of having a fight with Charlie on his way out of the dining room.

Were you there? Did you see anything that contradicts that?"

"I wasn't there," Bernardo said. "I'm sorry."

I sat back, defeated. Rats. I thought we were on to something.

"But there is something else I should tell you," he said. "You said that Charlie got a text and immediately left. That text was from me."

I jumped up and planted a big smooch on Bernardo's cheek. "Finally, some positive information. Come on." I grabbed the poor man's hand and pulling him toward the door. "We have to tell Deputy Armstrong this right away. This will get Mike off her radar."

"I don't see how," Claire said, throwing her usual wet blanket on my excitement. "Even if Bernardo admits he sent Charlie a text message last night, that doesn't prove that he and Charlie actually connected."

I just hate it when people are logical. It spoils everything. I shot her a dirty look and plopped back down on the sofa.

But Claire was just getting warmed up. "My husband, Larry, is an attorney back in Connecticut," she explained to Bernardo. "If this was an actual trial where he was the prosecuting attorney, and you were on the witness stand, I'm positive his next question would be, 'Did you and Charlie see each other last night? And, if so, was it at the beach?' Then he'd watch your body language to see if your answer was truthful. So, that's what I'm asking you. Did you meet Charlie at the beach last night?"

Bernardo shifted his position a little. I'm sure he was ready to grab his room service cart and boogie the heck out of here. Then, he made direct eye contact with Claire, and said, "Charlie and I did meet at the beach last night. We talked in the pavilion for about twenty minutes. He was going way over the budget we had agreed on for the pilot episode of the television show, and I needed to rein him in. When I left, Charlie was still there. Alive."

"I wonder how Deputy Armstrong will react to *this* information," Claire said, looking very pleased with herself that her questioning had gone so well.

"You just jumped to the top of her list, no matter how rich and important you are," I added, for good measure.

"She already knows," Bernardo said. "I met with her a few hours ago and told her everything." He looked at me apologetically. "She asked me if I'd seen anyone else on the beach. I told her I only saw a couple snuggling on a blanket, but I wasn't close enough to identify them."

Thank goodness!

Bernardo looked thoughtful. "Come to think of it, I just remembered I heard the sound of a car last night while Charlie and I were talking. But that must have been from the causeway, not the beach."

He glanced at his watch. I couldn't help but notice it was a Rolex. I wondered if any of the hotel employees had picked up on that. "I have to get back."

"Please tell Deputy Armstrong about the car," I said. "It may not be important, because I guess cars are always zipping up and down the causeway, even at night. But the timing may be significant." I hope.

Bernardo nodded. "I'll find her right now. Again, Carol, please accept my apologies for causing you so much distress today. Being a concierge is a lot more complicated than I thought it would be."

Chapter 43

I don't need Google. My husband knows everything.

"Golly, this was good," Nancy said, licking her fork for emphasis. "I feel better already. There's nothing like a combination of sugar and caffeine to cheer me up."

"It's too bad we didn't think to order this when Carrie was here," Claire added. "I bet she hasn't had a thing to eat all day. Poor thing."

"You really should talk to her, Carol," Nancy said again. "She's probably in her villa alone sobbing her eyes out."

"She may be in her villa," I said, "but I don't think she's alone. I'm pretty sure Mike is still with her. In fact, Carrie's one of the things we argued about this afternoon. Remember, she's the one who convinced Mike to lie to Deputy Armstrong."

"Well, I'm sure Carrie only had Mike's best interests at heart," Nancy said. "She was protecting him, plain and simple."

"I don't agree with you," I said, outraged that Nancy still couldn't see my point. "Carrie wasn't protecting Mike at all. She was making things worse for him."

"Now, Carol," Claire said in that pseudo soothing tone of voice that always drives me nuts because she sounds so much like Jim, "you're overreacting. Again. Bernardo has provided Deputy Armstrong with some pretty damaging information about his own activities last night. An argument over money is a pretty powerful motive. I think Mike's in the clear."

"And don't forget about the car Bernardo says he heard," Nancy put in. "That could be another clue. I'm sure Deputy Armstrong will find that significant."

"Assuming Bernardo actually heard a car," I said.

"Well, Deputy Armstrong did ask for your help this morning, Carol," Claire pointed out. "Why don't you see if she's still here and have a little chat? You do have some tasty tidbits to share with her."

I shook my head. "I don't dare. What if she asks me something about Mike? I can't afford to take that chance."

"I still think you should find Carrie," Nancy insisted. "Talk to her. She needs some mothering right now."

"I wonder what Carrie knows about her own mother's death," Claire said, a thoughtful look on her face. "It would be very traumatic to find out that your mom committed suicide, right?"

"According to the obituary Mary Alice read us, the suicide happened when Carrie was a baby, so she may not know how her mother died," I reminded Claire. "And I doubt that's the kind of information Charlie would have shared with her. If anything, he'd protect her from ever finding out. I don't think talking to Carrie tonight is a good idea."

"Honest to goodness, Carol, I could just shake you when you act like this," Claire exploded. "You need to either talk to Carrie or Deputy Armstrong. Tonight. Deputy Armstrong isn't looking for you. Carrie is. It seems crystal clear to me. Why are you so hesitant?"

"I don't know," I said. "I just am."

I thought for a few seconds and made a decision. "What the heck. I'll call Carrie. She may not even want to see me now."

"Thank goodness," Nancy said, handing me my phone and trying to pretend she wasn't listening to every word I said.

Fortunately, Carrie answered on the first ring. Just like she'd been waiting for my call. "Oh, Carol," she said, sobbing, "I'm so glad to hear from you. I don't know how I'm going to get through the next hours until Dad's memorial service. I miss him so much."

"What can I do to help you?" I asked, realizing that Nancy and Claire were right. Carrie was despondent and needed a mother's shoulder to cry on. It seemed that mine was her shoulder of choice.

"Can you meet me?" she asked. "At the beach pavilion? I want to go back to where Dad died. Maybe being there will help me. I suppose that doesn't make any sense."

"It doesn't have to make sense, Carrie," I said in my most

soothing voice. "If that's what you want, I'll see you at the beach pavilion in half an hour. We'll have a nice long talk." I ended the conversation before Carrie could start sobbing again.

"You're a good person to meet her," Nancy said; Claire nodded in agreement.

"I don't feel like a good person," I said. "I feel very guilty for dragging my feet about seeing her. You were both right. She really wants to see me. She didn't mention Mike, and I didn't bring him up, which, of course, you know, since you heard every word I just said."

"It's a nice night for a walk," Claire said. "Do you want us to go with you?"

"No, you two have done enough," I said. "I'll take the dogs with me. It's getting dark, so I think it's okay to bring them to the beach now. Their presence may soothe Carrie a little. I know that petting them always makes me feel better. And, heaven knows, we can all use the exercise. I'm not going to stay long. The park is probably closing soon."

Lucy gave me a look that telegraphed—loud and clear—that she'd had enough long walks for one day and her paws needed a rest. "After we see Carrie, I promise I'll feed you supper. Dogs do not live on Milk Bones alone," I said to her. "But first," I held up the leashes, "one more quick walk." Bribery usually works as well on my canines as it does on my humans.

"If you're sure you don't want us to come with you," Claire said, "I guess I'll try to find my wandering husband."

"If you should happen to see my own dear husband, tell him hello from me," I said.

"Don't be too hard on him," Nancy said. "He's working, remember?"

"Yeah, we all saw how hard he was working in the dining room this afternoon," I said with a grimace. "Come on, girls, let's go for walkies."

"I know, we should have brought a flashlight," I said to Lucy. Even in the dusk, I could tell she was giving me a dirty look. "We're going to be walking back to the hotel in the dark. Be sure you and

Ethel stick close to me and we'll be all right. No going off and exploring on your own."

I stopped and let the girls peruse a particularly fascinating piece of either flotsam or jetsam (I don't know the difference and I bet you don't know, either), then urged them along.

"Carol, over here." I saw a slim figure in white shorts and a tank top waving to me from the pavilion steps. Carrie, of course. I could certainly see why Mike was attracted to her. The wind from the Gulf of Mexico made her dark hair stream around her face. She looked like a sea nymph.

"Are you alone?" she asked.

An odd question, to be sure.

"Well, I have the dogs with me." I lifted up their leashes to show her as I climbed the pavilion steps. "They needed some exercise and I hoped I could get away with bringing them to the beach at this hour. Besides, I hate to be parted from them for very long." I laughed. "Stupid, I know. But I love them almost as much as I love my human family."

"I won't tell," Carrie said. "I love dogs." She sat down at a picnic table and put out her hand to pet Ethel. To my embarrassment, Ethel growled at her. Yes, gentle Ethel—who never woofs an unkind word at anybody—actually growled.

"I'm so sorry," I said, parking my derriere on a picnic bench and pulling the dogs' leashes a little tighter. "Ethel doesn't know you. I think you startled her. I apologize on her behalf."

"I guess I must be a horrible person," Carrie said, her eyes glistening with tears. "Even dogs don't like me. I really don't have anybody anymore. I'm all alone."

She jumped up. "Will you walk with me? I want to show you something."

"Of course I will," I said. "We all will. I can't leave the dogs here alone."

"Sure, that's fine," Carrie said, taking my hand and pulling me to keep pace with her. "I thought being here with you where Dad died last night would bring me some peace. Can you help me find some peace? Please! I'm begging you! I need to find some peace! You're the only one who can help me! Please, help me!"

By this time, Carrie was screaming at the top of her lungs. The next thing I knew, she'd grabbed the dogs' leashes from me and started to run away with them.

"You love these dogs?" she yelled over her shoulder at me. "Well, say goodbye to them. You're never going to see them again. They're coming with me. Forever. I'm going to take away your happiness, the way you took away mine. It's all your fault. And my stupid father's, who talked about you for years. His great grammar school love. It was your fault my mother killed herself! I hate you so much! But Dad wasn't supposed to die in the car! It was supposed to be you! You stupid person! You ruined that, too! You couldn't even die when you were supposed to! It should have been you in that car, not Dad! Oh, Dad, forgive me, please! It's all Carol's fault!"

It took me a few seconds to process what I was hearing.

Do something, Carol. Don't just stand there. You have to stop her.

But I was so stunned that everything seemed to be happening in slow motion. I couldn't move. Not a single muscle.

I caught a brief look at Lucy's face. She wasn't terrified at all. She was angry. And, unlike me, she could move. And move, she did. The little smarty made a quick end run around Carrie's legs, tangling her leash around her ankles, while Ethel went around the other way.

In no time at all, Carrie was trapped by the leashes and tumbled down the pavilion stairs onto the sand. She landed at the feet of my darling husband, holding a flashlight and looking as scared as I felt. "I talked to Nancy. She told me where you were," Jim said. "I decided to surprise you, but instead, you surprised me! I got here just in time." He wrapped me in a welcomed hug. "I heard everything Carrie said to you. Thank God you're safe, Carol."

He looked down at Carrie, trussed up like a Thanksgiving turkey at his feet, thanks to the quick actions of my dogs, who were now standing guard over her in case she made any sudden move to escape. "I texted Deputy Armstrong. She's on her way."

Carrie laughed out loud. I'd never heard anybody laugh that way. Then I realized that Carrie was losing whatever small grip on reality she had left. I knew I shouldn't feel sorry for her, but I did. "What the hell," she said. "I don't care what happens to me now. My life is over. It doesn't matter."

I was trembling so hard that I thought I'd never stop. "I didn't realize anyone could hate me that much," I said.

Jim looked at me with such tenderness that my heart couldn't stand it. "I love you so much, Carol. Even if I don't say it often enough. Mike loves you, too." He gave me a big smooch to prove it.

"Mike?" I repeated. "You've seen him?"

Jim nodded. "We finally connected a little while ago. He told me everything that happened. You were right. I should have talked to him sooner."

"Is Mike still mad at me?" I asked. I was almost afraid to hear Jim's answer.

"No, of course he's not still mad," Jim said. "He wants to apologize, and he's meeting us at the villa in a little while. That's another reason why I came looking for you."

Then Jim whispered in my ear, "I guess I solved the case instead of you for once, right, Carol?"

I wanted to remind Jim that Lucy and Ethel had played a pretty important part in the case, too. He just happened to be in the right place at the right time. But why bother? He was my hero, and maybe, from his point of view, he did solve the case.

And I knew he'd never let me forget it.

Chapter 44

I only drink wine to be sociable. And I can be very sociable.

"I never suspected Carrie for a single second," I admitted to Claire and Nancy the next morning. "But last night, after the whole horrible ordeal was over, I suddenly remembered the way she'd asked for my help in the first place. She said, 'Why did my father die?' What she really meant was, 'Why did my father die instead of you?' " I shivered, remembering the look in Carrie's eyes when she confronted me at the beach. "I don't think I'll ever get over what happened. I've read hundreds of mysteries; I guess last night was what's referred to in fiction as the 'black moment.' Believe me, when it happens in real life, it's black, all right. Black as death."

"Do you want to tell us more about what happened?" Nancy asked. I could tell from the expression on her face that she wouldn't quit asking me until she'd heard every single detail.

"I'll try," I said, biting my lip and attempting to put on a brave face. "But it won't be easy. If it hadn't been for the dogs, and Jim arriving just in time, I don't know what would have happened."

"At least you and Mike are reconciled," Claire said. "That's right, isn't it? All is well in mother/son land?"

"Yes, thank goodness. He was horrified when he found out what Carrie was really up to. Jim, Mike and I, had a long session with Deputy Armstrong last night after Carrie was carted off to jail. Mike came clean and told Armstrong everything, including the fact that it was Carrie who'd encouraged him to lie. She was setting him up all along. Just to get back at me and hurt me as much as possible."

I paused for a minute, then said, "I'm not sure if I'm supposed to tell you this, but apparently Armstrong was already suspicious of Carrie, especially when she found out there were no female servers in the hotel dining room that night. She realized it was possible that Carrie had made the call anonymously, but she couldn't figure out why she'd do it."

"That's what I want to know, too, Carol," Claire said. "Why did Carrie hate you so much? We all went to school with Charlie, and she didn't hate us? At least I don't think she did. Maybe she would have gotten around to us in time."

"Carrie blamed me for her mother's suicide," I said. "Even though I never even met the woman."

"But that's absolutely crazy," Nancy said. "Why?"

"Apparently Charlie used to talk about me at home a lot," I said. "About how I was his first real girlfriend, and how special I'd always be to him. When he insisted that his daughter be named after me, it sent his wife over the edge. Especially because she was already dealing with postpartum depression." I paused in my sad tale and took a large gulp of coffee. I needed the caffeine desperately.

"But Carrie was just a baby when her mother died," Nancy argued. "That doesn't make any sense. How could she know that her mother committed suicide…and because of you? I can't imagine Charlie telling her."

I shook my head. "He didn't. But Carrie was babbling nonstop in the patrol car on the way to the sheriff's office. Carrie's mother left a suicide note saying I was the reason why she had to kill herself, because Charlie never loved her the way he loved me. And Charlie saved the letter. Heaven knows why he did such a stupid thing. If he'd destroyed it, he'd probably still be alive. Anyway, Carrie found the letter a few months ago."

I started to cry. "I can't blame Carrie for hating me. Not really."

"Poor child," Claire said. "What a tragedy. It doesn't sound like she'll ever stand trial, though. I'm sure her lawyer will plead insanity."

"I guess when Jim and I were hired for *The Second Honeymoon Game,* and Charlie made such a big deal about it, Carrie saw her big chance for revenge. She decided she had to eliminate me," I said.

"But how?" Nancy asked. "How did she do it?"

"I don't have all the answers," I snapped. "I'm sure Deputy Armstrong will figure it out."

"Maybe Carrie switched cars at the beach," Claire suggested. "All those white Mercedes sedans looked alike to me."

"That makes sense," Nancy said. "Remember, Bernardo said he heard a car on the causeway. It could have been Carrie, driving to the parking lot and switching the car she'd rigged to explode for the one you and Jim took to the beach. She set the timer, or whatever she used, and left the parking lot in your car. Poor Charlie turned the ignition switch and, well, boom...."

"Maybe," I said. "I remember hearing that Carrie had fixed all the Mercedes so they operated on the same key. I guess it could have happened that way. But right now, I'm exhausted. I'm not going to try and figure it out."

Claire opened her mouth once more. "I hate to bring this up, but what about the television show? Is it still a go? And will there be a memorial service for Charlie today?"

I yawned again. "The memorial service is off. And, according to Jim, the television show's on hold indefinitely. Bernardo has pulled out his money, and Kurt Armitage is scrambling to find a new backer. Unfortunately, Bernardo's also taken back his private jet, so we may have to hitchhike our way back to Fairport."

My cell phone pinged, and I realized I had a text from Jenny. With an attachment. I squinted to decipher it without my glasses.

Thought you'd like to see how our home improvement project is coming along. You'll meet the finished project in twenty-eight more weeks.

Love, Jenny and Mark

It was a sonogram. We were having a baby!

Key Lime Pie—a Gift from Florida

Several years ago, Key Lime Pie was chosen by the Florida legislature as the Official State Dessert. And if you try these recipes, you'll immediately agree. Be sure to use real key limes. Their taste really makes a difference.

Enjoy!

White Chocolate Key Lime Pie with Coconut Graham Cracker Crust

A light and refreshing dessert to enjoy on a warm summer's evening. Your guests will think you slaved for hours, but it comes together in a snap, making a lovely presentation!

GRAHAM CRACKER AND TOASTED COCONUT CRUST:
1 ½ c graham cracker crumbs, approx. 9 whole crackers
3 T white sugar
$1/3$ c unsalted butter, melted
5 T shredded coconut, preferably unsweetened

FILLING:
$3/4$ c white chocolate chips, melted (Nestles works well, as does Ghiradelli's white chocolate melting chips)
14 oz sweetened, condensed milk (not evaporated milk)
8 oz mascarpone cheese, room temperature
½ c plus 2 T fresh squeezed lime juice (juice of appx. 5 large key limes)
1 T lime zest

1.) To prepare the crust: Preheat oven to 325. Combine graham cracker crumbs, melted butter, sugar and coconut in a large bowl and stir until well mixed. Press evenly into an ungreased 9-inch (preferably glass) pie plate, working part way up the sides. Bake 10 minutes or until golden brown. Transfer to a wire rack and cool completely. You can use a pre-made crust, but you'll miss the coconut, trust me!

2.) To make filling: Place chocolate chips in a small microwave-safe bowl. Microwave at medium power (50%) at 30 second intervals until melted, stirring after each interval. Stir until smooth. Combine melted chocolate and sweetened condensed milk, mascarpone, lime juice and lime zest. Whisk or beat with an electric mixer until smooth. Pour into cooled crust and smooth top. Chill at least 4 hours, or place in freezer for 15-20 minutes just before serving. Top/pipe decoratively with freshly whipped cream, or if preferred, serve whipped topping separately. Garnish with toasted coconut flakes and lime slices and/or zest.

Recipe provided by Sandra Tatsuno, Dennis MA

Fully Loaded Key Lime Pie (about 519 calories per slice)

CRUST:
Crush 2 c graham crackers until fine
Or a half and half mix of graham crackers and your favorite cereal (honey nut Cheerios works great but corn flakes or rice chex works well too)
Add ½ c softened butter
2 T sugar
Mix well and press into 9-inch pie plate
To bake: Bake at 350 for 10 minutes, let cool

FILLING:
1 14 oz can sweetened condensed milk
3 large egg yolks
½ c Key Lime juice
¼ c buttermilk
Add filling to cooled pie shell
Bake 350 for 10-12 minutes.
Cool and serve with whipped cream.

Gluten Free Key Lime Pie (about 510 calories per slice)

CRUST:

Crush 2 c gluten-free graham crackers or crunchy cookies of your choice crushed until a fine crumb

Add ½ c softened unsalted butter

2 T white sugar

Mix well and press into 9-inch pie plate

Bake at 350 for 10 minutes, let cool

FILLING:

1 14 oz can sweetened condensed milk

3 large egg yolks

½ c Key Lime juice

Add filling to cooled pie shell

Bake at 350 for 10-12 minutes.

Cool and serve with whipped cream.

Reduced Calorie Key Lime Pie (about 290 calories per slice)

CRUST:

Crush 2 c reduced-fat graham crackers crushed into a fine crumb

Add ½ c reduced fat butter substitute

2 T Splenda

Mix and press into 9-inch pie plate

Bake at 350 for 10 minutes, let cool

FILLING:

1 14 oz fat-free sweetened condensed milk

¾ c egg substitute

2 T Key Lime juice

½ c reduced fat Greek yogurt

Add filling to cooled pie shell

Bake at 350 for10-12 minutes.

Cool and serve with non-fat whipped cream

Recipes provided by Chef Paulette DiAngi, Osterville MA

About the Author

An early member of the Baby Boomer generation, Susan Santangelo has been a feature writer, drama critic and editor for daily and weekly newspapers in the New York metropolitan area, including *Cosmopolitan* magazine. A seasoned public relations and marketing professional, she has designed and managed not-for-profit events and programs for over 25 years, and was principal of her own public relations firm, Events Unlimited, in Princeton NJ for ten years. She also served as Director of Special Events and Volunteers for Carnegie Hall during the Hall's 1990-1991 Centennial season.

Susan divides her time between Cape Cod MA and the west coast of Florida. She is a member of Sisters in Crime, International Thriller Writers and the Cape Cod Writers Center, and shares her life with her husband Joe and two very spoiled English cocker spaniels, Boomer and Lilly. Boomer also serves as the model for the books' front covers, and Lilly is pictured on the back cover of this title.

A portion of the sales from the *Baby Boomer Mysteries* is donated to the Breast Cancer Survival Center, a non-profit organization based in Connecticut which Susan founded in 1999 after being diagnosed with cancer herself.

You can contact Susan at ssantangelo@aol.com or find her on Facebook and Twitter. She'd love to hear from you.

31003788R00127